TO DIE FOR

TO DIE FOR

Melanie George

ZEBRA BOOKS
Kensington Publishing Corp.

ZEBRA BOOKS are published by

Kensington Publishing Corp.
850 Third Avenue
New York, NY 10022

Copyright © 2002 by Melanie George

ISBN 0-7394-2966-3

First Printing: November 2002

Printed in the United States of America

To all the survivors out there . . .

One

"Man-killer at six o'clock."

That announcement brought Stefan Massari's head jerking up so abruptly one would think his editor-in-chief, Rick Faraday, had just confessed he was in the habit of carrying heads around in a duffel bag.

Damn. She was back. Her return was inevitable, of course, but a man could hope. It wasn't outside the realm of possibility that she had suckered another old man with one foot in the grave into marriage. She had done it three times already. And three times had not been a charm for her last husband, or the two before him.

Michaela St. James was a death sentence waiting to happen.

At twenty-seven, she had buried each of her wealthy husbands within six months of the nuptials, leaving little speculation about how they had found their end. Her kills were always clean.

Sex, her weapon of choice.

"Hot damn!" Rick hooted. "She's got on those spiky black Manolo Blahnik heels and that here-to-kick-some-male-ass red Armani suit. Hello, hard-on!"

"Do the words *ruled by your dick* mean anything to you, Faraday?"

Rick flashed Stefan an unrepentant grin over his shoulder. "None of my women are complaining."

"You mean the ones you pick up on Ninth Avenue?"

"Dream on, buddy. Just because you haven't had a date since the fall of Red China doesn't mean the rest of us aren't getting wrung dry every night."

Faraday's not-so-subtle reminder that Stefan was toeing the line of celibacy only capped off his already declining mood. He massaged his temples and wondered why he bothered sparring with Rick on the issue of women. The man was always chasing an erection.

He had met Rick while working for *Gentleman's Quarterly,* where Stefan had begun his career as a copyboy after graduating at the top of his class from the Columbia School of Journalism.

Then one day he had been lured away by the dream of taking a struggling new magazine and building the fledgling upstart into an industry giant.

Bastion was Lowery St. James's baby, and he had wanted only the best and the brightest the business had to offer. Lowery worked hard and lived hard, which had led to a fatal heart attack two months earlier, leaving his daughter, Michaela, to step into his shoes. She hadn't wasted a moment before making Stefan's life miserable, even while in Europe, where, until today, she had been "mourning," with her French lover.

Only minutes before Rick had announced her arrival, Stefan had been speaking with Francis Costello, president of Magazine Publishing for R. R. Donnelley & Sons, who had informed him that Michaela had decided the company needed to cut costs. Therefore, she no longer wanted the magazine printed on top-quality heavy-gloss paper but on a less-expensive grade instead.

Stefan had been furious, which is exactly why Micky had pulled her stunt. She didn't like being bested, and the codicil left in her father's will had royally chapped her ass.

Without the full consent of the members of the board, Stefan could not be fired, which thwarted her plan for revenge. If she'd had her way, he would have been out before the dirt had settled on her father's grave.

"That bad, huh?"

Stefan's irritated regard slid to Rick to find him shaking his head in mock pity, the gleam in his eyes conveying that he anticipated the coming fireworks like a hunter anticipated the hunt. That there would be an explosion was of little doubt. Who would walk away with fewer battle scars was another matter entirely.

"And here I thought not even the devil himself could intimidate Stefan Massari, let alone a hundred-and-twenty-pound pain in the ass like Micky."

"How the hell do you even know it's her? We're six stories up."

"I'd recognize those legs anywhere."

Yeah, most men who had eyes would, too. As a general rule, Micky favored short, tight skirts and disdained pantyhose. Occasionally, she donned a red power tie to remind the men she had castrated who had their balls.

Ever since Stefan had fended off her attempts to seduce him, she had used whatever weapon was at her disposal to pay him back, which, among her usual arsenal of ways to piss him off, also included hiking up her skirt and giving him a look-what-you-can't-have view of the wispy lace G-string nestled between her thighs, perhaps expecting him to come groveling for a fuck. Christ, if it would get her off his back, he might just give her the satisfaction of telling him to go fuck himself.

"You know, Stef," Rick said in a way that told Stefan he would be irritated by the time the man finished, "maybe if you stopped protecting your virtue like it's gold bullion in Fort Knox, you'd ease some of the stress that's giving you those unflattering scowl lines in your forehead. Give Micky a little stroking in the requisite erogenous zones and I bet she'll turn into a pussycat."

The fact that Rick articulated what Stefan had been thinking told him that he had just lowered himself to a whole new level. "Don't you have anything to do?"

"Fine. I can take a hint. But I wouldn't dismiss my idea simply because you're incredibly stubborn as well as being the most irritatingly noble bastard I know. Satisfaction's the name of the game, Stef. Getting Micky off your back could be as easy as getting her on her back."

Not even if it meant bringing world peace, Stefan thought as he watched Rick depart. Men were like Blow Pops to her, treated to a few teasing licks before she sank her teeth in, devouring one after the next and discarding them at a near head-spinning clip.

She had already managed to drive off his sales manager, Hale Turner. Hale claimed to have accepted another position at a rival magazine. Yet from the way the man couldn't look Stefan in the eye, he figured Micky had led Hale into committing an unfortunate mistake—one Stefan doubted *Mrs. Turner* would appreciate hearing about.

Simmering, Stefan shoved away from his desk and stalked to the window overlooking a million dollar view of Manhattan, the buildings stacked up like dominoes, peaks thrusting skyward, citadels vying for attention. A concrete and steel prison to those who had not been born into its hard-edged grandeur as Stefan had.

He caught a glimpse of his reflection in the glass and noted his grim expression. His secretary referred to it as his butts-are-gonna-roll look. And at least one would.

He had no intention of mincing words with Micky now that she was back. No conniving daddy's girl with crushed feelings and an ax to grind was going to undermine him.

And very shortly now, Stefan intended to bring that point home.

She was melting, every last electrolyte dissolving in a puddle at her feet as if all the sun's rays were directed solely on her, enclosing her in a concrete jar of stagnant, hot air and leaving her limbs feeling boneless.

Abby fanned herself futilely as she stood on the sidewalk watching the cabbie who had just deposited her at her destination give a crude hand gesture to a passing motorist before tearing off in a yellow blur, leaving her adrift in a sea of bodies.

The nervousness she had barely managed to hold at bay began to creep up on her as she turned and gazed up at the jutting Madison Avenue building blocking out the sun.

She forced herself to shake off her worries. It was a little too late for cowardice. She was here now.

Weaving her way through the crowd, Abby pushed the heavy revolving door with both hands and entered the vaulted atrium, which was a welcomed surprise, adorned as it was with the first bit of greenery she had seen since leaving home.

She didn't stop to speak to the receptionist, had the woman bothered to look up from filing her nails. Instead she headed for the elevators where a group of people already waited, churning with restless energy, eyes fixed to the blinking light that indicated the elevator's descent.

As soon as the doors cracked open, a flood of bodies surged forward, sweeping Abby along with them. It was either move or be trampled.

By the time the elevator doors opened onto the sixth floor, she had to pry herself from the back wall and shoulder her way through the two men blocking her path. With a sigh of relief, she made her escape.

Straightening, she blew wisps of hair from her face, feeling daunted now that she had arrived, her feet suddenly welded to the floor as she stared at the impressive double glass doors emblazoned with the words *Bastion Magazine* in fancy gold lettering.

She couldn't believe she was here. Years ago she had vowed never to return to New York. The place held too many memories, painful memories she wanted only to forget, but they had never fully let her go.

Perhaps that was the underlying reason she'd had to come, to exorcise those demons and be free at last. The past had taught her hard lessons while the present had taught her valuable ones about the swift passing of time, of life—and how fleeting both could be.

Since her mother's death, the peace and contentment Abby had waited for through the long years of her mother's decline remained elusive. She was restless, unfulfilled, searching for a part of her that was missing. She had been looking for a reason to run away when the call came.

The sound of a door closing down the hall jolted Abby. She pulled the cell phone from her purse and dialed the number she had scribbled on a piece of paper.

"Hello?" came a languorous, deep-throated voice from the other end.

"I'm here."

"Damn it, Pierre! Can't you see I'm busy? Entertain yourself, for God's sake. Here, play with this." A husky male groan followed that statement. To Abby, she said, "Do you remember everything I told you?"

"Yes."

"Good. Walk in there with confidence. That'll be

the only way you'll get any respect. I hope you dressed appropriately? I know you have that god-awful propensity for wearing clothes straight off the rack."

Abby could almost see the shiver that possibility induced. "My clothes are fine."

"All right. Now don't forget what I said. Keep an eye on that guinea bastard. I don't trust him for a minute. Stay in control, remain tough, and above all . . . keep Stefan Massari at a distance."

The next thing Abby heard was a dial tone. She put away the cell phone, feeling as if she had just been ordered to charge into battle, which very well might be the case.

Taking a fortifying breath, she squared her shoulders and breezed through the doors. A gleaming circle of red mahogany enclosed the receptionist who, unlike the first receptionist, was busy answering the phone and didn't even take notice of Abby.

Beyond the reception desk, a long hallway opened up, walls done in a paneling of the same rich mahogany as the desk, flowing nicely into a dark, sturdy Berber carpet that would hold up well under the barrage of workers jetting from one door to the next.

Abby pressed onward, hoping her anonymity would last until she reached the end of the hall.

It didn't.

She had only made it a third of the way down the corridor before people noted her presence. She tried to act as if she knew exactly where she was going when she was only half sure of her destination. It had been a long time, after all. Things change.

As her nervousness rose, so did her pace, and by the time she neared the end of the hallway, she was very close to running. It wasn't until she had steamed her way into the corner office on the right that she remembered there was also a corner office on the left.

Too late.

A dark head snapped up. Abby's gaze locked with fierce, unwelcoming eyes the color of a midnight tempest, skewering her to the spot—eyes that brought a painful jolt of memory of how they had passed over her twelve years ago without ever truly seeing her.

Words tumbled through her head, but she could not catch hold of a single one. She had thought herself prepared. But how could she have ever been prepared for him?

An explanation formed on her lips, but whatever words she might have uttered disappeared when he rose from behind his desk and started toward her, broad shoulders filling out his perfectly tailored navy jacket, hard, muscled arms bulging beneath the sleeves, black hair gleaming in the light.

Abby took an involuntary step back as he stopped before her, only inches separating them. "Let's get something straight," he bit out. "I don't care who you are, but I'll be damned if I'm going to let you waltz in here and screw up years of hard work."

Abby tried not to feel threatened, though the menace he radiated was palpable. "Excuse me?"

"Whether you like it or not, I'm here to stay. So get used to it. And I tell you now, Micky, if you ever pull another one of those stunts like you did with Donnelley, there'll be hell to pay."

"You've got it wrong. I'm not—"

He slashed a hand through the air, effectively silencing her. "I don't give a rat's ass about whatever you have to say. I'm doing the talking now."

All right, Abby thought, trying to remain calm in the face of his escalating anger. Let him talk. Obviously there was something he needed to get off his chest. Sooner or later he would figure out that she wasn't Michaela. People had gotten them confused before.

That was the downside of being a twin.

Two

Abby waited as Stefan continued to chew her out for some imagined sin. She was grateful he had chosen to blow off steam by pacing back and forth rather than facing her directly. She doubted she could have made it through the confrontation. She knew her limitations.

Having that menacing gaze off her gave Abby the opportunity to collect herself and stave off the rising tide of panic welling inside her. She was here. With Stefan. And he was just as handsome as she remembered.

Twelve years was a long time. She had been a gawky, moon-eyed teenager the one time they had met, and Stefan had been the stuff of a young girl's fantasies.

Now that he had matured, he was even more breathtaking. Abby remembered how she had looked into his eyes and known he was not the kind of man who would ever purposely hurt anyone, that he would never be like her father, who had so easily cast aside his family when they no longer suited his lifestyle. If Lowery St. James had taught Abby one thing, it was that men betray . . . and they leave.

And that's exactly what her father had done. Betrayed his wife and children and then left. De-manded a divorce one day and moved out the next, taking an apartment in the city with his mistress.

Micky had remained with their father in New York while Abby had chosen to go with her mother to her grandparents' farm in Idaho. Neither of their choices had been a surprise. Micky craved the flux and flow of the big city while Abby preferred the simpler life.

In many ways, Abby had lived vicariously through her sister, listening to her tales of grand parties, trips, shopping—and men, lots and lots of men. Even Stefan.

Micki had confided all the intimate details of their heated affair. She claimed to have broken off the relationship when Stefan became too jealous and possessive.

"He frightens me, Abby. Sometimes I fear for my life. I wouldn't put it past him to have murdered Dad just to get his hands on the magazine. He's ruthless and single-minded. He'll do just about any-thing to get what he wants."

Abby didn't doubt that Stefan was the type of man who went after what he wanted, but he wouldn't go so far as to kill someone to get it.

"Dad died of a heart attack, Micky. Nothing sin-ister."

"There are ways of making murder look like a simple death."

Her sister sounded so sincere, Abby could only wonder what else had transpired between her and Stefan to make her believe he could possibly be ca-pable of murder.

"You know Dr. Miller had been telling Dad for years to stop smoking and drinking so heavily," Abby reminded her. "Besides, the Stefan Massari I remember didn't seem the kind of man who would resort to murder."

"And how do you know so much about his character?" Micky sniped. "Jesus, Abby, don't tell me you're still harboring a crush on the man?"

"Of course not!" Abby replied a bit too vehemently, regretting having confided that particular secret to her sister when they were younger.

"Good, because you'd be setting yourself up for a big fall. Stefan would never be interested in someone like you."

Abby didn't delude herself by pretending not to know what her sister meant. A man like Stefan would want a woman like Micky. Someone sexy and exciting and glamorous, and Abby had never been that kind of woman.

"Whatever you do, Abby, don't let the man get too close. He's a heartless son of a bitch with some very unusual tastes in the bedroom. In other words, the big, bad wolf. And you don't even rate as Little Red Riding Hood. I can handle him. But you . . . well, you're too damn nice for your own good."

That statement seemed to be the sum total of Abby's life. How many years had she longed to be less nice? To be wild and carefree.

To live.

After her mother had died, she had harbored that dream, tucked it safely away, believing the world would become new again someday and she could start fresh.

But the call had changed everything.

"Are you listening to me?" Stefan barked, the harshness of his voice rattling the calm Abby had been striving to achieve.

She met his hard, uncompromising gaze, and tried not to flinch. "Yes," she lied. "I heard everything you said."

He glowered, looking as if he didn't quite believe her. Then he resumed stalking the length of the room, speaking tersely about net costs and gross returns.

Abby found herself studying him, covertly observing the way he moved, with a sleek, masculine grace that proclaimed he was in charge. That, too, had remained unchanged. He was still a commanding presence.

"And another thing," he bit out. "Wear some pantyhose. This is an office, for Christ's sake."

That comment startled Abby, unexpected as it was. She glanced down at her bare legs, noting with a renewed sense of self-consciousness how much skin the skirt revealed. Trying to find a suit in her sister's closet that had not been embarrassingly short had been a chore, and Micky owned not a single pair of pantyhose. Abby had already made a note to get some. If Micky hadn't drummed it into her head that her style of clothing was less than appealing and that she needed to present a corporate image, she would have worn one of her own outfits.

"I was hot," she replied, wishing he would stop staring at her legs.

He grunted and then turned his back on her

once more to continue his tirade about someone named Donnelley and the cost of paper.

And Abby waited.

How was it possible that he had yet to see the differences between her and Michaela? And it was not merely the physical aspect: the ugly little mole on Abby's upper lip or that her hair was an indescribable shade somewhere between brown and red while Micky's hair was long and blonde.

Micky had presence, commanding people's attention as though it was her right. She would never have tolerated anyone yelling at her.

"Well?" Stefan growled, turning abruptly and impaling Abby with the full impact of those eyes, leaving her slightly unbalanced. "Don't just stand there staring at me as though you don't know what I'm talking about."

"I don't," she managed to get out, endeavoring to meet his gaze squarely and not squirm under the intensity of his regard even though her palms were clammy and her heart beat like a trip-hammer.

"Come off it, damn you! I'm not in the mood for any of your games."

Abby flinched at the blast. What a time for her to realize she was out of her element and completely unprepared to take on an angry Stefan Massari, who she had little doubt was formidable when he wasn't irate—but who was completely forbidding when he was.

"I'll come back when you're feeling calmer," she murmured, wanting only to get out of there.

She turned to go, but Stefan came barreling around the side of his desk like an enraged bull who had just seen red. Stepping in front of her with less than five inches to spare between them, he towered over her, his nearness and radiating anger singeing Abby clear through as black eyes, harsh and unyielding as granite, bore into her.

"Don't press me today, St. James." His voice held all the warmth of an ice-filled crater as he took a step closer, trying to intimidate her and succeeding more than he would ever know. "One day you'll push me too far and you won't like the end result."

Abby dared not breathe, dared not think of how close he was, how paralyzing the effect of his nearness. She tried to squelch the fear threatening her, panic rising like a mammoth wave inside her, old memories seeping through the cracks, coloring the present.

"Now," he metered the word, "your office is over there." He pointed to the door directly across from his. "Go to it. And stay the hell out of my way." He leaned down close to her face and added in a dark voice, "If you even sneeze in my direction, Calcutta won't be far enough for you to go to hide."

The dizziness came on Abby swiftly and without warning. Her chest tightened painfully, her breath rasping in short pants. Her vision began to blur and thoughts scattered like leaves in a high wind as blackness swam before her, enfolding her within its numbing embrace.

Stefan lunged for the girl as her eyes rolled back in her head and her legs buckled beneath her, catching her just before she hit the floor and lifting her into his arms.

He stared down into her pale, flawless face and

gritted his teeth. What the hell was wrong with her? Was this another one of her tricks? It would be so like the witch to pretend to faint just to blink open her eyes and laugh at him, mocking him for being a gullible jackass.

Great. Now what? If there was one woman in the world he should have let faint dead away, it was this one. But even though the right half of his brain knew Michaela was public enemy number one, and that only a silver bullet or a stake through the heart would do away with her, the left side had to go off half-cocked and act the savior. Damn it!

Disgruntled, Stefan stalked over to his black leather couch and deposited his burden. He realized he had a perfect excuse to toss a glass of water in her face, but unlike Faraday, he had been raised better than that.

Stefan eyed her. What had the little shrew done to her hair? She had shorn off the long, blonde locks that were her crowning glory. Now her hair was a copper color cut straight to her shoulders.

Stefan was loath to admit that the change had almost knocked him on his ass when she had first entered his office. The new look made her appear more approachable, sweet rather than siren. Definitely not such a bitch, which had very nearly kept him from blasting her as she deserved.

Scowling, Stefan headed into the bathroom concealed at the back of his office and grabbed one of the two monogrammed hand towels from the rack.

Wetting one down, he returned to the unconscious form on the couch, and none too gently, slapped the cloth across her forehead. He may not have the option at the moment of pitching her into the corridor, as would be his preference, but neither did he have to enjoy bringing her around.

"I see you've taken my advice," a voice drawled.

Stefan's gaze swung over his shoulder to find Faraday standing behind him, arms crossed over his chest, a smug half-grin on his face as he ogled Michaela's prone form with his usual copulatory leer.

"You must have given it to her good if she's already passed out."

"She fainted," Stefan replied tersely. "Case closed." His expression warned Faraday to let the matter drop.

Rick shrugged. "Whatever you say." He jerked his chin toward Stefan's desk. "I left this month's dummy for you. The issue looks to be one of our best."

"Fine. I'll look at it later."

Rick nodded and then felt it necessary to remark, "Girl's got great tits," before departing, leaving an unvoiced retort on Stefan's lips while causing his reluctant gaze to drift toward that part of her anatomy, where the soft mounds pressed against the silky fabric of her pristine white blouse.

"Get a grip, man," he muttered to himself. Then he lightly slapped her cheeks. "Wake up."

She made a throaty sound and turned her face into his fingers, her lips brushing innocently across his palm. The contact gave Stefan an unexpected jolt.

He snatched his hand back as her eyelids fluttered open. She stared up at him with dewy lavender eyes that appeared surprisingly guileless. "What happened?"

"You fainted." Stefan rose abruptly from the couch, needing to put some distance between them and gather his wits.

"Oh." An embarrassed flush heated her cheeks as she sat up, her silky hair framing her jaw, making her eyes appear even larger and more luminous. Something about having those eyes focused entirely on him was a little nerve wracking.

Christ! What was the matter with him today?

Stefan turned away from her and moved to his desk, shuffling his papers and hoping she would get the hell out of his office.

"The staff meeting is tomorrow morning," he said brusquely, though why he reminded her, he didn't know. She never attended. "Eight A.M. sharp." He glanced up. "That's Eastern Time. Not South Pacific."

He expected a scathing retort to his sarcasm, especially since she had been uncharacteristically quiet this whole time. But no caustic barb was forthcoming.

She simply rose from the couch, a bit unsteadily, which concerned him when he didn't want it to, then walked across the hall to her office and closed the door, leaving Stefan with one gnawing question.

What the hell had just happened here?

Abby spent the rest of the afternoon avoiding Stefan as best she could and endeavoring to forget her humiliation over fainting in front of him. Stress, she told herself, not wanting to dwell on the incident or her reaction to Stefan, which had been acute and disturbing.

She couldn't tell him the truth about her identity in his current state. He glowered whenever he caught sight of her, which kept her a near-prisoner in Micky's office, where Abby tried futilely to get down to the business of learning about magazine publishing in all its facets. There was a lot she needed to do. She only hoped she had enough time to accomplish it all.

In an attempt to understand the reason behind Stefan's upset and why she hadn't been warned she might be walking into a war zone, Abby phoned Micky.

"Who is R. R. Donnelley & Sons?" she queried her sister.

"They're our printer," Micky replied in between sips of her wine as she lunched at one of the numerous outdoor bistros lining the Champs Élysées. "The company is spending astronomical sums on paper."

"So what did you do?"

"I protected our interests." Micky's tone clearly conveyed that she didn't appreciate having to explain herself. "I called Donnelley and told them we wanted a less-expensive paper. We don't need that heavy, high-gloss stuff. It's wasted glitz."

That answer puzzled Abby more than clarified things. "I know I'm not an expert, but I think glossy paper makes the magazine look classier, more upscale and substantial. Besides, the company is doing very well. I'm looking at the P and L right now. Profits were above average last year and we seem to be doing even better this year. So why worry about saving a few dollars on paper?"

"You've got one thing right. You're *not* an expert. So I'd appreciate it if you didn't question my decisions. *I* have been the one working there, not you."

Abby wasn't prepared to argue the point at that moment. "Fine, but shouldn't you have at least consulted Stefan? He is the publisher after all."

"We don't owe Stefan Massari, or anyone else for that matter, explanations about what we choose to do with the magazine."

Abby didn't agree with her sister, but she let the matter drop. Until she understood more about the workings of the magazine, arguing was of no use.

Besides, her stay here was only temporary, constructed to suit a single purpose. She had vowed to do what she had come to do so that she could move on. And wasn't that what she knew best? Doing what she had to do?

If only moving on could be as easy.

Three

The next morning, Abby stood in the threshold of the conference room wondering if her blouse was missing a button or if her lipstick was smeared because everyone was staring at her. She glanced at her watch. Only two minutes past eight.

She would have arrived at least ten minutes ago if her taxi hadn't gotten stuck in a bottleneck on one of those slim side streets where inconsiderate truck drivers seem inclined to double-park.

"Sorry I'm late." She hustled to the only vacant chair, gracing the gentleman beside her with a brief smile of thanks when he slid a sheaf of papers toward her that read: TODAY'S AGENDA.

Glancing up, she found Stefan scowling at her, a warning look in his eyes, which she had already grown accustomed to in such a short period.

After the fiasco the day before, Abby had decided the best course of action was to maintain her distance as Micky had suggested.

Ignoring the man, however, would be more difficult, especially dressed as he was in a stunning gray suit, pristine French-cuff shirt with gold cuff links, and a red tie that only accentuated his bronzed face and chiseled jaw.

He possessed the kind of casual elegance that most men could never hope to achieve, epitomizing both raw masculinity and the mien of a high-powered executive, although Abby could just as easily picture him gracing the pages of *Bastion* as a model or a wild adventurer base-jumping in some remote Ecuadorian jungle as she could in a boardroom.

She forced herself to look away, choosing instead to let her gaze skim over the rest of the room's occupants, perhaps searching for an ally, a friendly face, neither of which she found. Either people averted their gaze when she glanced in their direction or they regarded her with thinly veiled animosity. Why?

Like Stefan, they believed she was Micky. Abby had been so rattled that she hadn't told anyone the truth. She had thought to address the group at the end of the meeting, but now found herself curious about what had caused all this anger.

"Where were we?" Stefan asked gruffly, bringing Abby's gaze back to him. He leveled her with one more cautionary look before glancing down at the papers in front of him.

"B2B, Stef," a statuesque blonde across the table from Abby replied. The woman then turned cool, appraising green eyes in Abby's direction, regarding her for a moment before flashing her a completely ingenuous smile, one Abby remembered well from her youth.

Carol Elliot. The woman her father had left his wife for, tearing a family apart and placing a permanent wedge between Abby and her father.

Abby had never truly forgiven her father for his

callous treatment or forgotten the sting of his be-
trayal. She had simply buried what she didn't want
to face.

She wondered if coming face-to-face with Carol
was what she had feared more than her father's
ghost. Either way, she would struggle through this
newest challenge as she had all those in the past.
With a numbed heart.

Abby's attention was diverted as Stefan resumed
the topic her arrival had interrupted. "As I was saying, we all know that barely a week passes without a
press announcement heralding the intention of another company to launch a new business-to-busi-
ness eMarketplace or trading exchange.

"Often these marketplaces are industry specific
with competitors joining forces to aggregate their
purchasing power. Although increasing, they are
operating both vertically and horizontally."

Abby noted how effortlessly Stefan commanded
the room, and she suspected that same self-confidence flowed into his personal life as well.

"The level of media exposure recently witnessed
is justified by industry analysts who estimate that pro-
curement professionals buying online will rise from
around thirty-five percent today to ninety percent by
2003. I want *Bastion* to be on the cusp of that explosion. We need to get a better, more diversified niche
in the market, expand our online presence.

"Larry"—he glanced at the gentleman sitting to
the right of Abby, who had passed her the papers—
"I want you to find out more about the benefits of
eProcurement and the areas it impacts in the mar-
ketplace—cost and risk."

"Will do, boss."

Stefan then turned to an older, balding gentleman across the table from her, next to Carol. "Bill, I'd like you to get me more comprehensive and accurate data on international eCommerce."

"Right-o."

"Carol," he went on, "I want you and your marketing team to get the pivot points for an Internet strategy and forecasts, incremental revenues, low price points, and the benefits of developing market share early."

"Already on it, Stef." She graced him with a dazzling smile, her face still unlined even though Abby figured the woman must now be in her late forties.

"Good. Now let's move on to CTP."

Abby had learned the day before that CTP meant computer-to-plate and had something to do with digital ads. The previous afternoon, she had tapped into the information guru, Micky's secretary, Patty Henley, and had taken home several good resource books, as well as previous issues of *Bastion* and that month's dummy, as the preproduction issue of the magazine was called.

Stefan placed a transparency on the overhead with the heading *CTP, Past and Present.* "I'm sure you all remember that we hesitated in getting involved in this area of printing." The smile he flashed around the table was genuine and all of the twenty-odd department heads responded to it. "There were an equal number of pros and cons, but I think time has dispelled our worries on that front.

"Cost has gone down and acceptance of this new method has gone up among our advertisers. We've also demonstrated that we can produce accurate proof files by simply retraining people from film to digital. We haven't sacrificed quality, as some thought. Instead, we've gotten a sharper reproduction, which, in turn, made our advertiser happier with the end result. And for you ad folks who have a few clients who are still resisting the change, remind them of the cycle compression, which gives them extra time to submit their ads. Any questions so far?"

His gaze circled the table, but never stopped on Abby, as if to say she was excluded from the discussion. If she had understood more of what he had just said, she would have lobbed a hundred questions at him that would make him think twice about dismissing her again.

"Your turn, Rick." He gestured to the gentleman seated next to him at the head of the table, sandy blond hair, darkly tanned and almost as tall as Stefan, though not as broad.

Most of the previous day, Abby had felt Rick Faraday's eyes on her. Every time she turned around, he was there, always solicitous, but his gaze had a tendency to roam down her body, which made Abby extremely uneasy.

"I'll be brief," Rick said. "I just want to cap off the advertising portion of this meeting by making a few bullet points, things to stress to your subordinates. First, advertisers decide to buy based on overall perception, editorial fervor, past performance, new trends, value-added, and a number of assorted whims.

"Second, figures for paid circulation don't really influence advertisers. They want reader involvement, more polls, votes, charity auctions, reader-contributed articles that tell us what the consumer is thinking, what they want to see, what they're tired of seeing.

"Third, and most important, target your A-team advertisers with special research. Remember who pays our bills and treat them well. Align them as partners and not merely as someone who's selling something."

An open forum for questions followed Rick's address to the group. Abby remained quiet, trying to absorb everything, grudgingly admiring Stefan's knowledge and the way in which he shared it.

The men and women assembled regarded him with something akin to awe, which seemed at odds with the fierce man Abby had been confronted with the day before and who differed from the picture Micky had painted of him over the past few years.

Abby glanced up then and found the object of her thoughts regarding her intently as the rest of the group shot ideas and observations back and forth.

Though his look was by no means sexual, Abby felt as if the air had been pumped out of the room. He quirked a black brow and she realized she was staring. She quickly glanced away to regain her equilibrium and cover her mortification.

Stefan didn't miss the blush that chased across Micky's cheeks before she averted her gaze. He might have been flattered had he thought her response genuine rather than the result of picturing him buck naked and fucking her in some highly complicated Kama Sutra position.

The woman had a way of raping him with her

eyes. He now understood how females felt who were on the receiving end of a boss's leer. Like a sex object. But no one was groping him unless he was a willing participant, and if the other party was Michaela, then he wasn't willing.

Stefan distrusted everything about her presence in the room and wondered what she was up to, for certainly she was planning something. The girl was a born troublemaker.

Something he couldn't quite grasp nagged at him, and he found himself watching her much more than he wanted to, and in ways that were beginning to annoy him, like his occasional fascination with the way her silky pageboy cut made the ends of her hair skim over her shoulders.

His gaze narrowed suspiciously as she turned to converse with his layout manager, Larry Zelinski, when she hadn't deigned to look in the man's direction before.

Stefan suspect she was hatching a scheme to commit another faux pas with one of his staff, creating what he now referred to as the Hale Turner Syndrome, a spreading epidemic that made his employees resign, a particularly destructive disease that would continue if he didn't find a way to put a stop to it.

He remembered a particularly ugly scene a few weeks earlier when Micky had been coming on to one of the new interns, Danny Matthews. He was twenty-three years old, just out of college, tall, good-looking, and an office playboy second only to Rick.

Fresh meat to Michaela.

One morning, apparently after Michaela had

shown young Danny a wild night, he had been standing around with several of the guys in the break room doing what most kids his age do. Boasting about his latest conquest.

Stefan had been getting coffee and not paying much attention to the conversation. But a burst of laughter shifted his interest back to what was being said.

"So, Dan, was the widow as hot in bed as we've heard?"

Sounding smug, Danny replied, "Let's just say there's a reason the Navy categorized her as a friendly port."

More adolescent sniggering followed and Stefan gritted his teeth. He may not like Micky, but he wouldn't allow any woman in his office to be maligned.

When he'd turned around, intending to pull Danny aside and ream his ass out, he found Micky standing in the break room doorway, the look on her face telling Stefan she had heard everything. Her gaze zeroed in on Danny, whose face paled when he spotted her.

"Pack up your Pokemon lunch pail, you little prick. You're fired!" Then she spun on her heel and stormed away.

All hell had broken loose after that as a torrent of curses spewed from Danny's mouth. He started after Micky and Stefan had been forced to block his path.

He attempted to cajole Stefan's sympathy by using that man-who-has-woman-trouble spiel, but Stefan had no intention of intervening on his behalf. The decision had been one of the first

Michaela had made that he had actually agreed with, though he had known something like this would happen sooner or later.

"All right," he said, forcing the disastrous event from his mind, wanting to bring the meeting to a close and get the hell out of Micky's presence before the temptation to shake loose her hidden agenda overwhelmed him. "Let's move on to the dummy."

Stefan noticed the interest on her face at his announcement and he thought: *Here it comes.* This must be what she had been waiting for.

Though she did virtually nothing to assist in the production and management of the magazine, she loved having any opportunity to tear apart everyone's hard work. Normally she directed her sarcasm and criticism at him alone claiming that, as the man in charge, it was his fault whenever something went wrong.

Stefan didn't mind her tirades, as long as her hand grenades weren't lobbed at his people. Today, however, she must have fixed numerous targets in her sights to make up for lost time. His mind kicked into full alert.

Together the group leafed through the pages, discussing each facet, compliments handed out for a segment well done and general input on pieces that needed some tweaking.

All the while, Stefan waited, knowing something negative or caustic would be forthcoming from her. His gut clenched as the first remark fell from her lips, though what she said wasn't at all what he expected.

"This is really wonderful."

Stefan had never experienced a silence as complete as the one that followed those four words. If she had been looking for an effective way to shut everyone up, she had accomplished her goal.

His suspicions grew. She hated everything they did, always complaining there weren't enough male models in the ads or they were dressed too conservatively, that they should have more advertisers whose campaigns showed more skin.

But Stefan had always disliked such ads, found them exploitative and indicative of sending a mixed message or the wrong message entirely.

Micky had found that particular character trait out of date and annoying. She was fond of telling him he had to move into the new millennium.

"Sex sells, baby," was her favorite saying, a statement that seemed to be the continual refrain touted throughout the industry. But Stefan didn't intend to bend to that school of thought simply to appease someone else's ideals. As long as he ran the magazine, he would publish it his way.

"These articles are really great, too," she added then. "Very insightful. This one on Ernest Hemingway's grandson is especially good."

Stefan knew he was staring, but he couldn't seem to do much about it. She liked the Hemingway piece? Of all the things he expected her to hate, that was it.

"It's too bad there isn't a female version of *Bastion,*" she remarked with a thoughtful cant to her head. "You know, a magazine using the same principles, but geared toward women."

Her comment caught Stefan completely off

guard, setting off his internal alarms and effectively slipping under the cloak of suspended sensibility he'd been experiencing as he awaited her zinger.

Could she have somehow found out he had been talking to Janelle Harrison, CEO of *Posh* magazine? *Posh* was geared solely to the female market, but Janelle felt Stefan had ideas that would infuse new blood into the company. She had been trying to lure him away for over six months.

He had never thought about leaving *Bastion,* but since Micky had taken over, the idea had grown more appealing to Stefan. He didn't want a good magazine to go to shit just because of Micky's animosity toward him.

Besides, he admired Janelle. She was extremely savvy, as well as being a dead-on marketing whiz. And unlike Michaela, she pulled no punches. With enough capital, she could take the magazine to the top.

Stefan eyed his boss, wondering what she was up to. Her expression was surprisingly guileless.

"So what would you like to see in such a magazine?" he asked, deciding to bait the trap and see what he pulled up.

She nibbled her bottom lip, giving his question some thought. "Well," she said, "I'd like a magazine that doesn't make me feel there's something wrong with me or try to sell me things I don't need—products the magazine and the manufacturers feel I must have if I want to be the perfect woman."

Stefan noted a few female heads nodding in agreement. But what really took him aback was that she had said something that was not only insightful but valid as well.

"Anything else?" he prompted, surprised to discover he was interested in hearing her reply.

She didn't hesitate, nor did she disappoint. "I'd prefer a magazine that treats me as if I'm unique, that tells me I can wear a yellow blouse with a green skirt if I want to and won't insult me by insisting brown lipstick is in and my favorite red lipstick is out, or that I should shed those ten pounds because, really, how can I live another day without perfectly lean thighs and a butt so firm it can deflect enemy missiles?" She blinked and then flashed a chagrined smile. "Oh, boy, did I just say that?"

Something amazing happened then, a round of laughter burst forth, and as much as Stefan tried to keep the smile from his face, he couldn't.

"I can see the article heading now," Heidi Parker, assistant art director, said with amusement. "The Missile-Deflecting Butt Workout. Eight Weeks to Battle Stations!"

Another round of chuckles flew around the room, and before Stefan knew what had happened, the atmosphere had changed and people were actually responding to Micky. What's more, for the first time he could remember, he experienced something he had never felt in relation to his boss.

The faintest twinge of grudging respect.

"May I talk to you?"

Abby's attention was jerked from the notes she had taken at the staff meeting to the person now framed on the threshold of her sister's office. A leaden knot settled in the pit of her stomach as her gaze clashed with those of the last person she wanted to see.

Carol Elliot.

When they had faced each other across the conference room table, Abby had been insulated from her feelings because there had been other people around. And when she had been home tending her sick mother, thousands of miles had separated her from grim reality.

But now she had none of that. It was only she and Carol, and the memories Abby had always held so tightly inside threatened to choke her, as though she had suddenly found herself in the deep end of the pool and water was closing fast over her head.

"What is it?" she asked in a tone she had never heard from herself before, cold, remote . . . bitter.

Uninvited, Carol entered the office and shut the door behind her, and when her gaze returned to Abby, her expression held the same chill that Abby knew was reflected on her own face.

Gone was the indulgent smile Carol had mockingly bestowed on her earlier. Here was the vindictive woman Abby remembered from those few times her mother had forced her to go to New York, claiming it was important she spend time with her father. What her mother didn't know was that her father was always too busy for her.

Carol came to stand in front of her desk. Abby knew the woman didn't realize she wasn't Micky. But when had she ever taken a good look at her?

Seen the pain in her eyes? Or deigned to say she was sorry for what she had done?

A wisp of paper appeared in Carol's hand before she tossed it in front of Abby. "You haven't signed this," she said in that well-remembered cool voice, the one that always let Abby know she was a burden her father unfortunately had to tolerate.

Abby didn't need to look to know what was before her. The check for her father's yearly endowment to the Met. "You're right. I haven't signed it." Her voice hardened as she added, "Nor do I intend to."

"What do you mean? Your father donated money every year."

"My father is dead now, so I imagine he could care less about contributing to the arts." Abby paused deliberately. "Unless there's some other reason you want me to sign that check? Some personal gain? Good seats front row center, perhaps?"

Carol's lips thinned to the point of obscurity. "I want you to sign it because it's what your father would have wanted."

"Really? I would have thought if he had wanted that he would have put forth his wishes in his will."

Abby had never believed she could harbor such malice inside her, but she did—and the force of it frightened her. She wanted to lash out at Carol, fight a battle her mother had never been able to— and now never would.

She felt cheated, robbed. Wronged. The anger had festered inside her and the ugliness needed a way out before it consumed her, dragging her down into a suffocating dark place.

"You do remember my father's will, don't you? I

guess you thought for all your years of dedicate service that he would leave you something. I'm sure it must have hurt not to get a penny. But don't feel bad. Neither did his other women."

Carol's face mottled with rage. "You little *bitch!* You just can't stand the fact that your father loved me and not that ugly sow you called a mother!"

Abby rose abruptly from her chair, so fast it hit the wall behind her. Carol actually took a step back, and Abby recognized a savage satisfaction in the coldest part of her heart.

"Don't you dare talk about my mother," she said in a voice of barely suppressed fury. "You have no right to even speak her name."

"I don't even know her name!" Carol spat. "Your father never uttered it once. Mine was the only name he spoke—in and out of bed."

The invisible blow spiraled out of nowhere sending Abby reeling. She picked up the check on the desk and tore it into little pieces, letting it float through the air like confetti in a particularly ugly parade.

"You'll get nothing more from this family. Just be glad I don't fire you."

"You can't fire me," Carol sneered. "If you do, I'll slap a lawsuit on you so fast you won't know what hit you!" Then she spun on her heel. At the door, she turned. "I'd advise you to watch your back. You'll find I'm a formidable opponent. Your father made the mistake of forgetting that. I won't let that happen again."

"Are you threatening me?"

A hint of a smile curled the corners of Carol's lips, showing teeth like a baby shark. "Let's just say

I only rattle once before I strike." Then she threw open the door, leaving Abby dazed by the impact of what had just transpired.

Her heart was beating so fast, so out of control that she thought she just might die. What had she done? What could have possessed her to dredge up the past and throw it around so callously?

Her legs shaking, Abby moved to the window, hugging herself close, not understanding the monster inside her that she had just unleashed. She had never given the hurt free rein. She had always kept her emotions tightly contained.

It frightened her, this side of her that she couldn't control. It was as if she had stepped into the dreams of her youth, the only place she found surcease, where she could allow herself to scream and no one could hear her.

She shivered, wanting to hate her father for putting her through this. And she wondered why, even now when he was dead, that she continued to expect something he had never been able to give.

"Is everything all right?"

Abby tensed at the sound of Stefan's voice. She could not face him right now. She had nothing left in her, no way to fight his strange allure, no way to cover her fear. Carol had stripped her defenses and Abby needed time to find the comfort of forgetfulness, to cloak herself with the face she showed to the outside world.

"I saw Carol storm out of here," he said when Abby made no reply. "Is there a problem?"

"No."

She offered nothing more and Stefan noted the

brittle way she held herself, so tautly a strong breeze might snap her in half. He told himself to leave, that whatever rift had just fractured the ground between her and Carol was none of his business.

But instead of departing, he found himself moving across the room toward her. She stiffened when she heard him approach and he half expected her to tell him to get out, but she said nothing, and that quiet sense of desperation wrapped around him, leaving him unable to dredge up the comfortable distance he always kept squarely between them.

"Do you want to talk?"

She shook her head and turned away. He thought he had seen tears glimmering on her lashes, but that was impossible. Michaela St. James never cried. She was too hard, too impenetrable to do something entirely human as cry. Yet the possibility that she had been on the verge of weeping unsettled Stefan.

He noticed the framed photo sitting on the window ledge in front of her. He couldn't recall having seen it there before, but he recognized the face. René St. James. Her mother.

She snatched up the photo, clutching it to her chest as if it were a talisman warding off the living damned as she looked at him with eyes full of pain and reproach.

Never had Stefan felt so out of his element as he did at that moment. Conflicting emotions warred inside him as he stood before a woman he had always disliked and wondered when she had become so complex, so full of contradictions that he didn't quite know what to do. He struggled for the right words, though he had no idea what they were.

"Your mother was a very beautiful woman," he murmured, searching for the Michaela he knew within the lost lavender eyes staring at him as if he were another harm in a world full of constant threats.

"Don't." She spoke the word so softly it was almost inaudible.

What did she want from him? And why did he feel even the smallest desire to comfort her? This woman had staked herself as his enemy. She had no damn right to look this vulnerable, to turn him inside out when everything before this moment had been so cut and dry, so clearly understood.

"Fine," he replied shortly. "Forget I said anything." He turned to go, but her whispered words stopped him.

"You don't even know who I am, do you?"

Stefan stared unseeingly at the wall, telling himself to continue walking, that she was manipulating him to suit her purpose. He knew exactly who she was, and he would not fall prey to her games.

So why then did her question wrench at him? And why did it seem she was asking something different? Something that left him groping for an answer and beating himself up over an imagined disappointment.

Before he could reply, she whispered in a choked voice, "No one ever sees me," and then raced past him out of the room, leaving Stefan to rein in a strange, inexplicable urge to go after her.

Four

"What in the name of God is that racket?" Stefan demanded as he stormed out of his office, where he had been in the process of very successfully getting nothing done, as had pretty much been the case since the staff meeting a week ago.

The tension inside him had been building as he waited for Michaela to revert to form, hoping she would so that he could shake off whatever was bothering him and stop looking toward her office door and thinking about the sadness he had glimpsed in her eyes.

No one ever sees me.

When Stefan closed his eyes at night, he kept hearing those words, wondering what they meant and why he even cared.

His secretary, Gretchen, who Stefan knew could see right through him and who understood, without asking, what, or rather *who,* had caused his churlishness, glanced up at him.

"Sounds to me like someone is singing," she said.

That was what it sounded like to Stefan, and if he wasn't in such a volatile frame of mind, he might even be inclined to admit the voice wasn't all that bad.

He stalked across the hall, refusing to allow the thought to creep into his mind that he had been looking for a reason to check in on his boss.

He opened her door without knocking . . . only to stop dead in his tracks at the sight that greeted him.

Shoes that Stefan suspected had cost at least a thousand dollars were thrown negligently off to the side and an equally expensive jacket was tossed over the back of her chair, leaving her clad in a white silk blouse and a black skirt that actually went to her knees.

He glimpsed delicate headphones and a hand-held CD player, telling Stefan why she hadn't heard him enter. Her back was to him, allowing him to watch her dance unnoticed.

With all the sexual things she had done to get his attention in the past, only this remarkable and deceivingly innocent display incited his senses.

Angry with himself for enjoying the way her hips swayed, Stefan lifted his fist to pound on the already open door, but changed his mind at the last minute. Instead he propped a shoulder against the jamb, waiting as she slowly, but inevitably, gyrated in a circle.

Abby froze as soon as she spotted Stefan lounging in the doorway, his casual pose conveying he had been there long enough to witness her way of relaxing.

She struggled to regain her composure, hating how unnerved she became in his presence. As much as she wanted to deny it, he frightened her. He was physically intimidating, and even though she knew they were in the office, knew she was safe, some demons were hard to shake.

She had yet to confess her true identity. Under her guise, she felt untouchable, locked securely behind a wall of anonymity where no one could find her, and if she remained hidden, then no one would see through to her cowardice.

And perhaps deep down she had begun to hope that by staying in Micky's apartment and wearing Micky's clothes and sitting behind Micky's desk that some of her sister's self-confidence and strength and fearlessness might rub off on her.

Now, looking at Stefan, her emotions wrenched in an inescapable tangle, Abby understood there were places she would always fear to tread. Dark, dangerous places that existed in a man who both frightened and fascinated her.

Her hands trembling slightly, she removed the headphones. "Was there something you wanted?" she asked, feeling as though she were a thousand little pieces that couldn't find a connection.

"You're wearing pantyhose."

The remark came out of nowhere and made Abby acutely aware of her body—and the intense focus of Stefan's regard. His gaze drifted over her with interest, something disturbing and forbidden flickering in his gaze. She told herself that he wasn't seeing her. He was seeing Micky.

"You seemed to have a problem with it."

"Since when has my having a problem with anything ever mattered to you before?"

"Are you looking for an argument?" Abby prayed

he wasn't. She didn't know if she could endure another bout of his temper.

"I don't know what I'm looking for," he replied in a muted voice, leaving Abby faintly puzzled, and wondering if he could tell she felt the same way. "I see you're having lunch."

She glanced at the sandwich on her desk and then back to him, asking hesitantly, "Would you like some?"

Stefan halted in the process of berating himself for whatever imbecility had keep his feet rooted to the floor instead of decamping as soon as the problem had been rectified. Now, at least, he had an excuse for his inability to move.

Her offer.

Would he like some? Why? Had she poisoned it? There could be no other explanation, and he had no intention of believing her friendly gesture was genuine. Such a mistake would only serve to make him look like a bigger fool than she already mistook him for—right before an ambulance transported him to the hospital to have his stomach pumped.

"Thanks. I'll pass."

She nodded and moved behind her desk, still in her stockinged feet. She regarded the sandwich dubiously before taking a tentative bite.

She hazarded a glance in his direction, saw him still there and looked away, leaving Stefan to wonder why he had yet to turn on his heel and depart. She had stopped singing and all was quiet once more. So why the hell was he still leaning against the door frame as if the entire building would cave in should he leave his post?

God if he knew.

Everything about her suddenly seemed new, fresh. Had he never seen her eat a sandwich before? Then again, when had he ever given a damn? She could have inhaled tacks for all he cared.

His thoughts were diverted when he spotted a drop of mayonnaise dotting her upper lip. She appeared to have no idea it was there but its presence was driving him mad. He wished she would lick it away.

He managed to count to six before his control broke.

Then he strode over to the desk and swiped his thumb over her top lip, removing the offending condiment—and revealing a tiny black mole that captured his attention.

Shaken by his interest in that small beauty mark, he took a swift step back, absently rubbing his mayonnaised thumb across his forefinger.

"You had something . . ." He scowled, angry with himself for behaving like a bumbling idiot because of a tiny black dot.

Christ, he had to get the fuck out.

Swinging on his heel, he stalked to the door. On the threshold, he turned and growled, "Whatever game you're playing, St. James, it's a dangerous one."

Then he disappeared, missing the shaken look on Abby's face caused when he had abruptly touched her.

"You look like crap, my dear."

Abby glanced up from juggling the apartment

keys and a bag of groceries to see Ida Gelman standing in the hallway adorned in her signature multicolor robe, clutching a cigarette in one hand and a glass of gin in the other.

Abby had met Ida the night she had returned from her first disastrous day at *Bastion*. Ida had been chasing a ferret down the marble-lined hall-way.

"Come back here you little rat bastard!" she was bellowing when Abby stepped off the elevator, her stunned gaze following the path of a beribboned ferret as it scurried between her legs, its owner barreling toward her, garbed in fluffy slippers, an outrageously colored kimono, and sporting a green facial mask.

Abby had caught the escaping animal before it climbed aboard the elevator, which earned her Ida's not-easily-expressed gratitude and a friend Abby hadn't expected but who was welcome nonetheless.

Since Pisser's capture, Ida had been a fixture in Abby's life. Bold, blunt, and brassy, Ida cursed with a fluency that bespoke of her upbringing in a mixed neighborhood on the Lower East Side, though she learned to curb her tendencies long enough to catch the eye of a wealthy land developer who lavished her with all the things money could buy.

Addicted to tobacco, she had a smoker's voice, deep and craggy, which made her sound like she gargled her words through a long funnel. She was also the gossip of the building and had already filled Abby in on every tenant on their floor.

"Apartment C is Jerry Kessler—notorious F.A.G.
Apartment F we have Harold and Maude Toller.
Swingers. Watch out for Harold. The man is all
hands. Apartment D is the British ambassador
Jonathan Stewart and his wife, Margaret, who both
possess enough snotty wherewithal to think everyone is beneath them. Their daughter, Jessica is a
lesbian—and you are just her type. And in apartment B we have the playboy, Brett Cullman. Aim-
less ne'er do well of monied parents." Then Ida
leaned closer and said in a muted voice, even
though they were alone in the hallway, "And whatever you do, keep far away from apartment H."

"Why?"

"That's our hermit, Stanley Fisher. One of these
days we'll be hearing about him on the news saying
he went berserk and shot up a local MacDonald's
or that he dropped a brick out his window onto
someone's head or that he was a serial killer."

From that moment on, Ida had taken her under
her wing, clucking over the way Abby ate, saying she
was too skinny, that chicken soup could cure any
ailment, that she needed to get out more, and was
she interested in a nice Jewish boy?

Ida was the only person who knew Abby's real
identity even though Abby hadn't said a thing.

"How did you know?" Abby had asked her.

"Your aura, darling. Your sister's is a rather unpleasant shade of blue bordering on the black,
while yours is a pale pink." Then she took a long
drag of her cigarette and blew a billowing ring. "Besides, your sister would never have worn those
shoes with that suit."

Smiling in remembrance, Abby turned now to greet Ida, the usual cloud of smoke following in her neighbor's wake. Ida eyed her for a long moment before commenting far too astutely, "Is that luscious morsel giving you trouble again, dear?"

Abby didn't need to ask who Ida referred to. Stefan. Abby had confided the trouble she had been going through with him and Ida felt it her duty to ask that same question every night.

Abby suspected that if she came home looking a bit less frazzled, Ida might not be inclined to inquire. But Stefan did frazzle her, and on more than one level.

Abby averted her gaze and opened the apartment door. "Nothing I can't handle, Ida."

Ida followed her inside and closed the door. "You still haven't told him you're not Micky." It was a statement not a question.

Abby set her groceries on the marble island in the kitchen and stared at the bag, feeling a headache begin to build behind her eyes. It seemed each day the pain was a little worse, a little longer. Stress, she told herself again. Memories. Carol Elliot.

Stefan.

"He wouldn't care either way." He treated her as if he saw the ruination of mankind etched on her forehead. Abby knew it was better that way. Maintained the barriers.

"He must be blind if he can't tell. You're not at all like your sister. You're a stunning woman and any man would have a hard time overlooking you."

Abby began to pluck items from her grocery bag. "That's very nice of you to say."

"You should know by now that I do not say things to be nice. Frankly, I detest the word." Ida placed her hand over Abby's as she laid a tomato down on the counter. Veins stood out beneath Ida's thin skin and dark spots warred with diamonds for attention. She waited until Abby glanced up to ask, "What are you afraid of, my girl?"

"Nothing," Abby replied a bit too quickly.

"Come. Sit down." Ida dragged her over to the glass kitchen table and pushed Abby into a seat. Then she took hold of both of Abby's hands, turning them palms up.

"What are you doing?"

"Trying to understand you. I'm a bit of a mystic, you see. I had to find something to do with myself after my darling Bernard died."

"How about a job?"

Ida slanted a thinning gray brow. "Are you offering?"

Abby doubted there were any jobs at *Bastion* that would fit Ida's unique personality.

Ida gave her a good-natured smile. "I didn't think so." Then she wrapped her hand around a clear, sparkling stone hanging from one of her necklaces; a huge gem that caught all the light and that Abby thought might be a diamond. "It's a crystal," Ida said, as if reading her mind. "It brings inner peace and divine harmony."

Ida took a few deep breaths, slowly in and out. "I'm feeling centered now. Open. The vibrations are strong. I'm sensing that someone's karma is not in tune with the universe." She proceeded to study Abby's palms, nodding her head and mixing in an occasional *hmm*. "You're clearly troubled. Many things weigh heavily upon your mind."

She peered at Abby through a thick coating of black mascara. "You harbor some deep resentments and there is a pain that holds you in its grip." A worried frown creased Ida's already wrinkled brow. "What is it about this pain, Abby, that haunts you so? Can you tell me about it?"

Abby felt her throat close, no words would come. She shook her head and tried to pull her hands away, but Ida wouldn't relinquish her hold.

"You've come to New York for more than one reason," Ida continued, trying to read something on Abby's face, something Abby didn't want her to see.

"You can't have read all that in my palm." Abby attempted to sound light, but heard the note of desperation in her voice.

"I didn't. I see it in your eyes. You know you can talk to me, don't you?"

Abby nodded, hoping Ida would drop the subject.

Ida hesitated and then released Abby's hands. But her neighbor wasn't through with her yet. "So do you like him?" she asked, switching subjects with mind-boggling ease.

Abby sagged back in the chair and pretended she didn't know who Ida was speaking about. "Him who?"

Ida wasn't fooled by her act. "That luscious hunk of an Italian you work with, of course. If I were ten years younger, I'd take a crack at him. I imagine he's a superlative lover. Gentle, thorough . . . well-endowed."

Heat scorched Abby's cheeks at the vision Ida's words evoked and she quickly rose from the table, not wanting her friend to see her reaction.

"I was going to make a salad," she said. "Would you like some?"

"Healthy food gives me gas, but I'll take a refill on the gin."

Abby poured Ida another glass, then went about distracting herself by preparing her food and listening to Ida regale her with stories of her son and daughter and her last trip to Israel.

By the time Ida was on her fourth gin and Abby had finished her salad and was sipping a glass of white wine, Ida had returned to the topic of Stefan.

"You must admit, the man is gorgeous. I don't think I've ever met a male with that much magnetic pull. Must be pure testosterone in his veins."

"You've met him?"

"Once, a number of years ago when my darling Bernard was still alive. He was having dinner with your father at the Oak Room and your father invited us to join them. Lowery and Bernard had a few business dealings over the years, you see. Anyway, every female eye in the room was riveted to the man—even mine." She winked. "Can't believe a woman hasn't snatched that boy up. Guess he hasn't met the right lady yet."

"I guess not." Abby didn't want to think about Stefan or his magnetic pull, which she felt every time he glanced in her direction. She was afraid of him, yet lured to him at the same time.

"Why don't you put yourself out there and see what happens?" Ida then said.

"Put myself out where?"

"In front of the boy."

The boy. How far from accurate that was. "I'm in front of him all the time."

"Ah, but you probably haven't sent any signals."

"Signals?"

"You're such an innocent. Perhaps that's why I like you so. Life has yet to jade you."

Abby choked back a bitter laugh. Life had jaded her in many other ways, but she could not bring herself to dispel Ida's illusion. "I think you're missing something, Ida."

"And what's that?"

"He doesn't like me."

Ida's laugh was deep and full-throated. "With that magnificent face, exotic eyes and fabulous bosoms you have? Impossible! How big is your waist, my girl? Twenty inches? Twenty-two? What man would not want to wrap his big hands around that? Signals, dear heart. You're not sending signals. The first time you bat your lashes the man will be hard as a stone."

Heat suffused Abby's cheeks, and she wanted to plug her ears, to blot out Ida's words, to eradicate the images they evoked, and the shame of emotions that were so natural to other women, but which carried pain for her.

"Imagine that body in bed next to you, encompassing you, wrapping you in all that heat. I can picture him in a skimpy loincloth, a little oil on that huge chest, standing in a grotto, beckoning me with one finger. If only my heart was stronger." She sighed.

Abby tried not to squirm in her chair as Ida painted vivid pictures of Stefan, visions that had come to Abby in her dreams with increasing frequency since she had arrived in New York, sometimes dispelling her nightmares.

She gazed out the window into the dark night. "I doubt he's lonely for company, Ida." Abby had seen the way the women in the office looked at him, with hungry eyes. Perhaps had she seen her own expression, she might have noticed the same thing.

"Oh, I don't doubt the boy gets propositioned, but from what I remember, he had a great deal of character. I don't think he jumps at every piece of fluff that wiggles her tush in front of him. But you, my girl, are far more than fluff. Why not give it a try? What's there to lose?"

There was so much to lose that Abby felt on the precipice of a yawning black chasm.

"Are you still a virgin?" Ida asked then.

Abby recoiled from the question, a black-and-white flash of memory searing her brain like a burning strobe light, threatening to release the specters of her past that always stalked at the periphery of her mind.

"Ida . . ." The word came out a plea, but either it was not heard or was ignored.

"Certainly a girl your age has been made love to?"

The question unlocked a floodgate, a door Abby had kept bolted for many years, a memory she had told herself was only a nightmare and had never truly happened.

But it had . . . Oh God, it had.

It was six years ago. She had been a sophomore at Idaho State. Jimmy Bodine was a senior and the school's star quarterback.

He had come upon her late one night in the school's nearly deserted parking lot. Suddenly and without warning, he'd slammed her car door shut as Abby was about to get in.

She'd swung around to find herself trapped between his two mammoth arms. "What are you doing, Jimmy?"

His gaze raked her in a way that made her insides grow cold. "I see you lookin' at me when I'm on the field."

Abby had watched him a few times while he was at practice. She had always sat far up in the bleachers hoping not to be noticed. He was so tall and broad, his black hair sweeping his shoulders, his face bronzed by the sun, and eyes so dark they were nearly as black as his hair.

She had been so lonely, so full of despair that she had substituted Jimmy in her dreams, unable to have the man who truly wreaked havoc during her sleep, in those long hours after midnight when nothing else battled for her time.

"I . . . I wasn't watching you. I was watching the game."

"Bullshit." He leaned closer. "Everyone knows you're hot for me . . . the sweet, untouchable ice princess. Won't let anyone get between her thighs." He took a length of her hair between his fingers. "But you'll let me, won't you, baby? You know I'll give it to you good."

Abby's throat dried, her heart beating in dull, thick strokes. "No . . . I . . . I just wanted to be your friend."

He laughed, a booming, dark, horrible laugh that chilled her. "Friends? Oh, no, princess. We'll be more than friends." He grabbed a fistful of her hair and yanked her forward. "Much more."

Then his mouth smashed down on hers, cutting off her cries as he ground his pelvis against her, jamming her back against the door handle. She tried to shove him away, but he was too big, too strong. Her hands pressed against his chest, but she couldn't budge him. She raked her nails down his neck.

"Bitch!" he exploded, grabbing hold of her wrists in one hand and slamming her back over the hood of the car.

"Jimmy, don't!" she pleaded.

"Shut up!" he hissed, meaty fingers curling around the top of her blouse and tearing it down the front. Then he plunged his hand beneath her cotton bra. "Oh, yeah," he groaned.

Shoving her thighs apart, he pulled her forward against the hard bulge in his pants. Abby felt as if she stood outside herself as his head dropped forward and his mouth latched on to her nipple.

He jammed a hand beneath her skirt and grabbed her panties, yanking them down. Then he shoved her skirt up to her waist, and in the next instant, he stuck his finger inside her.

Abby screamed and he clamped his hand over her mouth. "Make another sound and you'll be sorry." He pressed farther inside her. "Damn, you're dry as dirt," he growled. Then a cruel smile curled his lips. "Don't worry. I've got something that'll get you wet." Then he unzipped his jeans and stroked himself. "Like what you see?"

Abby's head rocked back and forth on the hood of the car as tears poured down her face. "Jimmy," she choked out between sobs, "please don't. *Please.*"

He ignored her, holding her wrists tightly above her head with one large hand while he positioned his erection between her thighs, pushing against her, paying no heed to her cries.

"Hey!" a voice called out then, coming from some distance away. "Hey, what's going on over there?"

"Shit," Jimmy swore, low and fierce. "Fuckin' security guard." But he didn't let her go immediately. Instead, he licked a wet path up her throat and put his mouth next to her ear, his breath hot and smelling of beer. "Say one word about this and you'll be sorry, princess. It'll be your word against mine, and they'll never believe you. I'm a god in this school." His laughter was dark and dirty as he flicked his tongue over her nipple, making Abby draw further inside herself. "Until next time." Then he'd disappeared into the darkness.

Abby never said a word. She was too ashamed, too full of guilt, believing she had done something wrong to warrant the attack, even though deep down she knew she hadn't.

Nearly four years passed before she felt strong enough to go out with a man. Brian was a teacher at the elementary school where she had worked part time, unable to put in more hours as she needed to be home to take care of her mother. He was reserved, gentle, and not physically intimidating. Big men scared Abby, reminded her of how little control she'd had that night against Jimmy.

She and Brian had dated for almost a year, but Abby had never allowed things to get serious, for the intimacy to progress. Two months before she came to New York, she had broken the relationship off, knowing there was no future for them. She was defective, hollow. Something was missing—and he deserved better.

Until she had seen Stefan again, she didn't believe a man would ever have the power to move her, to make her wish she wasn't broken or wonder what it would be like to let herself go, just once.

To be free while there was still time.

Five

"God damn you!"

The booming voice startled Abby, causing her to drop the watering can she was using on the plants she had brought into the office.

She whirled around to find Stefan looming in the threshold. The breath hitched in her throat as she saw the rage on his face, eyes dark and violent, his expression utterly devoid of human civility. Never had she seen him look like this, not even on that first day when he had taken her to task for Micky's interference with Donnelley.

The door closed behind him with a deceptively soft click.

He stalked toward her and Abby's palms began to sweat, thoughts of fleeing tumbling wildly through her mind. Her gaze flew to the door. But Stefan stood squarely between her and freedom.

When he stopped before her, barely a foot of space remained between them. Abby pressed back against the filing cabinets, her mind flashing images of Jimmy Bodine even as she tried to tamp the horrible memories down, a litany repeating in her head. This was not college or a dark parking lot.

She was not helpless. Stefan was not Jimmy. He would not hurt her. He wouldn't.

But in the face of his towering presence, those things were so hard to remember.

"You did it again, you little . . ." He clamped his mouth shut, a muscle working in his jaw as his fought for some semblance of control. "Christ, every fucking time I let myself believe you'll behave yourself, that you won't cause any more trouble—that perhaps you've changed—you make me look like a giant asshole. Why can't you let it rest?"

Abby's chest ached with the strain of having to hold the fear inside. "What did I do?"

"You know damn well what you did," he answered tightly, his words edged with rage. "You interfered with Handover."

"Handover?" Abby had never heard the name before. Then it dawned on her. Micky must have done something else. "I didn't do anything."

"Don't lie to me! You called him and told him that you wanted him to cut our rates by five percent for *Bastion*'s distribution in the front-line racks. God, I can't believe you! Don't you friggin' understand? We have contracts! The world doesn't bend just because your spoiled ass wants it to. There are rules! I warned you not to do this again. I goddamn warned you!"

"But I didn't—"

"You won't walk all over me, princess."

"Don't call me that!"

"I'm not one of your husbands."

"I told you, I didn't do it!"

He ignored her. "You keep yanking my chain and

expect me to take the abuse. I'm tired of your spiteful shit! Are you that horny that you can't find another man whose balls you can bust?"

"I'm not—"

"Come off it!" He slammed the palm of his hand into the file cabinet behind her.

Abby jumped.

A quick knock sounded at her office door before it opened. Patty stuck her head in. "Is everything all right?"

"Fine," Stefan ground out, not bothering to look at Patty.

Abby's gaze locked with the brown eyes of the only ally she had in the office, wanting to beseech Patty not to go, yet she couldn't bear for the girl to see her cowardice.

"Everything's fine," Abby told her, even as she ached to take the words back. "Thank you."

Patty hesitated, then nodded and shut the door.

Stefan raked a hand through his hair. "Damn," he growled under his breath, drawing Abby's attention back to him, making her acutely aware of how close he stood to her. "I didn't mean . . ." He shook his head. "Christ, you make me nuts."

Abby fought the urge to slide her back along the file cabinets and get away from his overwhelming nearness. He was too close, too big, too frightening in his current state.

She tried to inch away, but his large hand clamped around her upper arm. "I'm not through with you yet."

Though his hold was not punishing, Abby jerked

from the touch. "Don't." The fear began to rise within her again, threatening to choke her. "Please."

He gave a harsh bark of laugher. "Jesus, that's a new one. You've been trying to get me to touch you since the moment I walked through *Bastion*'s front door. Now you're going to act like Pollyanna? What game are you playing?"

Abby shook her head because no words would come. She didn't move any farther, but when he closed the small gap between them, she felt herself shrinking back and hating herself for it.

She forced herself to breathe. "What do you want?"

"What do I want?" Christ, how much plainer did he have to be?

Stefan wanted to rattle some answers out of her, but she stared at him as if he scared the shit out of her. And damn it all if he didn't believe he did. Ever since her return, she had been turning him inside out, making him want to throttle her one minute and soothe whatever the hell plagued her the next.

When he wasn't careful, he could almost believe she was truly as vulnerable as she looked, and that maybe he understood what she meant when she had said that no one ever saw her.

Prior to her father's death, she had taunted and teased him in small ways, nothing too overt, too much at risk should Lowery get wind of her behavior. Not that Lowery was a shining example of morality. But he ran his business with a firm hand and would tolerate no one, not even his own daughter, fucking with it.

After Lowery's death, however, the kid gloves had

come off and Stefan had not only seen more of Michaela than he cared to, but he also thought he knew the kind of woman she was—the kind he stayed the hell away from.

But the past few weeks, he had glimpsed another side of her, full of contradictions and uncertainty and a painful vulnerability that nagged at him like a constant toothache.

Vulnerable women had always drawn out his protective instincts. He wanted to help, to be some kind of stupid knight-errant and fix what was broken. But rarely did he get further involved. Rarely did he think about letting his lips and body soothe the hurt.

But he did now. God, he did now.

The way those violet eyes regarded him, asking him to keep his distance, yet seeming to beckon him closer were nearly his undoing.

Satisfaction's the name of the game.

Rick's words came back to haunt Stefan, and for a brief moment, the thought of giving in to Michaela's desires danced through his brain.

He couldn't deny she was a riveting woman, possessing the kind of beauty that made other women not only uninteresting but irrelevant, her body infused with an electric vitality that was hard to ignore. She had a way of fully occupying the space in which she moved.

Christ, have you lost your mind?

The last person Stefan intended to satisfy was Michaela St. James. Her attractiveness did not make up for the fact that she believed ordinary rules didn't apply to her and that walking over people was acceptable.

But why couldn't he find that woman in the eyes staring so hauntingly into his at that moment? And why couldn't he stop himself from moving toward her, closer, until barely a breeze could blow between their bodies.

"Please," she whispered. The word was a raw plea, but for what, Stefan didn't know.

"I don't like what you did." He pinioned his hands on both sides of her head, his gaze dropping to her lips. Soft pants issued from her lush mouth, and then a slight whimper as he edged closer.

"I promise I won't do it again."

She made promises after she had vowed she hadn't done anything. He knew she had, and now her words only confirmed it. But suddenly the problems with Handover no longer seemed quite so important.

"Prove it," he challenged, even as he wondered what he was doing.

She shook her head and put her hands against his chest. "No."

Stefan barely felt the pressure she exerted, so absorbed was he in that sweet black mole above her lip, a spot he'd been fantasizing about in his dreams, envisioning his tongue sweeping over it, then pressing his lips to it, before slipping his mouth over hers.

Before he realized his intention, the fantasy became reality. His head dipped and he touched her there.

"No," she whimpered, turning her head away, only for him to capture the sound in his mouth.

Stefan groaned at the first taste of her lips and

the press of her breasts crushed against his chest. He skimmed a hand down her waist to cup the sweet curve of her buttocks, pulling her tighter against him, a fist of desire slamming into his gut with the impact of a ninety-mile-an-hour fastball.

It took his hazy brain a moment to realize that she was not moaning with the same passion he felt . . . she was crying.

Stefan jerked back, the blood draining from his face as he looked into her anguished eyes. "Oh, Christ . . . oh, Jesus Christ." Her small body was wracked with silent sobs. He tried to pull her close to comfort her, but she fought him. "Ssh, *cara mia,*" he said softly, wiping a hot tear from her cheek and hating himself when she flinched from the contact. "Don't . . . please don't."

"Get out," she wept.

He deserved her scorn. No matter what she had done to him, the pushing, the prodding, the constant warring . . . none of it compared to his taking something she had not offered.

"Forgive me," he whispered before turning and leaving.

Stefan stared absently out his office window, a photo clutched in his hand, a face in his mind's eye that was still as young and beautiful today as it had been five years ago, a face that had never looked the same even after the bruises and scars had healed from the vicious beating it had sustained.

His hand unsteady, Stefan lifted the photo and held it against the glass, the pain that sluiced through him as strong at that moment as it had been the day his sister, Maria, had died.

Emotions wrapped around Stefan's throat, threatening to choke him, and he thought, as he had so many times before, that he should have protected her better, that somehow he had failed her.

But how could he have known she would be savagely raped in Central Park? How could he have changed what happened? Yet no matter how many times he told himself he was blameless, the impotent rage continued to fester inside him.

He remembered his sister's excitement the summer she turned eighteen, about to start her first year of college. Never had Stefan felt prouder of any of his accomplishments than being able to afford to put his sister through school so she wouldn't have to scrape and struggle the way he had.

He didn't blame his parents for being poor. They had done everything in their power to provide for their children, and Stefan had wanted to do something in return. If his parents wouldn't accept any money from him, then he could at least help his siblings.

Four years Maria had been dead. The shame left in the wake of her brutalizing attack had sent her spiraling further and further into despair until living was too painful and she took her own life.

God, how he missed her. Some memories were so vivid, so fresh, as if there had never been a passing of time. What he remembered the most about her was how beautiful her hair had been, long and thick and black, hanging to the middle of her back.

Their mother would braid it into a thick rope when it became too unruly, and he used to yank it just to annoy her when they were kids.

Joey Canto, his old childhood friend, had told him that he would marry Maria someday and forbid her to cut her hair, even though if he had made that demand to Maria's face she would have clocked him in the jaw.

The fucking bastard who had raped and sodomized her had chopped her hair off, hacked it into ragged sections, and then, as if he hadn't done enough, he'd slashed her throat and left her for dead.

When they captured the prick a month later, Maria was told she would have to testify against him, that she'd have to sit in front of the man who had taken her innocence, her hopes, her dreams, and tell the world what he had done to her—in detail.

The day before the trial, eight months after the attack, Maria slit her wrists in the bathroom of her college dorm—and the man who had victimized her managed to plea-bargain his sentenced down to three years for what he had done. Three fucking years!

Stefan had received a month in jail for vaulting over the barrier separating the courthouse observers and the defendant and breaking the son of a bitch's jaw before the police had hauled him away. Stefan only wished he had killed the piece of shit. For his sister's honor, he would have done it.

So what would Maria think of him now, after the way he had acted with Michaela? After his lust had gotten the better of him, a lust that had never come over him with such force, and never with Michaela. Christ, he didn't even like her! Or at least he hadn't felt anything remotely resembling interest until these past few weeks.

Why had she done it? Why had she called Handover? And why did the realization that she had taken another backhanded swipe at him hurt him more than make him angry?

But even more confusing was what happened the day after their encounter. Handover had called and told Stefan that Michaela had phoned and explained her mistake, saying that her actions had been prompted by a misunderstanding on her part and that she was sorry for having caused any trouble.

Sorry. Michaela had apologized. If that wasn't a shot out of the dark. First she had instigated the problem and then fixed it, leaving Stefan more baffled and guilt-ridden than he already felt. What would make her do such a thing? The woman had never apologized for anything.

"Stefan?"

Jerked from his thoughts, Stefan swung around, not realizing how forbidding he looked as he faced Michaela's secretary, Patty Henley, who stood in the open doorway regarding him tentatively.

"Sorry to disturb you," she said. "Maybe I should come back later?"

"No. Now is fine." Stefan forced back thoughts of his sister, put the memories away until something else triggered them, as life so often did. He pocketed Maria's photo, laying his hand over it for a moment before walking back to his desk and sitting down on the corner. "Shoot."

Hesitantly, Patty stepped into his office, a small linen-colored envelope in her hand. She held it out to him, and for some inexplicable reason, Stefan thought it was a note from Michaela, finally telling him what she thought of his shitty behavior. He had been expecting some kind of blast, had hoped for it. What he had received instead was silence, three days of her absence from the office with the excuse of sickness.

Stefan turned the envelope over in his hands. "What's this?"

"An invitation to my wedding. I would have mailed it to you, but . . ." She paused, her expression chagrined.

"But you didn't think I'd be interested in coming."

"I know how busy you are," she rushed out, "and I didn't want you to feel obligated."

"You know I would never feel that way." Instead he would have felt the way he always did at weddings. A keen sense of exclusion, as if a wife and children and backyard barbecues belonged to a different realm, one he would never be a part of.

"I know you wouldn't have," she said, looking apologetic. "And I realized I would have felt horrible if I hadn't invited you. If you decide to come, you can bring a date—if you want to," she quickly added, coloring slightly.

A date. The last female Stefan had been with in a fashion that remotely resembled a date was Janelle Harrison. He'd had a drink with her a month earlier, and that was simply to discuss business, although Stefan had gotten the impression it could have been more if that was what he had wanted.

Janelle was a beautiful woman, sexy, genuine, and he had felt a certain amount of attraction to her. But something had been missing. He imagined another man wouldn't have passed up the opportunity, certainly not Faraday. But Stefan wasn't Rick. He didn't work that way. Never had.

Perhaps his reluctance stemmed from his desire to be more than another good time. He'd had plenty of those wild, reckless nights in his youth. Now he wanted a woman who needed him—and Janelle wouldn't, not in that way, not to fix a plumbing leak, not to mow a lawn, not even for a shoulder to cry on if she was having a bad day. Fact was, Stefan wanted a woman who wasn't so perfect.

He glanced up and smiled at Patty. "I'd love to come," he said, hoping his lie wasn't obvious.

"Wonderful! I'll put you down for two people just in case you want to bring someone."

He wouldn't. "All right."

"Great." She turned to go.

For some reason Stefan couldn't quite fathom, he stopped Patty with a question he had wanted to ask for three days. "Have you heard from Michaela?"

Since the incident in her office, she had not come into work, claiming illness. Stefan had a different theory. Avoidance. Could he blame her?

"Yes, I heard from her" Patty replied. "Just a short while ago."

"How's she feeling?"

"Better, I think. Though I don't really know what's ailing her."

Stefan did. Him. "Did she give you any indication as to when she'd be back?"

"No. But every day she's asked me to send work home to her."

She did? That was news to Stefan, and a facet of his boss he couldn't gauge. Before her trip to Europe, she had barely worked while in the office, let alone brought anything home. At least as far as he knew.

"I hope you haven't been using your personal time to take stuff to Michaela?" That wouldn't surprise him. Michaela rarely concerned herself with how something she wanted affected anyone else.

"Oh, no." Patty shook her head. "I offered, but she declined, so I've been using a messenger." When he fell silent, she prompted, "Is that all?"

"Huh? Oh." Stefan nodded. She turned to leave, but before she got to the door, he stopped her again. "Are you sending something home to her tonight?"

"Yes, I'm getting a box together now. I plan to include a wedding invitation for her as well. I didn't know she would be back from Europe so soon, so I hadn't sent her one either."

A hint of a blush reappeared at her admission, telling Stefan that she had left both of them off her list, most likely with good reason. He couldn't blame her. He and Michaela were warring factions most of the time and he sincerely doubted Patty wanted her wedding ruined.

"Would you bring the box in here when you're finished?" he asked. "I have a few things to add to it. I'll call the messenger service when I'm through. Is it the same place we always use?"

She nodded. "Ask for Mark."

"Fine. I'll do that. Thanks."

Once Patty was gone, Stefan stared at his closed office door and wondered what the hell he was thinking about doing.

She had a Peeping Tom.

At first, Abby thought she had been mistaken as she looked through her sister's telescope, assuming the device was there so that Micky could enjoy the Manhattan skyline since her apartment was situated on the sixtieth floor of Trump Towers.

Abby had paid the telescope scant attention, tired as she was each night after returning from work, barely managing to eat before falling into bed. But after several days of inactivity, she had become restless, and as she waited for the messenger who would deliver the items she had requested from Patty, Abby had decided to put an eye to the lens.

A mistake.

She gnawed her lower lip, debating what she should do next. Perhaps her eyes had deceived her? The room she had viewed had been steeped in shadows, after all. And certainly no one would be so brazen as to stare into her apartment knowing she was there.

Abby decided to put her speculation to rest, hazarding another glance through the telescope to see if the man in the building across the street was still staring at her through his telescope.

He was.

She frowned. Now that he had been caught red-handed, why didn't he stop looking?

Abby stepped away from the telescope, rubbing her arms to chase away the chill brought on by this new development. She decided there was only one thing she could do. Cover the windows, as they were without curtains. The task would keep her mind and hands occupied while she waited for the messenger. But what could she use as a drape? The windows were large and would require a lot of material.

She headed down the hallway in search of something she could use and found a linen closet stuffed with fancy Egyptian cotton sheets. A twinge of conscience caused her to hesitate, knowing how costly they were. But aside from calling in an interior decorator, what other choice did she have?

Before she changed her mind, she scooped the sheets from the closet and went in search of a stapler. When she had at last dug up the elusive stapler, she returned to the living room with her supplies.

In the kitchen, the microwave chimed three times, telling her the water for her tea was ready. She let the tea bag steep for a minute and then grabbed the milk carton from the fridge.

She was just pouring the milk, when a black blur hurtled at her head. She let out a quick scream, her cup overturning and the milk container bouncing against the counter, sending a plume of liquid spewing all over her shirt.

She turned narrowed eyes to the cause of the turmoil. Micky's Persian cat, Sheba.

The feline perched daintily on the granite

counter regarding Abby with mocking eyes while
licking one perfectly coifed paw.

"Bad cat," Abby scolded, which earned her the
cat's equivalent of cold disdain.

Abby couldn't figure out why the cat disliked her
so. Sheba had been menacing her since the first
moment Abby walked through her sister's front
door to discover the pampered feline hissing at her
from the top of a headless sculpture of Eros.

With a sigh, Abby snatched up a kitchen towel
and wiped off her face. Then she surveyed the dripping mess around her before dropping to her
knees to clean up.

Once she was finished, she realized she was
clammy. She frowned down at her wet shirt, the
only one that wasn't in the wash. Well, she could
grab something from Micky's drawer.

Hastening to the bedroom, Abby rifled around in
Micky's bureau for a T-shirt, which turned out to be
a difficult task, considering her sister's attire tended
to be expensive and skintight.

Abby lifted out a see-through red teddy. Her
cheeks grew hot just looking at it. And yet, in a
small part of her mind, she wondered what it would
be like to feel free enough to wear such a thing, to
want a man to look at her body, to know desire
without thinking she invited abuse.

Hesitantly, Abby held the lingerie in front of her,
trying to picture herself in something so daring,
so provocative, baring a hint of her nipples, the
faint curve of her breasts, the nest of curls between
her thighs.

She caught her reflection in the mirror and

hated herself, her thoughts, the needs that pounded away inside her. She quickly thrust the teddy in the drawer and forced the images from her mind as she resumed her search for a T-shirt.

Finally, she dug one up at the bottom of the last drawer. Hastily, she donned it and then returned to the living room where she eyed the black dining room chair with the fancy white damask cushion dubiously. The furniture possessed that fragile appearance of the fashionably expensive, meant to be admired but not sat on. But unless she suddenly had a growth spurt, she had little choice.

Climbing up on the chair, she began stapling the sheets in place. She got two windows done and dragged the chair to the third, where the telescope was situated. She intended to move it, but decided to take another peek across the street, hoping the man had gotten the hint.

What she saw made her gasp in horror, the blood draining from her face as the man unzipped his fly and delved a hand inside to stroke himself.

The sight sent a shock wave through her body and her mind rebelled at being subjected to another man using her for his sick pleasures.

Rage boiled up inside her . . . and the fear. She didn't want the fear anymore. For just this short while, she wanted to be free.

That need blinded her to any potential danger as she raced toward the front door intending to find the man and confront him, even as she knew she would not make it farther than the elevator.

Six

Insanity at the highest rung.

That was the thought careening through Stefan's mind as he stood outside Michaela's apartment, as he had been doing for nearly ten minutes, alternately lifting his hand to knock and then shoving the offending hand back in his pocket.

He silently cursed Hans, the security guard, who generally made getting past him more difficult than slipping by the Berlin Gestapo in 1939. But Hans had remembered Stefan from his frequent visits with Lowery, and Stefan's name still remained on the list of acceptable visitors.

What the hell was he doing here? he asked himself for the twentieth time. What form of mental incapacitation had brought him to this spot? A place he never expected to be even if the Lord blessed him with a life span of one-hundred-twenty years.

Apologies. He owed Michaela one.

She didn't deserve how he had treated her. He had no right to touch her, kiss her . . . or to enjoy either. Any other man in his office who had done what he had would have been fired.

Frankly, he was surprised the ax hadn't fallen on him already. Michaela had been looking for a reason to get rid of him and he had handed her a perfect excuse to go to the board and get him ousted. And if it came to that, Stefan would not deny his role in the incident nor fight the consequences.

But he hadn't come to Michaela's apartment because he was worried about losing his job. He had come because apologizing was the right thing to do.

Deep down he knew he had used his size and his rage to intimidate her. He had been so angry, so damn disappointed that she had screwed everything up after making him see something he liked in her that he had lost his head, acting no better than the kind of men he detested.

Stefan forced the thought aside and adjusted the box under his arm. He was just about to ring the doorbell when the door swung open and a copper-haired vision slammed into him, knocking the box to the ground.

Wide violet eyes, filled with the same fright Stefan had witnessed only a few days earlier, clashed with his—and the next thing he knew, she was pounding her fists on his chest.

"Go away! Leave me alone!"

"Stop it! I'm not going to hurt you!" Stefan tried to gently restrain her, capturing her wrists, but she struggled wildly, kicking out at him.

He hadn't meant to back her up against the wall. He'd only intended to subdue her, calm her, keep her from hurting herself. He didn't realize his mistake until she went stock-still, the color draining from her face.

"No." The word was barely a whisper, but it sliced

through him with the force of a white-hot blade. He
jerked back as if he'd been burned.

He didn't know what to say, how to erase the fear
in her eyes. He couldn't find the words to tell her
how badly he felt about what had happened between them, to speak the apology he had come to
give. It all seemed trite, worthless now. But he had
to find a way.

So he spoke to her in Italian, whispering words of
apology, of regret, and then sweet, nonsensical
things that seemed to soothe her even though she
didn't understand him. He spoke from his heart
and the language did not matter.

She watched him with eyes as deep as a Sicilian
sea and fringed with the thickest lashes he had ever
seen. Why had he never noticed the beauty of those
eyes, the depth? And why did she have to look at
him as if he'd suddenly become her salvation instead of her tormentor?

And why, why did she have to wrench at his heart,
his very soul with a fragility that nearly undid him?

A hint of a smile touched his lips when he
glanced down at her bare feet, her toenails painted
pink. She curled one foot over the other as if embarrassed to have been caught shoeless.

Stefan was rocked by the realization of how much
she affected him, of how much he liked her this
way, her hair slightly disheveled, her worn jeans
caressing her thighs like an old lover, the frayed
hems teasing those beautiful bare feet. When she
looked as she did at that moment, he could not
dredge up the dislike he'd always felt for her.

He forced himself to remember that nothing had

changed. She was still the same woman who had been causing him trouble and endeavoring to make him miserable in any way possible.

Elevating his gaze from her feet, Stefan noticed her eyes were fastened on his chest, staring as if something there fascinated her. She glanced up suddenly, found him watching her, and quickly looked away.

Stefan shook himself from his daze, thinking of frozen glacial streams in an effort to cool a rising heat inside him. He glimpsed the box near his feet.

"I brought over the work you requested from Patty."

She regarded him for a long moment before saying quietly, "Why?"

Why. The question of the day.

Stefan shoved his hands in the pockets of his black denim jeans and shrugged. "I had time."

"Oh," she said in a small voice.

She reached for the box. So did he, laying his hands over hers as she went to pick it up. Her gaze leaped to his. Her face was so close . . . so close that he almost tilted the half-inch it would take to press his lips against hers.

As if seeing the intention in his eyes, she quickly straightened. "Thank you," she murmured. "I can handle it."

Reluctantly, Stefan handed over the box, but he couldn't bring himself to leave. "Were you going somewhere?"

A puzzled frown knit her brow, as if she had forgotten what she had been doing. Maybe his presence had distracted her as much as she distracted him. Then a hunted look came into her eyes and she nodded. What was going on?

"Barefoot?" he pressed.

"I forgot I wasn't wearing shoes."

"You must have been in a big hurry." Stefan leaned a shoulder against the door frame. "So where were you going?" He told himself it was none of his damn business and that he should go the hell home before he did something he regretted, but he didn't move.

She studied the box, and Stefan didn't think she was going to answer him. Finally, she murmured, "Across the street."

"What's across the street?" Every muscle in his body tensed as he waited for her to tell him she was going to meet her lover.

"There's a man . . ."

"I see." His jaw was so tight he thought it would snap. "Don't let me hold you up then." He pushed away from the door, but he had barely gone two feet before her words caught him.

"I saw him through the telescope. He was . . . doing things."

Stefan felt as if he'd been poleaxed. He faced her. "What things?"

She shook her head, unable to look at him.

Cautiously, he moved closer to her. "What did he do?" But he knew.

She made no reply.

"You weren't going to confront him, were you?" He hoped to God she said no. The thought of her confronting some pervert made his skin grow cold, images of his sister flashing in his mind, remembering what her attacker had done to her, what could very well have happened to Michaela had he not come along when he did.

"Were you?" he demanded when she didn't reply, his anger building.

"Yes."

"Christ, you're a damn fool!" He wanted to shake her for even thinking about doing something that stupid. He never expected the desperate savagery of her response.

"I won't let him frighten me! I won't be a coward again!" Her voice trembled with emotion. "I can't. Not again."

Her words rocked Stefan back on his heels. "What do you mean, again?"

"Nothing." She shook her head.

"Tell me." When she wouldn't look at him, he caught her chin in his hand. "Tell me."

"Please. Let it go." She curled her fingers around his wrist, a beseeching gesture. Stefan wondered if she realized she had voluntarily touched him—or how that small touch brought out every protective instinct inside him. "Please. I'm tired. I—I just want to forget about this."

It took every ounce of self-control Stefan possessed not to press her for an answer. But he suddenly noticed how worn out she looked. She had claimed sickness for the past three days. Perhaps she truly had been ill.

"At least tell me what the bastard did."

She caught her bottom lip between her teeth, hesitating. When she finally spoke, her voice held a slight waver. "He . . . touched himself."

Scumbag. "And where did he touch himself?"

She glanced away.

Christ, he felt as if he were dying, burning up. What was happening to him? "Look at me," he softly commanded.

Hesitantly, her gaze returned to him.

"Did he touch himself here?" He placed his hand on his chest, cursing the aching need he had to know what had happened.

"No." Her gaze flicked from his face to his chest and Stefan had to curl his fingers into his palms to keep from touching her, kissing her closed eyes and willing away what she had seen.

Yet a devil inside him, some warring faction, made him push—and he slid his hand down to his abdomen. "Here?"

"No." The word was half-plea, half-whisper, her chest rising and falling in short pants, motivated either by fear—or by escalating desire.

Every nuance of her face riveted him. Each of the myriad emotions that flickered in her eyes hammered at him. He didn't know what he was doing, what motivated him, but he couldn't stop.

So he slid his palm down farther.

"Don't." She grabbed his hand as it eased over the waistband of his jeans. "Please don't."

Stefan stopped, looking at her small hand wrapped around his much larger one, light skin to dark. The contact jarred him.

Jesus, what was he doing?

And what was she doing to him?

He couldn't believe the way he was feeling. Not

for his biggest adversary. He could not have been that wrong about her, that blind.

She was manipulating him, he told himself. That could be the only answer. Somehow, some way she had learned his weaknesses and changed the rules of the game, concocting some scheme while she had been away to keep him continually off balance.

She had played him for the fool so many times, and every time she cried wolf, he had believed her. He wouldn't allow himself to be duped again. And yet . . . her fear seemed genuine.

God, did she know what might have happened to her had she found this man? Of the things he could have done? What was she thinking?

A strained silence lengthened between them until at last she murmured, "Thank you for bringing the box. Good night."

Stefan's entire body grew taut as he watched her turn and head into her apartment. He was *not* going to let her draw him in. He was *not* going to believe the sadness he had glimpsed.

God, he would be utterly mad to allow himself to fall victim to Michaela's plotting; she was such an expert after all. Yet as he watched the door close, her pale face and wide eyes haunted him.

No gentleman would let a potential harm to a woman go unchecked, and that was the only reason, or so Stefan told himself, that he put his hand out and stopped the door from shutting in his face.

Startled, she swung around, dropping the box. She stared up at him with eyes like jewels, eyes on the verge of tears.

"I think I better check this guy out." He scooped

up the box and stepped past her before she could tell him to leave.

Stefan forced the vision of her sad eyes from his mind and tried to think rationally. He surveyed the living room, wondering why he was surprised by the overdone opulence. For some inexplicable reason, he had expected . . . what? Comfy chairs? Homey paintings? Perhaps the television going?

Or maybe a little music, he mused as a powerful recollection came to mind of the day he had found her singing in her office.

Everything in the place shouted the Michaela he knew, from the expensive Italian marble floors to the abundance of naked male statues in every style and shape imaginable.

Stefan turned, half expecting to find her poised against the door sporting a catlike grin that let him know he had been duped, that she had finally gotten him exactly where she wanted him.

Instead, he found her still framed in the threshold, eyeing him warily.

"Where do you want this?" He held up the box.

She hesitated. "On the cocktail table is fine."

Stefan nodded and deposited the box on an art deco–style peanut table that he suspected cost as much as some people made in a year.

That table brought back all the reasons he had never truly liked Michaela, the way she tossed money around, the way having that money made her act superior to everyone.

She had never had to work for a thing in her life. Lowery had given her whatever she wanted, except perhaps the one thing she had really desired. Complete control. Over his fortune. Over his business. Even from the grave, he had thwarted her.

Stefan had met plenty of Michaela's type, women who looked down on those who were not their social equals, more so if they were poor, as he had once been. He had never realized just how much of that poor kid still lived inside him until Michaela had ground his face in it.

He noticed the book lying open on the table then. *Wuthering Heights.*

He reached down and picked it up. The cover was worn, the pages dog-eared as if had been read over and over again. Next to the book were the remnants of a hamburger, a pickle, and a flickering vanilla-scented candle.

Something about the setup seemed lonely to him, out of context. He could more easily picture her dining on chateaubriand, an extra-crisp endive salad, and a dessert of plums in brandy, topped off with a vintage bottle of 1972 Perrin Réserve, Côtes du Rhône Roughe at Le Cirque than this.

He glanced sideways and saw her watching him, remaining at a distance, which rubbed a raw spot inside him. He held up the book. "You're reading this?" His voice held the bite of incredulity.

She nodded. "It's my favorite. It's . . . I've had it a long time." She looked as if she wanted to snatch the book away from him, as if by his touching it he was corroding something, leaving his mark where she didn't want it.

Not wanting to further upset her, he laid the book down. "The story is rather tragic from what I recall." Tragic and darkly romantic, a tale of undying love, even beyond death. Not something he'd expect Michaela to ever waste her time with.

"Life is rather tragic," she murmured in return.

Her remark was made without emotion, seeming to hold no hidden meanings, yet Stefan felt its impact. Did her comment have something to do with the loss of her father?

Or did it have more to do with her mother? Stefan remembered how she had clutched the framed photo to her chest.

He felt compelled to test the waters once again. "I was sorry to hear of your mother's passing."

She made no remark, and her eyes gave nothing away, no clue as to how she felt about her mother's death. It was as if she had shuttered herself off, blanketed her emotions.

"The telescope's over there." She nodded toward the windows behind him.

Stefan took the hint and forced himself to drop the subject for the time being.

Turning, he noted the sheets covering half the windows. He was mildly surprised to find she had gone to such lengths to ensure her privacy. He had never thought of Michaela as a private person, or one who wouldn't think a pervert was more amusing than frightening.

Leaning down, he peered through the telescope into what looked to be an empty apartment. "I don't see anyone." He glanced over his shoulder. "Are you sure you couldn't have been mistaken? Maybe you thought—"

"He was there." Her tone was adamant.

"Well, he's gone now." Stefan straightened. "If he

bothers you again, just call me—or contact the police," he added as an afterthought, wondering what had prompted him to offer himself up for service when only a couple of weeks ago he would have preferred to have his fingernails extracted one by one than to be in Michaela's presence for more than a second.

Stefan wasn't sure what to do at that point. Departing would be the obvious choice. Obvious, but oddly, not preferred. "I'd better be going." He would drive out to the marina and sit on the deck of his boat with his companion Jack Daniels and endeavor to forget this night.

"Thank you," she said.

Stefan nodded and forced his feet toward the door, struggling to block out the sweetness of her gratitude and the lingering worry in her eyes.

He had just made it to the foyer when a black ball of fur sprang out at him from nowhere, clinging precariously to his shirt for a moment before proceeding to wrap around his neck.

"Sheba!"

The cat paid its owner no heed but instead rubbed its furry head along Stefan's jaw, its rumbling purr vibrating through his skin. When Michaela came over to pluck the cat away, it hissed and batted a paw at her.

Stefan stifled his amusement and stroked the cat's plush tail. "It's all right. I don't mind."

She appeared chagrined over her pet's less-than-loving attitude. "She can be touchy."

"Yes, I can see that." Stefan suspected the cat

had decided there could be only one diva—and she was it.

"She's been rather difficult recently and hasn't been eating well."

"Is she sick?" Stefan stared into the cat's puffy, pampered face and thought he had never seen a healthier feline.

"I don't think she's sick as much as finicky. I put down her food and she just meows incessantly up at the cabinet that holds the tins of beluga."

Stefan would do the same thing if he were a cat. "Where's her food? Maybe I can get her to eat." And maybe a troop of pigs would do a rendition of *Riverdance* in Rockefeller Center. What the hell did he know about a cat's eating habits?

His once formidable adversary nibbled her lower lip, bringing Stefan's gaze to the plump ripeness of her mouth and sending a jolt of desire slamming through him.

"Are you sure you don't mind?" she asked tentatively.

"Nope. Lead on." He waved her ahead of him, which turned out to be another mistake as his gaze trailed down her T-shirt-clad back and lingered on the sway of her hips.

To distract himself, Stefan stroked the Persian and eyed the huge kitchen with its stainless-steel subzero refrigerator, etched glass-door cabinets, granite countertops, electric range with barbecue, two full-size ovens, and under-the-shelf microwave.

The room would have had an austere feel to it if not for the various plants and flowers strewn about. They seemed out of place, a contradiction—almost like Michaela herself, Stefan was coming to discover.

She scooped a can of cat food into a crystal bowl emblazoned with Sheba's name on it. Then she turned and handed it to him. "Here you go."

With some finagling, Stefan managed to unwind the cat from his neck. Then he placed her in front of the bowl. As soon as he did, Sheba began to eat.

"She doesn't seem to be having any problem now." He watched the feline devour the food and then he glanced at Michaela, whose incredulous gaze was fastened on her cat, leaving her in profile and giving Stefan an unguarded moment for his gaze to wander over her smooth cheeks, a pert nose with the barest dusting of freckles across the bridge, full lips, slightly tipped eyes. The light reflected off her straight, shiny skein of copper hair, catching hints of gold mingled with red fire.

"Incredible," she said.

"Yes," he murmured.

She turned to glance at him and Stefan cursed his uncharacteristic ogling. He thought this was where she would show him the door. Instead, she regarded him for a long moment, her expression contemplative.

"I was wondering . . ." She paused, biting a corner of her lip, something Stefan had come to realize she did when she was nervous. But why was she nervous? She had never been that way with him before.

"What were you wondering?"

"Well, I had an idea . . . for the magazine."

He raised a brow, not sure he was going to like

where this was going. Michaela's ideas and his generally clashed.

"What's the idea?" He kept his voice purposely neutral as he leaned back against the counter, trying not to think about how adorable she looked in that big shirt—or the words written on the front.

She moved past him, toward the table in the corner of the room that held a grouping of plants. She busied herself plucking dead leaves instead of looking at him.

"Well, I thought it might be interesting to do bios on our advertisers. You know, give some background on their company, who they are, what they are. Make them seem more accessible to the readers."

Stefan stared, certain he had lost the ability to blink. "Go on."

"I also thought the bios might appeal to the advertisers, too. Give them some additional coverage and show them in a different light. And we could charge a reduced fee at first to entice them. Even at a lowered price, we would still increase our advertising revenue and in turn be able to expand other areas of the magazine."

Stefan was impressed. Not only was her idea a good one, genuinely insightful and doable, but he'd be damned if he hadn't even thought of it, and such things were his job.

"I like it."

A hesitant but thoroughly engaging smile tilted up the corners of her lips. "Really?"

"Really." He returned her smile. "I think it's

sound, easily integrated into our advertising program, and damn smart. Good job."

The way she looked at him then, eyes bright with joy, face lit up, Stefan would have thought he had just hung the moon for her instead of merely telling her that her suggestion was good.

She looked so sweet, so damnably innocent standing there with her watering can and a handful of dead leaves that a surge of unexpected hunger blasted through him, and at that moment, he could not conjure up a single reason to resist the impulse.

"Come here." He beckoned her with a single finger.

The smile slipped slowly from her face and was replaced by a guarded expression.

"I promise I won't bite." But he would kiss her, had to kiss her.

Haltingly, she moved toward him, holding the plastic watering can in front of her as if it would ward him off. She stopped almost three feet away.

Gently, Stefan took hold of her wrist and tugged her forward until barely a foot separated them. Her eyes were glued to his face.

As if the air did not thrum with sexual tension, he calmly opened her hand and let the leaves fall into his palm. He tossed them into the garbage. Then he went for the watering can, which took a bit more coaxing to get her to release, though he finally managed the task.

His gaze roamed over her face, memorizing each freckle, the exact slant of her brows, the uniqueness of that tiny mole, studying her lips with rapt fascination. Then his regard inched lower, over her shirt, and the words he had wanted to say all night whispered forth.

"Kiss me."

Seven

Abby remained utterly still, feeling as if she could not get enough air into her lungs, like she stood on the edge of a precipice and one deep breath would send her tumbling off into oblivion.

She told herself that Stefan was making a request not a demand, tried to assure herself of that even as her mind railed that she should have known better than to let him into the apartment, to let any man get too close.

But when his eyes lifted to hers, the turmoil inside her began to diminish, and she found herself transfixed by what she saw in those dark depths, intensity tempered by restraint, like an unseen hand steadying her.

A lock of blue-black hair fell across his brow and Abby experienced an unexpected longing to sweep it back, to fan its cool, silky strands between her fingertips. She had never felt this way before, so completely lost in another person.

Whenever she looked at Stefan, something strong and frightening coursed through her, leaving her paralyzed with conflicting emotions. She wanted to see something other than anger or mistrust in his eyes, to know if the promise of comfort and protection that she had glimpsed was a vow he would willingly give.

"Kiss me." The deep timbre of his voice blew heat across her skin and raised the fine hairs on her arms.

It took a full minute for the haze to clear from her mind and realize his gaze had dipped to her chest. She glanced down and noted there was something written on her T-shirt. Her heart did a slow, painful thump as she read the two words.

KISS ME, it said in bold letters, a huge pair of puckered red lips beneath it.

Abby closed her eyes in mortification. She hadn't paid any attention when she had pulled the shirt from her sister's drawer.

She couldn't bring herself to look at him. What must he be thinking seeing such a thing? Had he taken those two words as an invitation to touch her?

"Look at me," he softly commanded, his words sending a shiver over her flesh.

Slowly, Abby elevated her gaze and was impaled by hot, dark eyes.

"Do you want me to leave?" he asked.

Her answer should have been automatic, immediate, yet it did not come.

In many ways Stefan terrified her; those large hands could hold her captive, pin her down against her will. He had the power to do things to her she didn't want—and pay no heed to her cries to stop.

But the way he looked at her . . . now, in the hallway, in her office, twelve years ago, made Abby think he would not purposely hurt her. But did she know what she was doing? Did she want to know?

Not then. Not yet.

"No, I . . . I don't want you to leave."

The way the corners of his lips turned up slightly at her reply did strange things to her insides. His thumb lightly stroked across her cheek, like the brush of a feather, a rush of warmth following in its wake.

"Kiss me," he repeated in a husky baritone, and this time she knew his request had nothing to do with her shirt.

He was asking her, not telling her. He was giving her the freedom to choose, to decide what *she* wanted. The prospect was heady, and all the fantasies that had lived in her mind about this man seemed possible, as if she need only reach out and take what she wanted. She could be in control. When was the last time she had felt in control? Had she ever?

He made no move, just watched her with dark, enveloping eyes. When at last they stood chest to chest, he remained motionless, bolstering her courage.

She laid her hands on his shoulders and rose on tiptoe. She felt awkward, uncertain how to proceed even though she should know what to do.

Her courage almost faltered, but the look in Stefan's eyes gave her confidence. She tilted her head slightly to the side and haltingly pressed her mouth to his, hesitant, light, a tentative brush, then another. He did not rush her, did not question her inexperience, but waited until she had found what she sought and then let her revel in the discovery.

Nothing could have prepared her for the sweet

sensations that floated through her, flooding her senses, lessening the hold of the demon inside her that had so long kept her in its grip, leaving her wary of all men and shaken by the fear of what a look could do, reminding her of the consequences.

Light-headed, she pulled back, nervous yet exhilarated, feeling the stirrings of a long-sequestered need. She stared at Stefan's lips, wanting to trace their contour with her tongue, to press her mouth against the indentation in his chin and whisper along his jaw, to kiss the corners of his eyes and take away some of the fierce concentration so completely centered on her.

He bent his head toward her and Abby felt a dart of worry, but it drifted away with his husky murmuring. *"Che cosa state facendo a me?"*

Then his lips brushed against hers and Abby was lost to the sensation once more. Large fingers slipped into her hair, cupping the back of her head as his mouth slanted across hers with a thoroughness that swept the breath from her lungs.

He was so hot. His heat enveloped her, coiled around her, and when his hand settled on her waist, gently squeezing, a shiver of desire rippled from the inside out.

His palms slid down over her buttocks, bringing her tighter against him. Abby could feel the hard length of his erection, the clear proof of his desire for her. She felt dizzy with the knowledge, yet she held a part of herself back, afraid to let go of that tenuous control.

"Stefan . . ." His name tumbled from her lips, benediction and plea.

Stefan groaned low in his throat as she gave into him just a bit more, opening up like a spring bud as he coaxed her with his lips, his hands. She slipped her tongue into his mouth in an innocent exploration and he couldn't remember anything as provocative as the moment she relinquished another piece of her inhibitions. Her breathy whimpers were driving him mad.

Dear God, how he wanted to wrap her legs around his waist and plunge into her, deep and hard, hear her sweet moans escalate, grip her hair in his hands and run his mouth along her neck, find the wild pulse of her heart, to know by its rapid beat how he was affecting her, and then push her over the edge.

He didn't realize until after he felt her inner thighs draped against his hips that he had lifted her onto the kitchen counter. She had not resisted and that fueled his desire even more.

He placed his palms on the countertop, trying to bring himself back to reality, to feel the cool, smooth texture of that reality beneath his fingertips. The need to touch her everywhere was so strong he was afraid he would overwhelm her.

When she twined her arms around his neck and pressed the soft mounds of her breasts into his chest, his resolve unraveled. He cupped her buttocks, sliding her forward against his arousal. He had to taste her, sweep his tongue across that heated skin.

His fingers slipped beneath her shirt. He felt her stiffen, but her tension slowly eased as he gently kneaded her back, warming her to his touch. Everything she did seemed inexperienced, like high school fumbling, yet it incited his senses and sent his blood roaring through his veins.

Stefan knew she was far from innocent, far from the naive girl she seemed in his arms, but he let himself pretend, to believe no man had ever kissed her as he had or been allowed to touch her so intimately.

She flinched when his thumbs brush beneath the lush curve of her breasts. Her hands locked around his wrists, pushing his hands down as she pulled away from him.

She regarded him warily, her eyes glazed with desire, her moist mouth bruised from his kiss. His gaze lowered. Her pebbled nipples pressed against her shirt and Stefan had to close his eyes to contain the passion rifling through him, to keep from bending down and laving the tight bud right through the thin material.

"I'm sorry," he said, his voice raw and low. "I didn't mean . . ." He shook his head. How could he say he didn't mean to touch her? He had thought of nothing else since that day in her office when she'd looked at him with tormented eyes.

"Promise me . . ."

Stefan lifted his head when she said no more. "What, *cara?*" he murmured. "What do you want from me?"

"Promise me . . . you won't ever hurt me," she whispered.

Sweet God in heaven, she tore him apart, brought him to his knees. Who was this woman he had never known? And what terrible thing had happened to her?

Brushing his knuckles across her cheek, he murmured, "I promise, *mia dolce*. I won't hurt you."

She studied his face. Perhaps something there convinced her that he was sincere, for in the next moment, her fingers curled around the edge of her T-shirt, slowly lifting it, revealing herself inch by torturous inch, a delicious belly button, a flat stomach with a thin scar, the shadowy crease of the underside of her breasts . . . and higher until she revealed herself fully to him, her pink nipples drawn tight, her body trembling. Breathing became difficult.

"Touch me, Stefan."

Stefan needed no further prompting. He bent down to take one sweet tip into his mouth. She gasped as his mouth made contact, and the breathy sound she made spiked through Stefan like light through water.

His tongue curled around her nipple, his lips gently tugging. She clutched his shoulders, her back arching, pressing her nipple farther into his mouth.

Her hands fisted in his hair as he suckled one taut nub, then the other, wanting to lay her down, peel off her jeans and panties and taste her until deep shudders wracked her body.

With a low growl, he pressed her tighter against his groin, reveling in her deep-throated moan as he rolled her nipples between his fingers and then gently but relentlessly abraded the sensitive peaks with the tips of his thumbs, increasing the pleasure/pain before cupping each globe and soothing the hurt with his mouth.

Her fingers slipped from his hair, skimmed down his neck and toyed with the V of his blue chambray shirt before tentatively undoing two buttons and slipping her hands inside. Her exploration was whisper-soft yet grippingly erotic, turning him inside out.

His tongue trailed up her chest, along her collarbone, up the slender expanse of her throat, and finally, inevitably, returned to plunder her mouth as his thumbs swept feverishly across her turgid peaks, making him ache with the unrestrained passion of her response.

In turn, her fingers slid downward, making Stefan's gut clench as he waited, tense, simmering. She seemed to want to touch every part of him, as if by simply caressing him she would know him, memorize him. Lightly, she grazed his nipple, swirled away and then returned to gently tease.

He undid the button on her jeans. She grabbed his hand. "No . . . don't."

"Ssh," he whispered against her ear, drawing down the zipper. "Just let yourself go."

She continued gripping his wrists.

"I swear I won't do anything you don't want me to."

She stared deep into his eyes, as if searching for the truth, and once found, she gradually released him.

Stefan kissed her, a slow, lingering kiss as he stroked his finger along the edge of her panties. He eased back. She regarded him with passion-

drugged eyes. Then he glanced down, expecting to
see a wispy G-string and finding delicate pink cotton panties instead.

The sight of those panties were nearly Stefan's
undoing. Gently, he slid his fingers underneath the
waistband. She tried to clench her thighs together
but he stood between them, denying her. He kissed
her gently, coaxing her to relax.

He groaned as he separated her slick flesh with
a single finger, finding her clitoris swollen and wet.
"Watch me," he murmured as his forefinger glided
over the hot nub, rubbing back and forth. "Do you
like how that feels?"

She clamped her bottom lip between her teeth,
as if to keep herself from answering. Stefan wanted
to see her wild, out of control. He increased his
tempo, watching her body tighten even as she
opened further to him.

"Something's . . . happening," she softly panted.

"Let it happen." He spread her legs wider, dying
to press his fingers inside her, to slip into that hot,
tight sheath and feel her clench him.

"That's it, sweet," he whispered as her eyes closed
and her head tipped back against the cabinet. "Feel
what I'm doing to you."

She was holding back, refusing to let herself go.
Stefan would not be defeated. He took her nipple
into his mouth and suckled, increasing the pressure with his fingers until at last he succeeded in
pushing her over the edge.

Every muscle in her body tensed as the first deep
pulse came, followed by another and another. He
cupped her, wanting to drown in those hot convul-

sions, until he saw a single tear slip from between her closed eyelids.

Something primitive stirred to life inside Stefan. Something possessive, and dark, and threatening to eclipse his sanity. His desire was nearly pounding out of control.

He wanted to dominate her, lay her down on a bed, put her hands above her head and do as he pleased—for as long as he pleased, flick his tongue over those glorious nipples and then slip lower, between her thighs and lick the sugar right off her, have her writhe and moan and beg for surcease.

And that truth slammed into Stefan with the force of a sucker punch to his solar plexus, sending him stumbling back.

"Christ." He drove a hand through his hair, knowing he had to get out, that he couldn't stand there another minute and look at those sumptuous breasts, her skin flushed with her release, without slaking every ounce of his need on her.

It wouldn't be right . . . it would never be right.

"I'm sorry," he said in a raw voice, before turning and getting the hell out of there.

Eight

God, he was deranged, Stefan thought.

Completely fucked up in the head.

Why had he started this whole thing with Michaela? What could have prompted him to break a cardinal rule and kiss her? Not once, not twice, but a number of times. And not short kisses, but long, passionate, deep-throat kisses, his tongue sliding in and out in a rhythm he came damn close to repeating with another part of his anatomy, an act he would no doubt have thoroughly enjoyed . . . had it been any other woman.

Somewhere along the line he had fallen captive to a state of mind that he could only categorize as an anomaly-heretofore-unexplained, as mysterious as the fabled black hole, a vast endless emptiness he could only hope to be sucked into.

God willing.

Because to think he might have stayed in Michaela's apartment for any reason other than an honorable attempt to confirm or deny her claim that some pervert across the street was watching her was a variable too enormous to fathom.

But sweet Jesus, the way she had responded to him still caused Stefan's gut to knot painfully.

Now, a week later, he had become somewhat of an expert at deluding himself, anything to keep from facing the truth: that he had actually experienced a deep hunger for a woman he once wanted to strangle with his bare hands.

For seven days, he had been enmeshed in a two-step shuffle with Michaela, deftly skirting her perimeter, his face feeling as if it were permanently immobilized in a mask-like grimace, though less fierce-looking than the expression he wore at that moment as he watched Faraday slide into Michaela's office and ease the door closed behind him.

Rick had been sniffing around her since she had returned, even more so than usual. Normally, she led him around by the nose, the perpetual tease, dancing just out of his reach, and engaging in the type of dallying that might someday lead the wrong man to make the wrong move.

But maybe the wrong man already had.

I won't be a coward again.

Again. She had said again. Stefan couldn't help wondering if something had happened while she had been in Europe, because things had definitely changed, a tangible element he couldn't precisely define.

He braced his hand against the wall and stared at the closed office door across the hallway, thinking about sad violet eyes, long, slow kisses . . . and beating the crap out of Faraday.

At the sound of her door opening, Abby glanced up, tensing, thinking perhaps it was Stefan come to demand an explanation about why she was avoiding him, as if she had any solid reason other than feeling ashamed of her wanton, reckless behavior. How could she have let herself go like that? To risk the possibility of his hurting her?

But he hadn't hurt her, hadn't done anything she hadn't wanted, needed. Every time she thought about the way he had caressed her, where he had touched her, of what had happened when his fingers had slid beneath her panties, her entire body grew warm.

She could barely look at him for longing, for feeling the fool when she realized that he had only touched her because he thought she was Micky.

That realization made telling him the truth about who she was that much harder. He had unlocked something inside her, something she was afraid she'd never find again should she confess her sin and he discovered who she truly was.

Masquerading as Micky allowed her to hide behind a veneer and pretend she wasn't uninteresting Abby St. James, replete with her problems and personal tragedies, but rather someone who had no baggage.

But it wasn't Stefan who had entered her office, but Rick Faraday. Abby repressed a shudder. She didn't know what it was about the man that bothered her so much. He had maintained his distance, been polite, helpful, and gracious to the point of ingratiating. And yet, Abby couldn't shake the sense that things were not as they seemed.

"May I help you, Rick?"

"I have something for you."

An uncomfortable sensation fluttered in the pit of Abby's stomach as he closed the door and walked toward her. She very nearly jumped out of her chair when he swiveled it around so that she faced him. Then he knelt down in front of her.

"What are you doing?"

He slipped a hand into his pocket, extracting a small square box.

"Rick—"

"Don't say anything." Without warning, he grabbed hold of her ankle.

Panic rose in Abby's throat. "Don't!" She tried to yank her leg away.

"Relax." He then clasped a gold bracelet around her ankle, meticulously adjusting the tiny heart that dangled from it.

"I know it's not much," he said, glancing up at her. "But I wanted you to know how much you're on my mind."

Oh, God, Abby thought. She should have known there was more to the looks that Rick cast in her direction. He was in love with Micky!

He rose slowly; his gaze fastened on her lips. "I missed you terribly while you were gone. Did you miss me?"

"Rick, stop. You don't know—"

"You're still mad at me, aren't you? I told you those other women didn't mean anything to me. You're the only one I want." He leaned forward, bracing his hands on the arms of her chair, trapping her. "Please, Micky, say you forgive me." Before Abby knew what he intended, he leaned forward and kissed her.

"What the hell is going on here?" an ominous voice demanded.

Abby's entire body jerked from the force of Stefan's angry voice. She knew a moment of wanting to shrink from the harsh impact and hated herself for feeling that way.

Her gaze lifted and locked with his over Rick's shoulder. Words lodged in her throat as she saw the thunderous expression on his face.

"I repeat, what is going on here?"

Rick straightened casually. "Hey, Stef. Just keeping our star here from hurting herself. Her chair almost toppled over. I'd get it checked. Could be defective." Then he glanced over his shoulder and winked at Abby as if she had planned to be part of his deception. "Gotta run. Meeting with my group in five minutes."

Then he was gone, leaving Abby alone with Stefan.

He stood there, utterly unmoving, his features implacable, eyeing her as if she were something distasteful. What was he going to do? And why didn't he say anything?

"Are you just going to stare at me?"

That stirred him. Unfortunately, it didn't stir him to remove himself but forced him farther into the office, closing the door behind him, which raised the fine hairs on the back of Abby's neck.

With a slow, purposeful stride, he moved toward her. "I'm going to tell you this one last time, after that I can't promise I'll remain a gentleman."

Abby scooted the chair back on its rollers, feeling

dwarfed as Stefan came around the side of her desk and glared down at her.

As Rick had done only moments before, Stefan leaned forward, trapping her between two large, muscular arms, the seams bulging on his navy blue suit jacket. "If I see you sexually harassing another one of my employees," he said in a measured tone, "there will be hell to pay. Do we understand each other?"

Abby was hurt by his accusation. How could he think she would do something like that? And worse, right there in the office.

She had begun to believe that Stefan might be coming to understand her a little bit, that maybe he *did* see her. She hadn't expected the realization that she was wrong to be so painful.

"I didn't do anything." She tried to keep her voice modulated but a slight quaver filtered through. "Now please leave."

"I'll leave when I'm goddamn good and ready."

"You promised."

"What?" he demanded.

"That you wouldn't hurt me."

Jesus, Stefan thought, feeling as though he'd just been backhanded, the reminder of his vow barreling out at him from the dark and hitting him squarely between the eyes.

He had frightened her again, come across like a raving lunatic. That hadn't been his intention. He had simply wanted to ask her a question. The fact that he had been looking for any excuse to barge in was what gnawed at his gut.

"I'm not going to hurt you, damn it," he ground out.

She glanced away from him. "You already have."

Stefan gritted his teeth so hard he felt certain his jaw would crack. How the hell had she managed to turn this around and make him feel as if *he* were the one in the wrong? She was the one who teased every cock in the office—his included, which is what burned Stefan more than anything, were he honest enough to admit it. But at that moment, he wasn't feeling inclined toward honesty.

It didn't matter that she hadn't gone near any of the men in the office in the six weeks she had been back. A zebra didn't change its stripes that quickly. She was up to something, but he'd be damned if he could figure out what it was.

"I'd like you to leave," she said, not looking at him.

He ignored her and moved closer, their faces mere inches apart. Abby gripped the seat of the chair so tightly she thought her knuckles would poke through.

The expression in Stefan's eyes shifted. They were still dark and forbidding, but the heat was unmistakable. Abby shivered beneath the intensity of that look, remembering the feel of his mouth pressed to hers, his hands on her body, touching her everywhere, shockingly intimate, dangerously exciting, eliciting responses she never imagined possible.

His gaze made a slow sketch down her body, and she felt herself responding to him against her will, her nipples peaking, thrusting defiantly against her silk blouse, an ache building between her thighs.

And he had not laid a finger on her.

His perusal stopped at her bare feet, a scowl forming on his face. He reached down, and with the lightest touch, outlined the bracelet at her ankle with his index finger. She trembled.

"Did Rick give this to you?"

Abby hesitated, then replied, "Yes. But I plan to—"

"Save it," he bit out, stepping away from her, the look in his eyes cold enough to freeze her clear through. He shook his head. "Christ, what made me think you had changed?"

"Stefan . . ."

A muscle worked in his jaw. "Stay away from Rick," he ordered. "I'm not losing him like I lost Hale Turner. Consider yourself warned."

Nine

Abby stared out the window of her sister's apartment into the inky black night, the moon and stars swaddled in a woolly blanket of clouds, the windows of the city shining like golden diamonds.

The view should have moved her, should have made her feel as if she need only reach out and the whole world would be hers to command.

She had had faith in that dream once, but she had stopped believing when she was twelve years old and the realities of life had intruded on the small sphere of her existence.

Some philosopher once said that you could live a lifetime and at the end of it know more about other people than you know about yourself.

How true that statement was, for there were times when Abby understood herself least of all, times when she knew in her heart that she should have spoken up, forced people to listen to her, but something inside her always withered, shriveled into the single thought that no one would be interested in what she had to say.

But for a short while, she had believed Stefan was interested in her opinions. When he had listened to her suggestions and found them worthy, it had validated Abby in a way she had never experienced before.

And she felt she was coming to understand him, recognizing that his fierceness was a facade more often than not—just as she knew that Micky was causing trouble for Stefan out of spite.

Yet when Stefan got angry, Abby instinctively recoiled, and when her sister claimed she was innocent of harboring ill will toward Stefan, Abby believed her.

But neither Stefan nor Micky wholly occupied Abby's thoughts that night, but rather the person whose machinations had brought them all together.

Her father.

Or more appropriately, her father's letter, which had been sent to her in Idaho before the reading of his will. The message it contained could not have shocked Abby more.

Her hand trembled as she lifted the wrinkled paper that she had thrown in the garbage more than once, not wanting any explanation from her father now, when it was too late, refusing to accept some deathbed request for forgiveness or a purging of his guilt.

But each time she threw the letter away, she inevitably retrieved it, carefully smoothing out the sheet, not understanding the impulse that forced her to hold on to the last words of a man who had just walked away from being her father. Yet she knew she was not ready to be rid of this final vestige of him.

As she had so many times before, she read her father's letter.

Abby, if you're reading this, then I was too cowardly to set things right with you before it was too late. There are many things I want to say, sentiments I wish I could express, but I have never been very good with such things.

I know I haven't been the best father, but I have always loved you and I should never have let us grow apart. That was my fault, not yours. I always was a selfish man.

I think deep down I feared I would corrupt you somehow, belittle the beautiful person I knew you would become. Lord knows I didn't do well with Michaela. The more I gave her, the more she wanted. She was always searching for something I either didn't possess or I simply didn't realize she needed.

I guess I failed both of you. Please believe me when I say I'm sorry. You deserved better and I hope someday you will find a man who is nothing like me, who will love you without cowardice, without selfishness. I only want the best for you.

Now the time has come to let you know of my decision regarding the magazine before my will is read, though it was not an easy one for me to make. I thought long and hard and realized there was only one clear road for me to take, only one person whom I could trust to keep the magazine going when I was gone.

And that person is you, Abby. I leave you as sole owner of Bastion.

*I pray someday you will find it in your heart to for-
give me for all the pain I've caused you.*

Abby curled the paper in her hand as she had so
many times before, and whispered, "What have you
done?"

Even though months had passed since she first
read her father's letter, she still couldn't believe the
terrible decision he had made, and how, even at
the end of his life, he truly didn't see or understand
how much his actions could hurt the people he
claimed to love.

Micky had been devastated when she found out.
She had expected to assume controlling interest in
the company, and she should have. Micky had been
the one who had stayed with their father in New
York, who understood the magazine business. Not
Abby.

But Abby knew the reason she had been chosen
as *Bastion*'s owner over her sister.

Guilt.

Her father had always thought material possessions made up for love, that a harsh word or neglect could be soothed with a hundred-dollar bill.
But Abby had never been for sale and he had
known that. So he had inflicted his will on her in
the only way he knew how. By leaving her his pride
and joy. His magazine.

Abby wanted to throw it back in his face, tell him
that she had needed him fifteen years ago and didn't
want his bribe, rail at him that his wife had died with
only Abby by her side and not the man who had
once vowed to love, honor, and protect her.

If it had been possible, Abby would have imme-

diately signed the company over to Michaela, if for
no other reason than to have the satisfaction of
never fulfilling whatever it was her father hoped his
bequest would accomplish. But even in that he had
thwarted her.

He had stated in his will that she must spend at
least six months working at *Bastion* before she could
hand over controlling interest of the company to
anyone else, and the time must be spent within the
first year after his death or else the magazine would
be split up among the members of the board and
they, not Micky or Abby, would be in charge.

Abby knew how much the company meant to her
sister, and she could not simply abandon it because
of her feelings. This might be the only chance she
had to make things right with Micky and salvage
what remained of her family.

She had learned early on that there were no
guarantees in life and nothing should be taken for
granted. Where might she be in a year? Two years?
Tomorrow even? Two months ago, she would have
never believed she'd be in New York. Then she had
received a call that had changed her life.

As if the memory conjured up reality, the telephone rang, jarring Abby back to the present.

She hurried to the telephone next to the sofa assuming it was Micky calling her back. Abby didn't
look forward to the conversation, especially considering how badly the last one went, when she requested that her sister call Handover and fix the
problem she had created.

That was the only time Abby had used her position as *Bastion*'s owner to get Micky to do what she

wanted. She knew her sister resented her interference. She could only hope Micky would come to understand that by working against Stefan she was working against the company.

Abby picked up the phone on the fourth ring. "Hello?"

Silence.

"Hello?" she repeated a bit louder.

Still no response.

A sudden chill crawled up Abby's spine. She knew someone was on the other end of the line. Why wasn't the person saying anything?

She intended to hang up when she heard, "You're very pretty."

It was not the words alone that sent a shock wave through her body, but the bone-chilling mechanical hiss of the voice, the tone distorted by something that altered the sound.

"Who is this?" Abby demanded, trying to talk through the knot in her chest.

"I've been watching you."

Abby clutched the top of the sofa. "I'm hanging up."

"Don't hang up!" Rage poured through the line, stilling Abby's hand. Then a dark laugh echoed over the wire. "You don't want to make me angry. I'm not nice when I'm angry."

"What do you want?"

"You." The single syllable, drawn out in a long metallic whine, had the same effect as nails scraping on a chalkboard.

Cold sweat broke out on Abby's body. "Leave me alone."

"I can't do that. You're all I think about. When I close my eyes, I picture your sweet body on top of mine, riding me hard, moaning my name, telling me how much you want it."

The receiver nearly slipped from Abby's hands.

"I know what you're doing all the time," the voice then rasped. "You can't hide from me."

This isn't happening, Abby told herself. It was just a prank, a weirdo getting his kicks out of trying to frighten her. "So what am I doing now, then?"

"Scared?"

She was terrified, but she would not give him the satisfaction of knowing. "No."

"You should be. Now . . . come to the window. I have something I want you to see."

Abby's mind raced, remembering the shadowy image of a man across the street, watching her, putting his hands down his pants . . .

"I won't."

"Do it!" the voice barked, jarring her like the flick of a whip.

Shaking, she moved to the window and inched back the sheet.

"Look through the telescope."

Her heart hammering in her ears, Abby leaned down and peered through the lens. She glimpsed two figures in the vacant apartment. She could not make out the face of either person. But the shapes were that of a man and a woman. The woman was on her knees. Naked and blindfolded.

Hands bound behind her back.

Horror closed off Abby's throat as the man raised his arm and backhanded the woman, sending her reeling hard against the floor. Then before the woman had recovered, the man reached down and grabbed her hair, yanking her to her knees.

"Like what you see so far?"

"Stop it!" Abby cried. "What are you doing?"

"Keep watching."

Abby was paralyzed with fear, unable to move. It was as if she were trapped in a nightmare. No sound would issue from her lips. She was being dragged headlong into something she wanted no part of, but was helpless to stop.

The woman shook her head, saying something, pleading with the man.

Roughly, he grabbed the back of her head and hauled her forward . . .

Abby dropped the phone and stumbled back, the room beginning to spin, terror grabbing hold of her, trying to pull her down.

"No," she whispered. "No." She couldn't lose control. She had to focus. Had to help the woman. *Oh, please, dear God!*

She groped blindly for the phone, sickened by the deep guttural moans coming from the other end of the line, knowing the sound would haunt her as long as she lived.

She jabbed a finger down on the talk button, disconnecting and then reconnecting, barely able to hold the phone and keep herself from swirling into the beckoning darkness as she dialed 9-1-1.

"Here you go, ma'am."

Abby lurched violently as someone spoke to her,

the words melding with the memory of the horrible voice hissing to her over the phone.

She wrapped her arms tightly around her middle, trying to stop the uncontrollable shaking as she glanced up at the police officer now standing in front of her.

"I brought a blanket for you," he said.

Abby could only nod as he draped it around her. He seemed genuinely concerned about her, unlike the detective who had arrived shortly after him, who regarded Abby as though she were another nuisance in a night full of them.

"You can't remember anything about this man?" the detective queried.

"I told you. The light was dim. His face was in the shadows."

"What about the woman?"

Abby shook her head, having already gone down that road as well. "Nothing."

The detective sighed. Abby knew she wasn't being much help, but the shock of what she had witnessed kept her from noticing much. All she had wanted was to get someone over there to help the woman.

One of the other officers came into the room then, a middle-aged man with a slight paunch, followed by another detective with a thick head of gray hair and a world-weary expression.

"All clean, Jake," the newly arrived detective said as if he had expected it all along. "No one over there now."

"Did you do a sweep?" The man Abby knew as

Detective Tremonte rather than Jake asked, pocketing his small notebook and pen.

"Yup. Not even a mouse turd."

Tremonte turned back to her; his expression had changed from skepticism to full-blown disbelief. She wanted to scream at him that she wasn't lying, that there had been a man and a woman across the street. But she would not beg him to believe her.

Tremonte scratched his chin and glanced toward the window. "You look through that telescope often?"

Abby heard the unspoken question. He was turning the tables on her. Making her out to be a voyeur rather than a victim.

"No," she replied coldly. "I don't."

If he noticed the deep chill coming from her, he gave no sign of it. "You said this was your sister's place?"

"Yes."

He glanced around, his gaze lingering on the nude statues. Abby knew what he was thinking, that perhaps she had welcomed the violation that had been forced on her tonight.

Tremonte's skeptical gaze returned to her. "Maybe this guy's one of your sister's friends? You know, playing some kind of kinky game?"

Abby's entire body went rigid. "The man was beating a woman. Does that sound like a game to you, Detective?"

He shrugged. "Not for me, no, ma'am. But I can't say what other people find amusing."

Abby could do no more than stare at him in shock and disbelief, wishing he would leave, almost sorry she had called the police in the first place.

But that woman had needed her help. Abby was sure of it. She wasn't seeing things!

"Well, look," Tremonte said. "We got a call into the super to find out who was the last tenant in that place. Once I have some information, I'll let you know. Here's my card." He slipped her a business card with his number at the precinct. "If you see anything else going on, give me a call."

Numbly, Abby nodded, watching the men leave, glad they were going yet feeling her panic start to rise at the prospect of being alone again. She tugged the blanket tighter around her and rose unsteadily from the couch.

"Ma'am?"

Abby turned to find the police officer who had given her the blanket standing at her front door, knob in hand. "Yes?"

He gestured toward the lock on her door. "You might want to use this deadbolt tonight."

Abby smiled weakly at him. "Thank you. I'll do that."

She watched the door close after him, resisting the urge to call him back, to tell him that no lock would make her feel safe tonight. But he was gone. And she was alone.

Her gaze was unwillingly drawn back to the window, to the telescope that peered into the consuming darkness where a man still lurked.

Watching . . . and waiting.

She had the dream again.

Visions of heaven and hell.

Visions of her own death.

How long had it been since it had last come upon her, jarring her from sleep, leaving her trembling, and sweating, and frightened of every shadow? How long had she managed to run away from it?

Her breathing was erratic, her brow feverish. Darkness encompassed her, emptiness, no one there to drag her down into a burning pit.

She stared up at the canopy above her head, gathering the comforter closer to her, hoping to ward off the shivering that would soon depredate her.

All night she had thought about calling Stefan, wanting simply to hear his voice. But she couldn't call him. Not after what had taken place the day before, how he had accused her of coming on to Rick.

A noise out in the hallway brought Abby bolt upright in bed. Something had knocked against the wall. She told herself it was Sheba. The cat had bumped into something.

But why would Sheba be stalking around in the middle of the night? Every morning Abby found her curled up on Micky's bed, having marked her territory the first night Abby arrived, forcing Abby into the guest room.

Every sense heightened to a new awareness as Abby strained to listen for another sound, another movement, something to either confirm or deny she had heard anything. Silence reached her. Silence that was almost as terrifying as the noise, complete as it was.

She tossed the covers back, too tense to remain still. She needed to calm her nerves and she could not remain in bed.

Afraid to make a sound, she crept toward the bathroom, not turning on the light, which caused her to knock over the cup above the sink. The plastic tumbler banged into the counter and then toppled to the floor, sounding as loud as a gun shot to Abby's ears.

She groped for the glass, scooping it up and clutching it to her chest, sure she heard the sound of feet outside her door. Her mouth was dry, but she dared not run the water. She remained motionless on the cold tile floor, telling herself she was being silly, that she should leave the room and prove nothing was wrong. But her feet didn't want to move.

Finally, she forced herself out of the bathroom, quietly setting the cup on the counter. She stared at the bedroom door for long minutes before tightening her hands into fists, her fingernails jabbing into her palms, the pain confirming this was no dream.

Hands shaking, she grabbed a vase from the corner table and headed for the door. Taking hold of the knob, she swallowed a deep breath and yanked open the door with enough force to rattle the pictures on the wall. Nothing greeted her on the other side.

She briefly closed her eyes, stilling her nerves. Then she hazarded a glance up and down the hall, her gaze roaming over headless torsos and empty-eyed busts, the terror-stricken part of her certain that somewhere amid the statues stood a man, his face shrouded in darkness.

She flicked the light switch outside her door,

bathing the hallway in a muted yellow glow. Nothing sinister sprang out at her. Everything was as it had always been.

No one's there. You're safe.

Then a slight noise came from the other end of the hallway, like the sound of a foot on a creaky floorboard. Abby's gaze swung in that direction.

Nothing.

"Stop this," she whispered to herself, knowing the frightening events that had taken place earlier in the evening were what caused her fear, arousing the dream that had remained dormant for so long.

Abby stayed where she was until she had her breathing under control. The front door seemed so far away, as though she stared at it through a tunnel.

With hesitant steps, she walked toward it, needing to reassure herself that the locks were still in place. She glanced over her shoulder several times to scan the hallway behind her.

Everything was as it should be.

Reaching the front door, she leaned her forehead against it and dragged in a lungful of air, the tension flowing from her body at finding the deadbolt secured.

She returned to her bedroom, automatically locking the door behind her and then climbing into bed, pulling the covers up to her chin and closing her eyes, hoping the morning would come soon.

And when it did, all the fears she thought she had imagined swamped her as she found a single blood-red rose lying against the front door.

Ten

Abby sequestered herself in her office for most of the following day, trying to work, but unable to muster any productive thought.

She had called her sister that morning to tell her what had happened, hoping Micky would know something about what was going on and perhaps confirm the detective's assumption that she knew the man across the street, and that everything, even the rose, had been some sort of twisted, horrible joke. But her sister claimed to know nothing about it.

"That's New York, sis. People do sick shit. You've got to learn to toughen up."

Toughen up. Was that what she needed to do? Would that solve all her problems? Would she someday become so immune to indignities that she would simply look the other way?

Abby leaned back in her chair and closed her eyes. She was weary. Then again, she was always weary these days. Today, however, the weariness was in her soul more than her body.

The knock on her door barely seeped into Abby's consciousness. Her limbs felt heavy, drained of energy, and the lethargy was dragging her down.

She had drifted off to a state somewhere between awake and asleep until a light touch on her arm roused her. Her eyes snapped open and she glimpsed the hazy outline of a man standing beside her chair.

For one flashing moment, fear took hold of her, a split second floating between two worlds, believing that the nightmare had become reality. But the face she looked up at was not cloaked in shadows, but bathed in overhead light—and concerned.

"Are you all right?" Stefan asked, a slight frown pulling his brows together.

Abby blinked and shook away the lingering images in her head. "I'm sorry. I guess I was tired."

"I don't doubt it. You've been in here all day. Why don't you pack up and head home? It's almost six."

"Six?" Abby's gaze swung to her office window to find that twilight had settled over the city, a sight she would have found captivating had her mind not been consumed with other matters.

Stefan sat down on the edge of her desk. "Are you all right?"

"Fine."

"Anything you want to talk about?"

Abby could feel his scrutiny and knew a moment of wanting to confide, yet she wasn't sure where they stood after what had happened with Rick, nor did she think she could take another person telling her she had imagined things or that she had to toughen up.

"No." She shook her head. "Nothing."

"How come I don't believe you?"

"I have no idea." Having Stefan so close, her nerves feeling so frayed, Abby knew she had to leave before she gave into the urge to drop her head on his shoulder and cry.

She rose abruptly from her chair and started stuffing papers into her briefcase. She wasn't even paying attention to what she was putting in.

She grabbed her jacket from the back of her chair and moved around the side of her desk. "Good night. I'll see you in the morning." She didn't know where she was going. All she knew was that she couldn't go back to Micky's apartment. Not yet. Maybe not ever.

Before she made it to the door, Stefan blocked her path. Abby glanced up—and realized that was her first mistake. Looking into Stefan's eyes was always dangerous. It was as if he could see right through her, beyond her pretense, her hiding, and straight to her secrets.

"What's the matter?" he asked gently, yet with a bit of a gruff edge, as if wanting to know but wishing he didn't.

"I told you. Nothing." Abby tried to walk around him but he sidestepped her. "I have to go."

For a moment he remained silent. Abby expected him to keep prodding her. She steeled herself for it. Yet his question took her off guard. "Are you hungry?"

"Hungry?"

He gave her a crooked half-grin. "You know, for food."

"Oh." Food was the last thing on her mind. "No, I'm—"

"Good," he said, cutting her off. "I'm famished. I know this great little place with the best Italian food. I think you'll like it. The chef is a close friend and the lasagna can't be beat."

"But I'm not—"

He ignored her and grabbed her briefcase. Then he laced his fingers through hers and practically dragged her out of the office. Abby knew when she was beaten. Deep down, she was glad he had imposed his will on her. She really didn't want to go back to the apartment.

In the parking garage, he guided her to a stunning black Porsche 928. The car fit him. Sleek, racy, top of the line. And very powerful.

"Guess I should be glad the tire is flat on my truck," he remarked as he opened the car door for her.

Abby looked up at him as she slid into the passenger seat. "You have a truck?"

"Yup. An old Four-Runner that looks as if it barely survived reentry from outer space." He closed the door and went around to the other side and climbed in.

"Why does it matter what car you brought?"

He shot her a quick look as he pulled out of the parking space. "Just can't see you riding in a truck, I guess."

That was the craziest thing Abby had ever heard. "And why not?"

He shrugged. "Maybe because you strike me as the Jag type rather than the truck type."

"There's a Jag type?"

He hooked a left out of the parking garage and

seemed to make a point of not meeting her gaze. "Well, with all the fancy clothes you wear"—he glanced briefly at her outfit—"I always took you for a girl who'd appreciate Jags and Rolls Royces over a truck."

"Then you'd be wrong. I like trucks. Where I'm from—" Abby bit her tongue, almost letting it slip that she was from rural Idaho where everyone owned a beat-up truck or two.

When they stopped at a red light, Stefan turned dark eyes her way. "From . . . ?"

Abby changed the subject. "So where are we going?"

He regarded her for a moment, then said, "Little Italy."

"Little Italy?"

"Don't tell me you've never been there before?"

Abby could understand his surprise, considering Micky had lived in New York her entire life. But it was too late for her to pretend she had been to that part of town. "No . . . I haven't had the opportunity."

"I imagine it's not your type of place anyway."

"Oh? And what kind of place would that be? Does this have something to do with being a Jag type rather than a truck type?"

A faint, wry smile filtered across his lips. "Maybe. I guess I just can't see you meandering down Mulberry Street or dining at a small table in the back of Puglia's."

Micky certainly wouldn't, but it was on the tip of Abby's tongue to tell Stefan that that was exactly the sort of thing *she* would like. But that meant divulging the truth about her identity.

She knew she would have to own up to her deception, but she was just not ready to see everything end, to have him look at her differently when he discovered she wasn't who he thought. He wanted Micky, not her . . . and never had Abby wanted to be her sister more than she did at that moment.

She stared out the window at the passing scenery, wishing her life were different, that she was not so flawed, not so afraid. But nothing could change the past.

"I guess you've never been to the San Gennaro festival?" He didn't wait for her reply. "For ten days people stuff themselves on some of the best Italian food New York has to offer."

A festival. When was the last time Abby had done anything even remotely festive? Gone to a party and not felt the pressures of her mother's illness calling her back home? Never before had she felt such a deep ache for the loss of her youth, her innocence. Things that could never be recaptured.

"I could go for some fried calamari right now," Stefan continued. "And a fat sausage sandwich piled high with onions and peppers, topped off with a nice bottle of red wine, and a couple of cannolis."

"What's a cannoli?"

He looked at her as though she had just dropped in from another planet. "You've never had a cannoli?"

"No. What is it?"

"A pastry filled with sweet riccota and custard

rolled in a fried dough shell. You haven't truly lived until you've had one. I'll stop at Sperino's and get some before I take you home."

"That's not necessary."

"Don't argue with an Italian about cannolis." Then he downshifted the Porsche and pulled up along a curb.

Abby glanced out the window to find they had parked in front of a lovely, attached brownstone with an old-fashioned front porch. She could envision a group of people sitting around on a warm summer night talking about their day and reminiscing about the past.

Stefan came around and opened her door. Taking her hand, he helped her out. He stood so close Abby could see where he had nicked himself shaving that morning. She knew the strongest urge to touch him there, to feel his warm skin beneath her fingertips.

She shook off the thought and glanced up and down the block. "I don't see any restaurants."

"That's because there aren't any."

"But I thought—"

"I didn't say we were going to a restaurant. I said I knew a place with great Italian food—and no one cooks better than my mother."

The hinges of a screen door creaked then, forestalling Abby's question. She peered around Stefan's shoulder, catching a glimpse of a short, older woman coming out of the house.

"Stefano!" she said in an excited voice.

Stefan took Abby by the hand and led her up the

steps. *"Ciao, Mama."* He leaned down and kissed his mother's wrinkled cheek.

Mrs. Massari patted her son on the shoulder and smiled. She was about half Stefan's enormous height and Abby wondered how such a small woman had produced such a big man.

"Lei guarda bello come sempre," he said to his mother.

"Sono un disordine, ma lei sono un ragazzo dolce," she returned, self-consciously smoothing a few strands of graying hair back into place.

Stefan chuckled and turned to Abby. "My mother always thinks she looks a mess."

"I think she looks adorable," Abby said before thinking how that might sound coming from a stranger.

Stefan gave her a devilish wink and then leaned down to his mother. *"Pensa che lei guardi adorabile."*

Abby narrowed her gaze on his face. "You didn't just tell your mother I thought she was adorable, did you?"

"Yup." His grin broadened.

Abby felt a light hand on her arm and turned to find Mrs. Massari smiling up at her. *"Bell'ed intelligente. Mio figlio un uomo fortunato."*

Abby returned the woman's warm smile with one of her own and then looked at Stefan. "What did she say?"

Stefan's eyes were unreadable in the semidarkness of the porch, but something in his voice caressed her. "She said that you are not only beautiful but intelligent . . . and that I'm a lucky man to have you."

Abby's cheeks flushed with heat, an undeniable spark of electricity flaring between her and Stefan, the world around them disappearing in those few moments.

Then a soft chuckle from Stefan's mother reminded Abby they were not alone. Her blush heightened, and she quickly averted her gaze.

Stefan let out a low, husky laugh and took hold of her hand. "Come on."

As soon as Abby stepped through the front door, she closed her eyes and breathed deeply. The wonderful aroma wafting through the house made her mouth water. She couldn't remember the last time she had had a home-cooked meal.

"It smells delicious," she said with an enraptured sigh, opening her eyes to find Stefan watching her, the slumberous look in his eyes doing strange things to her insides.

He gave her hand a gentle squeeze and then guided her through the house, past billowy lace curtains, crocheted doilies, figures of the Virgin Mary and Jesus, a large crucifix on one wall, a brown tweed sofa and matching chairs, and assorted heavy furniture.

At a large oval dining room table that looked as if it could seat at least twelve people, Stefan pulled out a chair for her.

The two place settings on the table underscored the fact that dinner had only been intended for mother and son. Abby wondered why Stefan had suddenly felt inclined to invite her along. Whatever his reasons, she was glad he did. She hadn't wanted to be alone tonight.

His mother retrieved another place setting from an antique wood cupboard and handed it to Stefan to put in front of Abby. Then Mrs. Massari disappeared into the kitchen.

"I'll be right back," Stefan told her.

Abby had no intention of sitting there while Stefan helped his mother, so she got up and followed. The kitchen was a lemon-yellow color and looked as if it hadn't been remodeled since the 1950s, but it had a warm, homey feel, the kind that made a person want to sit down and chat for a while.

"What can I do?" she asked.

Stefan glanced over at her, a surprised expression on his face. Then that look changed into one of approval—and more, as his gaze dipped to her lips before making a slow, steady sweep down her body, heating Abby from the inside out. Then his mother said something to him over her shoulder.

A crooked smile curled the corner of his sensuous lips. "My mother wants me to tell you that no guest of hers helps in the kitchen. Only bad sons who neglect to tell their mother about the pretty lady in their life must work for their supper."

The words warmed Abby, and as her gaze held Stefan's, she felt the strongest desire to step into his arms and stay there for a while. She might have done so if he wasn't wearing two ridiculous looking oven mitts. She couldn't help chuckling.

"What's so funny?"

"Your mitts are cute."

His half-grin rode higher on his beautiful mouth. "You're cute." Before Abby had a moment to savor his compliment, he shooed her from the kitchen.

Back in the dining room, Abby retook her seat and exchanged looks with Stefan each time he came out of the kitchen with another plate or bowl, filling the table with enough food for six people.

Abby couldn't stop watching him, admiring the way he moved, how the muscles in his arms stretched the material of his shirt or how well his broad shoulders filled out that shirt, the way his black hair caught the light and shimmering paths of gold filtered through the silky strands.

He was very, very male and just looking at him made her feel weak, her mind conjuring up images of how he had touched her, made her body convulse with pleasure, something she'd never experienced before . . . but which she wanted to experience again.

Mother and son finally took their seats. Stefan piled a bit of everything on Abby's plate so that by the time he handed it back to her, the dish weighed about three pounds.

She slanted him an amused look. "Do you think I have enough?"

He glanced at her plate, and looking completely serious, asked, "Do you want more?"

"I was only teasing."

That slow grin that had the power to make her feel like she was melting crept onto his face. "I wouldn't tease a hungry man, sweet. You never know what he might devour."

Abby flushed, a common occurrence of late, and glanced away, pretending rapt interest in her fork, which made Stefan chuckle.

As they ate, Stefan took the time to explain each

dish to her. *Bruschetta al pomodoro* was an antipasto of grilled ciabatta bread, marinated chopped tomatoes, garlic, basil, and kalamata olives. *Veal pizzicagnolo* was veal medallions with eggplant, proscuitto, and mozzarella cheese. *Tagliatelle alla bolognese* was a thin, flat spinach pasta with meat sauce and parmesan. And for dessert, he told her there was a fresh batch of *canestrelli,* a type of sweet-dough cookie.

"I'm stuffed," she confessed an hour later, leaning back in her chair as Stefan's mother went into the kitchen to get a pot of coffee. "I feel like a Christmas turkey with all the trimmings."

"You don't look that way from where I'm sitting."

Abby's gaze slid sideways to find Stefan's eyes on her, warm and intent. He reached out and brushed her hair back, his knuckles grazing her cheek, sending a shiver through her.

She wanted to close her eyes and lean into his hand. The realization amazed her. She never thought she would ever desire physical contact from any man, but Stefan was changing all that, and Abby felt a mixture of fear and anticipation at the prospect of what it could mean for her.

"What's that look for?" he asked in a teasing voice.

The new emotions swirling inside Abby made her bold, though she sounded shy and uncertain when she spoke. "I think . . . I want to kiss you."

His gaze lowered to her mouth. "You think?"

"I . . ." She swallowed. "Yes."

"What's stopping you, then?"

If he only knew. But Abby didn't want to think

about anything but that moment, to behave as though she was like every other woman.

Unconsciously, she wet her lips, her body edging closer to Stefan's, her heart beating wildly in her chest as her eyelids fluttered downward. She could feel his warm breath on her cheek, smell the subtle textures of his cologne.

Then Mrs. Massari entered the room and Abby abruptly straightened in her chair, hoping she didn't look as guilty as she felt and wondering what had come over her to make her act so out of character. She could feel Stefan's questioning gaze, but she didn't look at him.

After coffee and far too many wonderful cookies, they all drifted into the living room. Abby was too full to sit, so she skimmed the perimeter of the room, her gaze drifting over the mementos, crevices crammed full of things Stefan's parents had kept of their children's accomplishments.

There were baseball, football, and soccer trophies with Stefan's name on them. Clearly, he had been an athlete, but that didn't surprise Abby. He moved with an efficient grace that lent itself to sports and that she found fascinating.

She picked up an oval picture frame; the photo within slightly yellowed with age. A handsome older man had his arm wrapped around a young boy's shoulders, and within that young boy's face, Abby captured glimpses of Stefan.

"That's my father."

Abby started as Stefan came up behind her. For such a big man, he moved like a wraith. "I have to put bells on you."

"Sorry." His expression was so boyishly endearing that Abby felt a rush of tenderness toward him. She had to force her attention back to the picture.

"Your father's very handsome." She could see where Stefan got his striking good looks.

"He used to tell us that all the women back in Italy were in love with him, but he only had eyes for my mother."

"How sweet."

"Yeah. He was a good man. I miss him a lot. He died last year."

Abby glanced at him over her shoulder. "I'm sorry."

He stared down at the picture. "My mother had a hard time at first, but I think she's getting better now."

"She's got you."

He shrugged and stuffed his hands in his pockets. "I try to swing by here at least twice a week to have dinner with her. She really loves to cook, and with all us kids on our own now, I think she feels out of her element."

Abby could understand that. She knew what it was like to feel set adrift. "How many brothers and sisters do you have?"

He hesitated, an emotion flickering in his eyes that resembled despair. "There were five of us. My brother, Dominick, is the oldest. He lives on the Jersey shore and races boats, selling them during the off-season. I bought mine from him."

"I didn't know you had a boat."

"I've got her moored at a marina on the Hudson River about fifteen minutes from the office. During the summer months, I sack out there a lot. I like sitting on the deck with a beer and nothing around me but sky. It's the farthest away I can get without going far. Does that make any sense?"

Abby understood exactly what he was saying. There were times she had ducked away from her house after getting her mother to sleep, when the desire for freedom had overwhelmed her.

She'd burst out the back door and run until her lungs felt as if they would explode. Then she'd collapse onto the ground and stare up at the stars for hours, wondering if it was heaven she glimpsed through those glittering pinpoints of light, feeling as if she were part of something bigger, something that belonged only to her. It was ridiculous, she knew. Escapism. But it was all she had then.

"It makes complete sense," she murmured, forcing her gaze away from Stefan's and returning her attention to the smiling faces in the photos.

"A hell of a motley bunch, aren't we?"

"Are you all still close?"

"Yes, but we don't get to see much of each other; our respective lives are rather busy."

"Who's this?" Abby pointed to one of the young men in the group.

"That's Anthony. He's the third oldest, or youngest, however you look at it. He's a priest for a parish in the Bronx. The area is fairly poor and often dangerous, but Tony has always been a supporter of the underdog."

"And this?" She slid her finger to a stunning woman who appeared to be about twenty-two when the picture was taken.

"That's my sister, Anna. She's a fashion designer. She just landed an apprenticeship with Versace and had to move to Paris. She wants to start her own line someday."

It was clear that each of the Massari children possessed a burning desire to succeed. She saw that strength in Stefan when he was standing before the department heads at the staff meetings. And he had put all that drive toward building *Bastion* into what it was today. Suddenly, she very much wanted him to know how grateful she was for his dedication.

"You've done a great job at the magazine," she murmured. "Thank you."

He regarded her for a long moment before softly replying, "My pleasure."

Abby had to force herself to look away or get lost in his eyes. She pointed to the remaining person in the photo. "Who's this?" The girl appeared to be the baby of the group, no more than sixteen or seventeen, huddling with her siblings on the front steps of the house.

When Stefan made no reply, Abby turned to look at him. His features had hardened, but his eyes . . . they were stricken.

"Stefan?" She reached out to touch him, but he stepped away, shaking his head.

"That's my sister, Maria," he said in a raw voice. "She's dead."

Dear God. That beautiful girl with the vibrant smile . . . was dead? What could have taken the life of someone so young and vital?

Stefan's mother entered the room then. She took

one look at the photo Abby held and then lifted her gaze to her son, murmuring something Abby didn't understand, but which transcended barriers and touched her heart.

Then she did what Abby so desperately wanted to do. She put her arms around Stefan and hugged him close. And together, in silence, mother and son comforted each other.

Eleven

They left fifteen minutes later, silence stretching around them as they drove away. Abby ached to ask Stefan about his sister, to discover what had happened to her, but he had erected a wall, warding off any questions she might ask.

She stared out the window, absently watching buildings roll by, wondering what might be waiting for her when she returned to Micky's apartment, and what she would do if the phone rang, and if she would be able sleep tonight . . .

And if another red rose would be perched in front of her door come the morning.

She was so absorbed in her terrifying thoughts that she didn't hear Stefan speaking to her. His hand against her cheek jolted her.

"Are you all right?"

"What? Oh, yes. Fine. Just . . . thinking."

"About?"

Abby shrugged and searched for something plausible. "Work."

Either he didn't believe her or it was a topic he didn't wish to discuss. A moment later he pulled the car over. "Wait here. I'll be back in a second."

Abby watched him disappear inside a store and

then noted what it was. A bakery. She had completely forgotten about his promise to get her cannolis.

A few minutes later, he reappeared, holding up two white bags. He slid into the driver's seat and winked at her, his dark mood obviously having lifted.

"You didn't have to do this."

"I wanted to." He dug a hand into one of the bags and plucked out a creamy pastry, looking very determined as he pressed it toward her mouth. "Take a bite."

"I can't. I already ate too much."

"Please tell me you're not one of those women who's always on a diet."

"No, but—"

"Good." He grinned. "Now eat."

He mercilessly teased her lips until Abby relented and sank her teeth into the sweet confection. Her eyes closed and she moaned in pure delight.

"Told you it was good."

"Heaven."

"You have a little powder on your upper lip."

Embarrassed, Abby went to wipe her mouth with a napkin from the bag. Stefan halted her. "Let me."

Before she knew what he intended, he dipped his head and licked the powder from her lip. Abby's breath locked in her throat and she automatically tensed, but the fear was fleeting.

She made a soft whimper of surrender and he captured the sound with his mouth, slanting his lips across hers with a hunger that left her breathless.

She stirred restlessly in his arms, pressing closer. He groaned low in his throat and deepened the kiss. Rivulets of heat flooded Abby's veins as she slid her palms up his shirt, taking pleasure in the way the muscles in his chest bunched and flexed with each move.

His mouth trailed down her throat and Abby tilted her head back to give him better access.

"God," he said in a husky rasp, "I've been thinking about this all night."

Deep down, Abby knew she had been thinking about it, too. Stefan made her feel things . . . sensuous, delicious things that she had never expected to feel. And when he cupped her breast, instead of recoiling, she pressed herself more firmly against his palm.

"Jesus," he swore a moment before he pulled away.

Abby stared at him through desire-glazed eyes. "What's the matter?" she asked, feeling suddenly ashamed. Had she acted too bold?

He raked a hand through his hair. "I feel like I'm eighteen again, making out like this in my car, only instead of being embarrassed by my behavior . . ." He looked directly into her eyes. "I'm wishing like hell that I had a backseat so I could make love to you."

His words were an erotic caress that every atom of Abby's being responded to, making her skin feel as if it stood on end. She had never wanted to make love to a man, never thought she would be able to let anyone touch her intimately. But something burgeoned inside her, a need, a desperate yearning to give herself over to what felt right.

Stefan must have taken her silence as censure because he gripped the steering wheel and cursed. "If you can believe it, I usually have more control. I'm sorry." Before she could tell him that she had liked what he was doing and hadn't wanted him to stop, he said, "So why were you upset at the office? Did you have another problem with Carol?"

His abrupt switch jarred Abby, bringing reality back with resounding force, along with the terrifying memories of the night before.

She glanced away. "No. Nothing happened with Carol."

"Well, something happened, and we're going to sit in this car all night until you spit it out." He cupped her chin, forcing her to look at him. "Tell me."

Abby didn't want to talk about it. She didn't even want to think about it. But Stefan looked determined. "The man . . . he . . . he called me."

Stefan stared at her in confusion, then a muscle began to work in his jaw. "Are you talking about the pervert across the street that you saw through the telescope?"

Abby nodded.

"Christ!" he exploded. "Why didn't you tell me?"

"I didn't think you'd want to know."

"Wouldn't want to know? Why the hell not? I told you to call me if anything happened."

"I just thought after what happened the other day with Rick you wouldn't want to hear from me."

"What happened the other day has nothing to do with this. Did you think I wouldn't come?"

"I didn't know what to think. I was so scared and confused." Emotions threatened to choke her, and tears brimmed on her lashes.

"I know. Ssh." He brushed a kiss across her lips. "It's all right."

Abby wanted to lean into him and absorb his strength, but she could not put the burden on him. He didn't deserve it. It was her problem and she would deal with it.

"First thing in the morning, you're changing your phone number," he told her.

Abby didn't argue.

"What did he say to you?" he then asked, his tone gentling.

Abby did not want to recite the crude words, so she skirted the question. "His voice was altered."

"Altered?" A sharp frown furrowed his brow. "What do you mean?"

"The voice sounded mechanical. The police said he could have placed something over the receiver."

"Jesus, you called the cops and you didn't think to call me? What aren't you telling me?"

Abby didn't want to ruin their night by relaying the whole horrible story. But she could see by the look in his eyes that he would not let the matter drop. He would keep on her until she told him everything.

"He . . . he made me come to the window and watch. He had a woman with his this time."

"Oh, Christ . . ." He reached over and pulled her into his arms.

Abby closed her eyes and pressed her cheek against his chest as she told him the rest of the story, the words choking in her throat and bringing tears to her eyes.

When she was finished, he lifted her head and smoothed his thumbs over the path of her tears. "You're not going home tonight."

Abby knew she shouldn't let him get involved, but she didn't have the strength or the desire to fight him. She had dreaded going back to Micky's apartment.

Twenty minutes later they parked in the lot for the marina. The moment Abby alighted from the car and took a deep breath of the warm, sea-sprayed night air, she felt as if she were coming back to life.

Stefan took her by the hand. "My boat is docked in the last slip at the end of the pier. You might want to take off your heels. They could get stuck in the boardwalk."

The idea of taking off her shoes sounded divine and Abby didn't hesitate. The pavement felt cool beneath her feet, and Stefan's fingers laced through hers made everything seem right with the world.

When they reached the end of the pier, Abby could only stare. "I thought you said you had a boat."

"That is a boat."

"That's not a boat. It's a luxury liner!" Abby estimated the sleek vessel had to be at least sixty feet long.

Amusement lit his eyes. "Let's just say it has all the creature comforts so you don't have to worry about eating beans out of a can for dinner."

As Stefan helped her onboard, Abby glimpsed the name of the boat. *THE MARIA*. A few hours ago, she wouldn't have thought anything of it. She knew better now.

They went up a short flight of stairs off to the right and onto another level with a set of double doors. As they moved along, Stefan appeased her interest about the boat.

"She's a nineteen ninety-five modified-V hull but with the versatility of a cockpit. She has a flybridge as well as a lower steering station and she's equipped with a twenty-four-mile radar, autopilot, hundred fifty watt SSB radio, two compasses, two depth sounders, intercom system, AM/FM stereo with twelve speakers . . . and two televisions."

Abby could only gape at the elegance surrounding her as Stefan guided her down a narrow set of stairs to a carpeted corridor.

"There are two double cabins and one single cabin with a total of six berths. The master and guest bedrooms have three separate heads with a shared shower."

He pointed out the boat's interior amenities then. A dinette with full-size refrigerator/freezer, a watermaker, microwave with oven, dishwasher, washer/dryer, hot and cold pressure water, and liquor dispenser.

"And should she catch on fire, there is a CO2 system and six fire extinguishers."

"And what if she springs a leak in the middle of the night?"

Stefan bent close to her ear. He felt warm and solid. "No worries. I'll save you." He pressed a light kiss to the top of her head. Then he stepped into the galley, retrieved a bottle of red wine from a rack, two glasses from the cabinet and took hold of her hand. "Let's go topside."

A few moments later, they emerged on the deck and Abby felt as if she were back home gazing up at the heavens as the night sky spread out before her, a crescent moon cutting a sliver of light into the darkness.

A gentle northerly breeze stirred the surface of the water, keeping the humidity low. The air smelled sweet and clean, as if it had been washed and hung out to dry. The sky was obscenely beautiful, salted with a panoply of stars sprinkled across black velvet, the world around them seeming to contract and billow.

Abby glanced up to find Stefan staring at her rather than the sky. Her body tingled. He pressed a glass into her hand and uncorked the wine bottle, a rich bouquet wafting upward.

He clinked his glass to hers. "Here's to new beginnings."

The idea sounded wonderful. A new beginning was just what she wanted, what she had hoped for after she had left childhood behind. If only things could be that simple.

She gazed out over the indigo water topped with lacy white peaks, something about the constant ebb and flow enticing her. Perhaps because the sea was so vital and constant, so enduring when other things faded, life, goals, the future. It reminded her of her past, her youth, dreams she had that had floated away with the tide until they were so far gone there was no way to recapture them.

A sharp pain suddenly twisted in her abdomen, reminding her that she was not as invincible as she wanted to be, and why happiness always seemed to remain just out of her reach.

She took a sip of her drink, praying the throbbing would subside, though relief seemed to take a little longer each time and would bring the fatigue and nausea by the morning.

For long moments neither she nor Stefan spoke. Instead they sipped their wine in companionable silence and stared out into the starry night.

The question of what happened to Stefan's sister continued to nag at Abby. He had looked so troubled and pained as he gazed at the picture of Maria that Abby's heart felt as if it were being squeezed.

"Stefan?"

"Hmm?" His tone was languid, and when he turned his gaze to her, his eyes were as dark and compelling as the water, nearly making Abby forget what it was she had wanted to say.

She stared down into her wineglass to refocus her thoughts. "I'd like to know about your sister . . . Maria." When silence met her request, she elevated her gaze to find Stefan regarding her through hooded eyes.

He put his glass to his lips and finished off the wine in a single swallow, then said, "What is it you'd like to know?" in a tone that suggested she might want to reconsider probing.

Clearly, he didn't want to talk about his sister. She could see it in the set line of his jaw and the rigid way he held himself. But for some reason she wanted him to know he could talk to her, that she would be there for him should he need her.

"I'd like to know what happened to her."

He poured himself another glass of wine, not looking at her. "She killed herself," he replied bluntly, flatly.

A slight gasp escaped Abby's parted lips and Stefan's gaze cut to her. He looked fierce and taut and miserable. "I'm sorry," she whispered.

She reached out to him, wanting only to console him, but he stepped back, as if having anyone touch him at that moment would be too painful.

"It was four years ago," he said, and Abby heard his bitterness and despair. He stared out at the water and took another swallow of his wine before his gaze slid back to her. "Don't you want to know why she killed herself?"

He seemed to be challenging her, his grip on the stem of the wineglass tightening until, with a crystalline pop, the glass snapped in half, a jagged shard bloodying his palm.

Abby pressed her lips tightly together, knowing that if she showed any emotion he would say no more. "Yes," she quietly said. "Tell me."

He looked dangerous, like a trapped animal seeking a target to lash out at. "She was raped."

The words were harsh, abrasive, meant to shock Abby, and they did; they tore all the way to her soul, making her own dark memories pound on the invisible door holding them back, screaming for release.

Stefan made a wordless sound, brittle and wounded. "Do you believe she blamed herself for what that bastard did to her?"

Abby understood far too well. How many times had she blamed herself? Told herself that she had done something to provoke Jimmy?

Tears began to fall, but Abby was not shedding them for herself but for a young girl who had thought life was no longer worth living, made to feel worthless by another human being, her despair so deep she believed the only way out was through death.

"Don't," Stefan said in a low, heartrending voice. "Sweet God, don't cry."

His arms coiled around her, pulling her tight against his hard frame. Then he leaned down and brushed a poignant kiss across her lips. She deepened the contact, her tongue tangling with his. He tasted of wine and heated male.

Remembering his injury, Abby forced herself to step back. She took hold of his right wrist, gently opening his fingers to see the damage the sharp glass had wrought.

She tugged Stefan behind her and headed for the galley. Once there, she turned on the cold water faucet above the sink and put his hand under the flow.

Gently she washed his wound. She had expected a single deep puncture mark considering the amount of blood that had been dripping. Instead, there was a long, thin cut running the entire length of his palm.

"You may need a few stitches." She glanced up, but he wasn't paying any attention to his injury. His gaze was focused solely on her.

"It'll be fine."

"Do you have something I could use as a bandage?"

He nodded and then led her out of the galley, down the corridor to the cabin at the end. As soon as he opened the door, Abby knew she had entered his domain.

An unexpected heat rose inside her at the realization and she forced her gaze away from the big bed in the middle of the room only to find Stefan reading her expression. Her chest felt tight, as if there wasn't enough air.

"Bandage," she managed to get past her lips, reminding herself as much as him.

Almost reluctantly, he led her to the bathroom. It was fully equipped with every necessity, yet there was only limited space, leaving barely two inches between their bodies. A single deep breath would press her breasts into his chest . . . and Lord help her, she wanted to take that breath.

She distracted herself by wrapping his hand. The space between them seemed to shrink while the temperature shot to sweltering. She had to get out before she lost what was left of her composure.

"There," she said hastily, tying off the binding.

Without another word, she whirled away. She had barely made it out of the bathroom when she felt Stefan's hand on her upper arm, turning her around to face him.

He stood in the threshold, his body filling the space, seeming to dwarf the entire room. He stared at her, long and hard, his fingers slowly running down her arm before releasing her, and when he did, Abby felt bereft.

She ached for him. Never, never before had she known this kind of soul-deep yearning, as if someone else was taking over her body.

"I want to kiss you." Stefan's words caressed her

like warm rain, and Abby felt a divine heaviness settle within her, a tautening at the remembrance of
his fingers touching her, spinning her in magic,
calling forth things her body had never done.

"Kiss me, then," she whispered, not wanting to
think, to worry, to die in little pieces.

He closed the short gap between them. The bandage seemed so insignificant wrapped around that
big hand . . . whose fingers reached for the button
of her blouse.

Abby's hand closed over his, stopping him. "W-
what are you doing?"

"You said I could kiss you."

"You can, but—"

He pressed a finger to her lips, then slid it down
her throat, over her collarbone, along the top of
her breast before saying in a husky rasp, "I want to
kiss you . . . here." Slowly, torturously, he circled her
nipple. The painfully hardened nub pushed against
her shirt.

Abby did not make a sound as he began to undo
her buttons, could not utter a word of protest, and
heaven help her, she did not want to.

Twelve

Cool air slid across Abby's heated body as her shirt dropped soundlessly to the ground. Stefan cupped her, his gaze so reverent, so gloriously male as he stared at her breasts that Abby thought she would die. Never had she understood the power of being a woman, of being desirable, and precious. Stefan made her feel that way.

He wrapped an arm around her waist, pulling her close. His tongue made an exploration of her skin, dipping into the hollow at the base of her throat as his fingers teased her nipples, gently tugging at them and then rolling the aching peaks.

Abby's head dropped back, which thrust her breasts forward, making the sensations that much more exquisite. Liquid heat began to build between her thighs.

He unbuttoned her skirt and oh, so slowly drew down the zipper. The material slid over her hips and puddled at her feet. He feathered kisses over her stomach, on the undersides of her breasts, his fingers kneading her back, cupping her buttocks.

He eased his fingers beneath the edge of her pantyhose, wanting to strip off another layer, lay siege to another one of her defenses.

Abby fought for rationality beneath the onslaught, trying to see her way through the sensual haze Stefan was so expertly creating with his hands, his mouth, his sweet reverence to every piece of flesh.

"Stefan . . ." His name came out a moan.

"Trust me. I only want to make you feel good." His hot breath fanned her skin and made her shiver.

Abby had to put her hands on his shoulders to keep herself upright as her mind whirled with sensations and vivid pictures of what he had done to her the last time, how incredible it had been.

"You want this, right?" he asked, as his mouth pressed kisses along her hipbone.

"Yes," she breathed as he tugged the pantyhose away and then skimmed his fingers up her calves, behind her knees, massaging her thighs, and finally toying with the sides of her panties.

"Say it, *cara.*" He pressed his mouth to her mound, kissing her through the thin silk of her panties. Abby wanted to feel his lips against her skin, no barriers, just flesh. "Tell me you want me to make you feel good." His fingers slipped beneath the crotch of her underwear and found her wet and slick, circling her nub then gently scoring it with his fingernail. "Say it," he gently ordered as he stroked her.

"Yes . . . oh, yes."

"Say the words and I'll give you anything you want." His erotic ministrations slowed, his finger barely touching her, making each whispering glide that much more exquisite, and making her that much more desperate for his touch.

Abby's legs felt as if they would no longer hold

her. "I . . . I want you to make me feel good. Please, Stefan . . . please."

He bore her down onto his bed and spread her legs wide, putting his warm mouth where his fingers had just been.

The first flick of his tongue against the engorged pulse point made Abby arch off the bed. He put his hands on the inside of her thighs and made her open even wider to him.

She was so crazed with need and desire she didn't even think to cover herself, to feel ashamed . . . because she didn't. She wanted to be devoured by the hot flames of his stroking tongue.

"Keep your legs open for me. That's it."

Abby would have done anything, anything for him as he drew the nub into his mouth, tugged and then licked to soothe, over and over again. And when his fingers flicked her nipples with the same intensity, Abby felt as if the entire world had disappeared and every fiber of her being culminated toward that bright, spiraling place he had brought her to once before.

Then he stopped and Abby nearly cried. "Stefan, no. Please . . . don't stop."

"Ssh." He put his hands around her waist and pushed her farther up onto the bed. Then his mouth came down over hers hard, hungry, demanding, his tongue sweeping into her while his fingers parted her folds and found her again.

There was no slow exploration with his mouth as he had done before, no trailing sweet kisses. Instead he went directly to her breast, suckling her, his midnight gaze holding her hostage as she watched what he was doing to her. His teeth gently bit down, and when she saw the tip of his tongue tease the distended peak, her entire world exploded into a warm flood tide.

"That's it, baby."

The pulses were so deep . . . so, so deep. He had promised, and, oh God, he had kept his word as convulsion after convulsion ravaged her body, leaving her drained in the aftermath of a pleasure unlike any she had ever known.

Stefan rolled to his side and brought her along with him. Abby pillowed her head against his shoulder and laid a hand over his chest, belatedly realizing he was still fully clothed while she was completely naked.

But even clothed, he was magnificent. His shirt had pulled free from his waistband, the ends trailing over his hips, which drew Abby's gaze to the bulge straining against the zipper of his pants. She knew a tenderness so strong it nearly burst inside her.

He had denied himself, restrained himself for her. She wanted to make him feel what she had felt, to be wild, mindless with unfettered passion. She had never had a chance to explore her sexuality. Her mother had gotten ill, and then Jimmy Bodine had tainted her for every man.

Yet in the warm security of Stefan's arms, she felt almost loved. But it would be pure foolishness to believe he felt anything for her. He thought she was Micky.

Abby desperately wanted him see *her,* to somehow know that she wasn't what she appeared. But how could he ever do that with her lie standing squarely between them?

He had given her so much that Abby knew she could no longer keep up the pretense. For better or worse, for heartbreak or happiness, she had to tell him. He deserved to know the truth. She should never have kept it from him this long. She only prayed he would not hate her after he found out who she really was.

She searched deep inside her for the courage to speak, but before she could say a word, Stefan did, turning his head on the pillow to look at her with eyes full of heated promise.

"Time for the truth," he said, taking Abby by surprise.

Could he know what she was about to say? Had he sensed all along that she was not Micky? Had her inexperience given her away?

If he had had a relationship with Micky as her sister had said, then certainly Abby had just proven to him that she was not the wild, sexy woman her sister was.

He levered up on his elbow and stared down at her. "I want to know what happened to you."

Abby frowned, confused. "I don't understand."

"Why are you afraid of men? Or is it simply me you're afraid of?"

Afraid of him? How could she ever have been afraid of him? It seemed so foolish now. How wrongly she had judged him. She knew now that even during the worst of his temper, he would never have hurt her.

"I'm not afraid of you."

"Then tell me who hurt you." He brushed the hair away from her face and Abby shivered in the wake of that gentle touch. "Tell me," he gently urged, as if knowing she would protest.

Abby could not meet his eyes. "It was a long time ago. Back in college." He didn't push her to go on, but instead continued his stroking, coaxing her with his light caress.

She could feel his intent gaze. He wanted to know; he really did. And didn't she owe him that much? He had confided to her about his sister and she knew how hard that had been for him. Then he had brought her as close to heaven as a mere mortal could, helped her to find a part of herself she had long believed dead.

"His name was Jimmy."

Stefan's hand stilled, and Abby could feel the tension coiling around him, the anger building, but she didn't know if it was directed at her or the man who attacked her. She was too much the coward to look at him and discover the truth in his eyes. Instead she pushed on, a need building in her to let out the ugliness.

She didn't realize tears were coursing down her cheeks until her story, so long kept secret, was finally out in the open, finally exorcised. And still, she could not look at Stefan, afraid of what she might see, censure, anger, disbelief. But he refused to be ignored.

His arms tightened about her waist, pulling her closer. "I'm so sorry you had to go through anything like that."

Abby shut her eyes, her heart twisting in her

chest. She knew he meant it, that he didn't accuse her, that he understood what she had gone through in a way many men could not. His own sister had endured the stigma of rape, had ended her life because of her despair, and Abby wondered how she could have ever doubted him.

For a long time he held her, no words passing between them, but none were necessary. A connection had been made, an invisible bond that had not existed between them until then, and as much as Abby wanted to finally admit her deception, she couldn't bear to see the hate in his eyes now that she had just been given her first glimpse of happiness she had known in so very long. She wanted a little more time to feel as she did at that moment.

"Let me get you something to sleep in," Stefan murmured, sliding out of bed and gently tugging the sheet up to cover her. Then he went to a chest of drawers and pulled out a T-shirt with a Columbia University logo on it. "Will this be all right? It's the best I have."

"It's fine. Thank you."

He handed her the shirt, standing uncertainly next to the bed. Abby suddenly felt shy, which was ridiculous in light of what had just happened between them.

"You can sleep in here," he said. "I'll sleep in one of the other cabins."

"You mean . . . you don't want to sleep with me?"

"I want nothing more than to sleep with you, but I'm afraid the last thing on my mind would be sleep." He leaned down and dropped a quick kiss on her lips and then he was gone.

Thirteen

Abby awoke the next morning to the sound of a seagull chattering to its mate.

A warm tingle flowed through her as she recalled in vivid detail all the things Stefan had done to her the night before in this bedroom . . . in this very bed. His bed. The way he had possessed her body, made her feel a slave to every silken caress. She had never believed anything could be so wonderful.

She sighed blissfully and hugged his pillow close. The faint scent of him greeted her, a little spicy, slightly musky, and very, very male. Abby would have been content to remain huddled beneath the comforter for the remainder of the day, but she had to get to work.

Yawning, she glanced over at the digital clock on the bedside table and shot upright in bed.

It was almost noon!

She scrambled out of bed. How could Stefan have let her sleep so long? Patty probably thought she had gotten run over by a taxi since she hadn't called in to say she was running late. What was the man thinking?

With no regard for how horrible she must look with her makeup gone astray and her hair uncombed and wearing only a T-shirt that went to mid thigh, Abby hastened from Stefan's cabin. The smell of freshly brewed coffee led her straight to the galley.

He glanced up from his newspaper at the sight of her and a languid, thoroughly devastating grin spread across his face. His gaze then moved down her body and back up again and Abby couldn't believe that short perusal could produce such a rush of heat, especially when she had come to give him a dressing-down for not waking her up.

"Good morning. Sleep well?"

"Do you know what time it is?"

"Somewhere around noon, I think. Coffee?" He rose from his chair to get a mug for her before she had even told him if she wanted any. She did. It smelled divine.

"And did it slip your mind that we are supposed to be at work?"

"Nope." Garbed in a pair of worn jeans that hugged every gorgeous curve, and a black T-shirt that molded the taut planes of his chest and broad shoulders, he strode over to her. Placing the mug in her hand, he swept a kiss across her lips and grinned down at her. "Have I told you yet how sexy you look in my shirt?"

As much as Abby didn't want to respond to that grin or the effect of his handsome face or explosive physique, her body began to tingle.

She forced herself to hold her ground, hoping her growing desire didn't show. "Will you be serious? I should have called into the office hours ago. Patty probably thinks I'm inconsiderate."

He raised an eyebrow at her last remark. "That's a first."

"What?"

"Well, you never seemed to care what anyone thought of you. You came and went as you pleased."

He was referring to Micky, and Abby realized he had given her another opportunity to come clean, and yet she couldn't. Not yet.

Was it wrong to want just a little more happiness? To need it so desperately she was willing to do whatever was necessary to hold on to it?

She had never comprehended how a deception could snowball until it was almost impossible to dig out of. For so many years she had dreamed of this . . . of Stefan, of freedom, and joy . . . and maybe love, things she had been denied for so long. Every time the words to confess rose to her lips, selfishness kept her silent.

"Are you all right?" he asked.

Abby nodded. "Fine. I just think you should have woken me up, that's all."

Stefan held up his hands in supplication, no longer smiling. "Forgive me. I thought you were tired and needed some rest." He turned his back on her then and Abby wanted to kick herself for ruining the moment with her waspish behavior.

He stood at the sink cleaning a few dishes and Abby felt an incredible tug at her heart just looking at him. She kept thinking that if she blinked, he would be gone, that she would wake up and realize she had been dreaming.

She padded across the short length of the galley, not thinking about what she was doing. Something else guided her, female instinct perhaps or a strange desire for preservation, for herself, the moment.

She pressed herself against his back, wrapping her arms around his waist, and laying her cheek against his smooth cotton T-shirt.

"I'm sorry," she murmured.

His fingers encircled her wrists and she thought he was going to put her away from him. A protest rose in her throat. Instead he turned in her arms so that they were facing each other.

Threading his finger through her hair, he pressed her head against his chest and wrapped his other arm around her waist, holding her tightly in his embrace, and Abby knew she was forgiven.

For long moments they stayed that way. Abby had never felt so content, so cherished. Stefan's warmth spread over her like a blanket, and for a few minutes, she allowed herself to believe all was right with the world.

Eventually, she glanced up and found Stefan's dark eyes boring into hers, heat in his penetrating regard that Abby immediately responded to.

"I missed you last night," she whispered. As little as three months ago, she would never have believed she would want a man in her bed, let alone crave his touch.

"I missed you, too." The words were a husky murmur that made Abby ache with longing. "I thought about you for hours."

Her heart swelled. "You did?"

He nodded slowly. "All I saw was your sweet body begging for my touch, your hands clutching my head as I stroked your nipples, those hot little whimpers telling me you liked what I was doing."

A blush heated Abby's cheeks and she focused her gaze on his chest. "I did."

He tipped her chin up. "I want to touch you again."

Breath lodged in Abby's throat. She wanted that, too. So much she thought she might die from the need.

She quivered as his big hand skimmed down her side, over her hip, to the edge of the T-shirt. She had not put her panties back on from the previous night, so his fingers made contact with the downy curls at the juncture of her thighs. Just that feather-light caress rocked her.

"Do you want me?" he murmured, and then decided to discover the answer for himself, easing a finger between her slick folds. "Oh, yeah. You're already wet." The words came out a near groan.

Abby didn't know what to think. "I can't seem to help myself."

His low chuckle was a sensuous thrum. "I don't ever want you to help yourself then." He stroked her with his finger.

Abby's eyes closed and her head fell back. "Stefan . . ."

"Do you want me to make you feel good again?"

"Yes . . ."

"And you'll spread your sweet thighs for me anywhere I want to give you pleasure?"

Abby moaned low in her throat as he stopped the erotic torture while waiting for her answer. "Anywhere," she breathed.

"Good girl." He walked her backward until she felt the edge of the dinette table. "Get on." She did as she was told. "Take your shirt off." With barely a shred of modesty, she lifted the shirt over her head, sitting naked before him.

"I want to see you," she said.

He nodded, but his finger never left her. Abby could barely concentrate on removing his shirt as exquisite sensations rifled through her body.

Once his shirt was off, Abby marveled at the sculpted beauty that had lain beneath his clothing, chiseled pectoral muscles, shoulders that were like melon halves, round and perfectly formed, arms that bulged, veins standing out, corded forearms.

And his stomach. Oh, sweet heaven. With every move he made, the muscles rippled and flexed.

Her gaze dipped to the jeans hugging his waist and the mystery that existed just beyond the single button enclosure and zipper. She wanted to touch him there.

Her fingers shook as she reached for the button and then eased the zipper down. White cotton briefs hugged him like a second skin, emphasizing his erection. The edge of the elastic waistband bulged, showing the very tip of his penis. He made no move to rush her along. Didn't force her to do anything, which gave her the confidence to do what she wanted.

She slid down the briefs and let the silky length of him spring free. He was magnificent, perfectly formed, and rock-hard. Without thinking, Abby wrapped her hand around him.

Air hissed between his teeth at her first tentative

contact. He swelled to even bigger dimensions as she stroked his shaft up and down.

The finger between her legs increased in tempo. His other hand cupped her breast, his callused thumb sweeping back and forth over her nipple. Then he eased a finger inside her. Abby immediately stiffened and drew her thighs together.

"I won't hurt you." The look in his eyes told her he meant what he said, and he had never lied to her before.

Slowly, Abby opened her thighs. Their eyes locked as he slipped his finger inside again.

"Jesus, you're so tight. I would have never thought . . ." He stopped, his gaze sliding away from hers, which made reality seep back into Abby's brain. It was about Micky. Always Micky.

"Never what?"

"Nothing."

"No, I want to know what you mean."

He looked grim and Abby knew the spell was broken. He stepped away from her, tugging up his briefs as she scrambled for her shirt.

"Tell me!"

"All right! Christ!" He raked a hand through his hair. "You've had three husbands. I guess I just thought—"

"That I'd be well used?" Abby didn't know why she was so indignant. Perhaps it was simply that she felt angry for her sister's sake, a need to defend Micky because she wasn't there to do it herself.

"Look," he said, trying to sound calm. "It was a stupid thing to say, to even think. I'm sorry." He turned half away from her. "Maybe I was just feeling insecure."

His confession took her by surprise. How could a man as beautiful and successful as Stefan feel insecure about anything? "I don't understand."

"Can we just drop it?"

Abby didn't want to drop it, but she did anyway. In truth, no matter what he had said, she didn't want to argue with him. She wanted to savor their time together.

He slipped on his shirt and went to grab her coffee mug beside the sink. He dumped the lukewarm contents and refilled the cup. Sinking one hand into the pocket of his jeans, he handed the cup to her. He looked chagrined and completely endearing.

"Thank you," she murmured, taking a sip. "I guess I better call the office."

"Don't bother. I already called."

"You did? Why didn't you tell me?"

"You didn't give me the opportunity."

He was right. She hadn't. "What did you tell them?"

"That we wouldn't be in today."

"We? Do you mean you told them that we were together?"

"No." He opened the refrigerator and took out a carton of orange juice. "I simply said we wouldn't be in. Gretchen has my cell phone number if she needs to reach me."

"But what if they think we're together?"

He leaned a hip against the counter. "I doubt they will."

"But what if they do?"

He shrugged diffidently. "Then I guess they'll think we're two adults and that what we choose to do is none of their goddamn business."

His reply was more forceful than Abby expected and she was curious as to why. Could her questions be causing him to regret what happened between them? The thought made her sick with despair.

"I'm going to take a shower."

Stefan nodded and watched her go, cursing his damn tongue for making that asinine comment about her husbands. But God, he had wanted her so bad he hurt. He could barely concentrate on anything else.

He couldn't remember the last woman who had made him this crazy. He felt like a teenager around her, wanting to do everything right and deathly afraid of doing everything wrong.

Christ, that was a revelation. Not long ago he had wished her to another continent. But over the past ten weeks he had seen a new side of her. She had become a woman he wanted to get to know.

He thought about the bastard who had abused her and felt that perhaps he finally understood why she had always acted like such a bitch, and why she had married men who were so much older than her. She could control older men. They wouldn't want much from her in bed, and they would be damn grateful for whatever they got.

Maybe the men were father figures. God knows Lowery had never seemed all that interested in his daughter. When he wasn't working, he was chasing a good time and a tight ass to warm his bed.

Maybe she hadn't really loved any of her husbands or known what it was like to feel passion. Every time Stefan brought her to orgasm, she seemed almost in awe, as if the whole thing were new to her.

Those were the things he wanted to believe, that with him, she had discovered the depths of her desire, the kind that claws at you until you're sure life will come to an end if you don't satisfy the need.

Every day she consumed more and more of his attention. Beneath the veneer she showed to the outside world was a vulnerable girl, sweet and smart, sincere and down-to-earth.

That morning, he had woken from a dream of a rambling house with a big piece of land, him outside trying to put together a jungle gym and her with their baby at her breast. He couldn't believe how much that dream had affected him.

Stefan was almost grateful when his cell phone rang, jerking him from his thoughts. He moved toward the dinette table where he had almost fucked Michaela like some mindless stud and answered the phone.

Abby was drying her hair when a knock sounded at the bathroom door. She opened it to find Stefan standing there, a cell phone in his hand and an expression that made her uneasy.

"What's the matter?"

"Patty called."

"How did she know to call you to find me? You said you didn't tell anyone we were together."

"I didn't. She was trying to reach you and decided to call me just in case I might know where you were."

Abby knew then that it must be important if Patty was trying to track her down. "What did she want?"

"She said the police were trying to get in touch with you. Apparently they went by your apartment last night and then called the office this morning."

Reality came back to Abby in a rush. For one glorious night, she had been able to shut out the memories of the horror she had heard and witnessed. But she should have known it would catch up with her eventually. Didn't everything?

"What did Patty say?"

"Just to have you get in touch with a Detective Tremonte."

The gnawing sensation threatening her stomach, Abby moved past Stefan into the corridor. "I have to go."

Stefan took hold of her arm. "Where?"

"To the police station, I guess." Abby didn't quite know what she was doing. So many thoughts were racing through her mind at that moment. Had the police found the man? Or had they discovered something far worse?

"All right, but I'm going with you."

"No." The word came out with more force than she had intended, but if Stefan came with her, he would find out the truth about who she was and Abby didn't want him making the discovery like that. She wanted to be the one to tell him. "You don't have to. I'll be fine."

As soon as she returned from the police station

she would tell him the truth—and then it would be over between them. It should have never begun in the first place.

"I don't want you doing this by yourself," he said, his hand sliding down her arm, his fingers entwining with hers. "I told you I was here for you."

Abby felt tears pricking behind her eyes. "I know, but I can't be afraid to leave your side. I refuse to let this man rule my life."

For a moment, it appeared as if Stefan would object. Then he heaved a sigh, looking none too happy. "Fine, but I'm driving you."

Abby knew further protest would appear suspicious. "I'd like that. Thank you." She went to move past him, but he still held her hand. She glanced up at him.

"Don't worry," he murmured, brushing his knuckles across her cheek. "Everything will be all right."

Tears threatening, Abby nodded and quickly pulled away, trying not to think about how that might be the last time he ever looked at her like that.

As the Porsche pulled out of the marina parking lot, Stefan said, "Let me have your apartment key."

Abby turned to look at him. "Why?"

"I'll go over and gather up some of your things while you're talking to the detective. I want you to stay with me until this problem is resolved."

"But—"

"The subject is closed to discussion."

Abby wondered if Stefan would still want her around once she told him the truth about who she was. She didn't want to think about it. She turned and stared out the window.

"Here." Stefan pressed something into her hand.

She glanced down to find a white a piece of paper in her palm. "What's this?"

"My cell phone number. I want you to call me the minute you're done with this Tremonte guy. I don't want you to leave the police station until I come for you. Do you understand?" His expression told her how serious he was.

She nodded.

"Good. Now is there anything in particular you want from the apartment?"

Abby thought for a second and then gasped. "Oh, no! I completely forgot about Sheba!"

"You mean the cat?"

"Yes. She's been alone for a whole day!"

"Don't worry. Cats are resilient. Do you have a neighbor who might consider watching her? I'd bring her to the boat, but there are too many dangerous spots a cat could crawl into and openings she might be able to get out of, and I can't picture that fur ball being too happy should she fall into the water."

"There's my neighbor, Ida Gelman. She lives two apartments down. Sheba seems to like her well enough. I can't really think of anyone else."

"Gelman. The name sounds vaguely familiar. I'll talk to her. I'm sure we can work something out."

A few minutes later, he eased the Porsche into a parking space in front of the station house.

Abby hesitated, not sure she wanted to go in now that she was here. What were the police going to tell her? Would it be good or bad? Did she dare hope they knew who the man was and he swore he would leave her alone?

"Are you sure you don't want me to come with you?" Stefan's question ended Abby's musing.

She forced a smile to her face. "I'm sure. I'll see you in a little while." Impetuously, she leaned over and kissed him, a kiss that said everything she couldn't.

Then she hopped out of the car, Stefan's confused gaze following her as she walked up the stairs leading to the precinct.

Fourteen

Sheba was clearly pissed to have been left alone.

With a shrill meow, the cat leapt from the head of a naked statue and flung herself at Stefan as soon as he stepped into the apartment.

The feline's claws raked his shirt as she climbed her way up his chest, promptly wrapping herself around his neck and bawling at Stefan in cat language, which, had he understood, probably would have blistered his ears with a litany of four-letter words.

"It's all right," he crooned, feeling idiotic talking to the cat, but the thing was smothering him in fur. "Uncle Stefan's here now and no one will forget you again."

As Stefan stroked the cat, he glanced around the apartment, once more struck by the almost decadent opulence, the rich furnishings, the unusual artwork. No matter how hard he tried, he just couldn't picture the woman he had come to know living here.

He headed down the hallway toward the bedrooms, an unrelenting Sheba in tow, thinking that perhaps all these trappings were another of Michaela's defense mechanisms, a way to mask who she truly was, which he had come to discover was surprisingly innocent, and very vulnerable.

He thought about the scum who had attacked her in college and wished he could go back in time and beat the shit out of the son of a bitch. Any man who would use his strength to harm a woman, to violate her, should be castrated and then riddled with bullets.

Stefan felt as if she had bestowed an honor on him when she had slowly opened up, letting go of her inhibitions in the same tentative way she had allowed him to undress her, one delectable layer at a time.

Lord knows, he wanted to make love to her, to the point he was about ready to chew through his own arm. But more than that, he wanted *her* to want to it, and he would wait until she was ready.

With some difficulty, he forced his thoughts back to the matter at hand. "All right, Sheba, lead me to your owner's toothbrush."

The apartment had three bedrooms. He glanced in one and found state-of-the-art exercise equipment. The second room looked like a spare, although the bedcovers were rumpled as if someone had recently slept there.

At the end of the hallway was the third and largest room with a huge four-poster Chinese sleigh bed swathed in a gauzy canopy. A dark burgundy and gold satin comforter adorned the top. The setup made Stefan think of a suite occupied by the sultan's favorite concubine. He immediately regretted the thought.

Unwinding Sheba from his neck, he plunked the

cat on the bed and put his mind to his task. He decided he would bring back a little bit of everything.

A door off to the side stood slightly ajar and he discovered it was an enormous walk-in closet with one entire wall dedicated to shoes. There had to be at least two hundred pairs, and all of them expensive.

Hanging from three rows of brass rods were dresses and suits in every style, color, and designer— Armani, Versace, Donna Karan, and countless others.

Again, Stefan was struck with the incongruity of what he saw compared to the woman he knew. And as he stood there in the middle of the closet something bothered him, a sensation that things were not as they seemed, which he had been feeling ever since Michaela's return, but couldn't pin down.

He shook off his unease and grabbed the Fendi suitcase he spotted in the corner. He only put two business suits in, and the most subdued he could find, a task that turned out to be surprisingly difficult.

He preferred Michaela the way she looked that night he had come to her apartment carting the box from work. She had been wearing jeans and an oversized T-shirt, looking adorable and sexy.

Stefan wanted more of those outfits so he searched the bureau. He frowned when he came across not a single pair of jeans. Did she keep them somewhere else?

Opening the top drawer, he was stunned by what he saw, a treasure trove of lingerie, silky G-strings and flimsy teddies. He knew underwear was one of the necessities he had to return with, and he had been secretly anticipating personally picking those items out.

He had been fantasizing far too much about the sweet cotton panties she liked to wear, the kind that made him think of hot summer nights and innocent groping behind the high school bleachers when copping a feel was the hottest thing to an adolescent with raging hormones.

But there was not a single pair of cotton panties to be found in either of the top drawers.

He lifted out a lacy thong and a matching bra with the nipple area cut out. With the items dangling from his fingertips, he remembered how he had originally believed Michaela was playing some kind of game with him, trying a different tack to seduce him, sweet rather than siren. He hadn't thought that way in a while because she had seemed so genuine. Damn it if he wasn't confused again.

"Don't move, buster!"

Stefan whipped around at the sound of a voice behind him to find a seventyish-looking woman standing on the threshold adorned in a boatload of jewelry and a flowing caftan in so many ultraviolet shades it was nearly blinding even in the dim light.

In one hand she held a broom, pointing the handle at him as if it were a sword. In the other hand she wielded an object with far more potential for bodily injury.

A butcher knife.

"You pervert!" Her disgusted gaze flicked to Stefan's hands and he realized he still held Michaela's thong and bra. Great. He did look like a pervert.

"This isn't what you think," he said.

"Tell it to the police. They'll be here any minute."

"Look, I can explain." He took a step toward her, feeling like a stalker hovering there in the shadowed corner of the room.

"Don't move, I said! I'm not some young innocent that you can frighten with stupid phone calls. Now put your hands over your head where I can see them."

Stefan decided simple compliance was the wisest course of action, so he raised his hands above his head. "You're making a mistake."

"No, *you've* made the mistake. You have terrorized that girl enough. Now you'll go to jail where you belong, you filthy lecher!"

Stefan nearly laughed. The scene was rather comical, after all. He was being held at broom-point by a woman who looked like someone's grandmother.

"Listen, ma'am." He went for the polite route, thinking of his own mother and what she responded to. "I'm not here to hurt anyone." He lowered his arm so that he could show her the apartment key, but she waved the knife at him.

"Keep your hands up!"

Stefan sighed. "Look, I got in here the same way as you. The front door. Did you stop to wonder how?"

She stared at him thoughtfully for a moment and then scowled. "You probably stole the key from Abby."

Abby? Who was she talking about? A housekeeper? "I didn't steal the key from anyone. Michaela gave it to me."

The woman squinted at him and Stefan wondered how she intended to fend him off if she
could barely see him. Thick-rimmed eyeglasses
hung around her neck, but she seemed oblivious to
them.

"Michaela?" She frowned. "When did she get
home?"

Stefan figured she was referring to Michaela returning to the apartment. "She didn't come home.
She's staying with me."

"Staying with you?" Her eyes widened in alarm.
"Oh, my God! You've kidnapped her, haven't you?"

Kidnapped her? "No! I'm helping her. I thought
it was too dangerous for her to stay here so I offered to let her stay with me."

"Then where is she now?"

"At the police station."

"The police station? Why?"

"They had some information for her."

"I don't believe you." Her gaze narrowed on his
face. "You're just trying to pull one over on me because I'm old—well not old-old, mind you, definitely not too old to testify against you at your trial.
And I hope they send you up the river!"

"Look, my wallet is in my back pocket. My name
is Stefan Massari."

"Massari?" She squinted at him again. Then she
slipped on her glasses. "Why . . . you *are* Stefan Massari! I'd know those broad shoulders and devilish
cleft anywhere."

Stefan chuckled. "May I drop my hands now,
ma'am?"

She blushed. "Of course! Of course! I'm so embarrassed. It's just that Abby has had so much trouble since she got here that I've kind of taken her under my wing."

Abby again. The old woman must be confused. "You wouldn't happen to be Mrs. Gelman, would you?"

"Yes, I most certainly am. Do you remember me, then? It was a number of years ago that my husband, Bernard, and I had dinner with you and Lowery, but you are very hard to forget, my boy. You're just as handsome as I remember. I bet you're still driving the girls wild."

Stefan smiled politely. "Now I know where I heard your name before. Lowery and I were at the Oak Room, I think. It was about two or three years ago."

The old woman beamed. "That's right."

"It's nice seeing you again. Although I wish it could have been under better circumstances." Stefan glanced pointedly at the butcher knife in her hand.

"Oh, my! How terrible of me." She plunked her weapons down on a table by the door and gave him a sheepish grin. "So sorry about all that. I've just been so worried about the dear girl. After that terrible incident the other night and then someone leaving a rose on her doorstep, I've been keeping an eye on her apartment. The whole thing makes me shiver. I have always loved New York, but it was so much different when I moved here with my family in nineteen forty-two. It's getting so a body can barely walk down the street anymore."

Stefan siphoned through her entire story to pluck out one thing. "Someone left her a rose?"

"Why, yes. Didn't she tell you?"

"No," he replied stiffly. "She didn't." That was so like her to keep information from him. She probably didn't want him worrying, and she would have been right if she thought he would. This put a new spin on things.

It had been one thing when the seditious fuck had called her, but to risk coming all the way to her door just to leave a rose? The man had wanted to terrify her.

On the other hand, maybe one of her ex-lovers had left the rose and not the creep harassing her? Either way, Stefan didn't like it.

Ida looked flustered. "Oh, my. I didn't know she hadn't told you. Well, I'm not going to regret the fact that you know now. The girl is far too prideful, doesn't want anyone to worry about her. But this is a serious situation."

"I agree. That's why she's staying with me. I just came here to get some of her things and ask if you would take care of Sheba for a while."

"Well, of course I will!" Ida readily consented. "As for the clothing, you're in the wrong room."

Wrong room? "This is the master bedroom, isn't it?"

"Yes, but she's not sleeping in here. Come with me."

Stefan exchanged glances with the cat and shrugged, trailing Ida as she opened the door to the room with the rumpled bedsheets. "I'll gather up some of her makeup and other womanly essentials while you get her clothes."

Stefan nodded and watched Ida disappear into a large bathroom. What would Michaela be doing sleeping in the spare bedroom? That niggling sensation prickled the back of his brain again.

He glanced around and spotted a pair of faded jeans thrown over the top of a chair. He picked them up with the intention of packing them, and in the process, a small white business card fluttered out of the back pocket. Stefan bent to retrieve it and glanced at the words written on the back in a flowery script.

Micky's cell phone #

He frowned, his confusion growing by the moment. Why would she have to write down her own cell phone number? Maybe she had been planning to give it to someone?

He flipped the card over and discovered it was an appointment card dated six months earlier for a Dr. Samuel Dressler, chief of Nephrology at a medical center in Idaho.

Something clicked in Stefan's head. Lowery's ex-wife lived in Idaho and Stefan recalled she had been sick for a number of years.

On the heels of that thought came another, something he had completely forgotten. Lowery had mentioned that his other daughter, Abigail, had been living with his ex since the divorce, a girl Stefan vaguely remembered having met once many years ago. She had been sweet, but painfully shy. The complete opposite . . .

Of her twin sister.

A horrible dawning stole over Stefan, pieces beginning to slip into place with sickening force, curious things that he had not been able to fit into the puzzle, all topped by Ida Gelman's own words.

It's just that Abby has had so many troubles since she got here.

Abby.

As in Abigail St. James.

The mystery that had been right in front of him all along now seemed so blazingly, blatantly obvious. Jesus, how could he have missed it? How could he have been so fucking blind?

It was not Michaela he had been kicking himself in the ass for wanting to make love to, thinking he had finally and irrevocably gone over the edge. It was her sister! *Her damn sister!*

Stefan felt as if he had just been castrated, that he had handed over his balls to a sloe-eyed girl who had lain naked before him and let him stroke her intimately all the while knowing she was deceiving him. The St. James sisters had a fucking knack for manipulation, but he only had himself to blame for falling into their trap.

Stefan had no intention of waiting until Michaela—no, *Abby*—called him from the police station. He was going to get her right now and let her know her masquerade was up. Was she even talking to a detective? Or was this whole bit about a stalker a fake, too?

He recalled how adamant she had been about going alone to the precinct. Could that have been another clue he had overlooked? Mrs. Gelman seemed to believe something was going on and had been willing to face off with an intruder to protect her young charge. But did the kindly old neighbor even know the whole truth?

Stefan felt steam rising off his neck as he thought about what might have happened to Ida had he truly been a psycho intent on harm, a state he suddenly found himself being dragged toward with the force of a deep-sea undertow.

Had the sisters planned this little hoax together? A bet to see which twin he screwed first? And here he hadn't screwed either of them. He had been trying to act noble and do the right thing.

Well, fuck nobility.

Do unto others, right? Why not deceive Abby as she had deceived him? Why the hell let her know that she had been unmasked? He had her right where he wanted, on his boat—and in his bed. He had already sampled her body, why stop now? What was it that Faraday had said? That getting Michaela off his back would be as easy as getting her on her back?

He might not have Michaela, but one St. James sister was good as the next. He would enjoy the upcoming days—and nights—slaking his anger and desire on her.

Then they would be even.

The ride home from the police station was made in silence.

Abby didn't notice that Stefan was exceptionally quiet or that he hadn't asked her any questions about what had transpired. She was too absorbed in her thoughts about what had been revealed during her meeting with Detective Tremonte.

As soon as she sat down in front of the detective's desk, she was summarily informed that he had heard back from the superintendent of the building where she had seen the man and woman and that he knew who was the last occupant of the apartment. There had been no buffer, no preamble before Tremonte told her.

"It's been owned by a woman named Carol Elliot for about ten years and is sometimes rented out on a month to month basis."

Carol Elliot. The news spiraled out at Abby like a gunshot in the black of night. She recalled Carol's last words to her in her office when she had first arrived.

I'd advise you to watch your back.

Abby had not taken the threat seriously. Although Carol had sent scathing looks her way since that day, they had not had another confrontation.

"The super says there's been no one living there for about four months," Tremonte had told her. "He couldn't recall if he had seen Ms. Elliot during that time. We can talk to her if you want. It's up to you."

Abby had told him she would think about it and get back to him. Then she had left, standing on the precinct steps in a daze for at least a half hour before numbly calling Stefan.

Could the blindfolded and bound woman have been Carol? Abby struggled to recall the woman's features, her hair or body type, but all she could remember with clarity was a female positioned on her knees and then seeing the vicious backhand that had sent her sprawling to the floor.

Perhaps the scene had been staged? Set up to frighten her? But why? What possible gain would Carol—if it had been her—have gotten from doing such a thing? It made no sense.

Abby was barely aware that the car had come to a stop in the marina parking lot until Stefan rapped on the passenger side window, her suitcase in hand.

Once onboard the boat, Abby headed straight for Stefan's cabin, and the bathroom within, feeling physically ill. The stress of the day had made her stomach feel as though it was being twisted in knots, her body telling her the problem could no longer be overlooked.

She didn't want to think about it, had avoided doing so to an unrealistic degree. But she had wanted so desperately to be normal for a while, not to allow any more heartache to touch her. And dealing with her problem required denial, and with denial came secrecy.

Besides, she had to come to New York for Micky, to set things right and hopefully restore the bond they had once shared before her sister's animosity toward her had blossomed into something close to hate, to close the wound sustained in the wake of their father's death, leaving Abby as sole owner of *Bastion*. She couldn't blame Micky for feeling bitter and betrayed.

All this time Abby had embraced an illusion. She should never have allowed herself to enjoy working at the magazine, to come to like the staff. To come to love Stefan. She had forgotten her reason for being here.

She turned the shower on, needing the warm water to wash away her shame, her regret, to soothe her troubled spirit and bolster her strength.

She savored the confined space of the tiny stall, closing her eyes and hiding from the world. She would have stayed there forever, but the water turned cold, forcing her back to reality. All she wanted to do now was crawl into bed and seek forgetfulness for a few hours.

But as she stepped out of the bathroom, she gasped as her gaze collided with Stefan's. He was lying on the bed, his eyes dark and unreadable as he studied her, his tanned skin standing out in stark relief against the white satin sheets.

Naked, but for the grim smile he wore.

Fifteen

Abby's feet were rooted to the floor, the adrenaline coursing through her resembling panic rather than desire, and she could not understand it. She had never been afraid of Stefan.

But as he lay there, fingers laced behind his head, huge arms making the pillow look small in comparison, his gaze roaming over her, she couldn't stop trembling.

"Come here." His voice was a whiskey-dark purr as he beckoned her with a single finger.

Abby's hand clenched and unclenched around the knot in the towel. "Why?"

His smile did not reach his eyes. "Because I want to lick your pussy."

Abby reeled from the crude words that fell from his lips like a slap, words that were so unlike him, as if he wanted to shock her.

"I don't want you to."

"Yes, you do. You like my tongue between your legs." His eyes were heavy-lidded, reminding her of a dangerous cat about to strike. "Now undo your towel and walk over here."

"No."

"Are you going to make me get up and take it off?"

Abby felt on the verge of tears. "Why are you doing this?"

"Doing what?" He stroked a hand over his penis, drawing her gaze to its enormous length. "I just want to make you feel good. Don't you want that?"

"Not if you're going to act this way."

"What way? You told me you'd spread your thighs for me whenever I wanted you to. Well, I want you to do it now. So come over here."

Abby shook her head. "Don't do this . . . not like this."

He ignored her. "Drop the towel, sweetheart."

"Stefan . . ." His name came out a plea.

A muscle worked in his jaw and he started to rise from the bed.

"You promised you wouldn't hurt me."

His body tensed for the briefest of moments, as if she had touched a nerve. Just as quickly, the restiveness was gone. "And have I ever broken my promise?"

He hadn't. Not once. "No."

"Good. Now do as I asked."

Abby hesitated, and then with shaking hands, she unwrapped the towel and let it drop to her feet, leaving her standing there naked before him. Never had she felt so exposed. She wanted to cover herself.

"God, you're beautiful." He sounded as if he hated the admission, as if the words were more curse than compliment. "Your nipples are already begging for me."

Abby knew it wasn't desire that had hardened her nipples, but the chill racing through her.

"Come here, baby. Daddy won't hurt you."

For almost a full minute, Abby's feet refused to move, but when he rose, as if to come and get her, she forced herself toward the bed, standing next to it but not sitting down.

Stefan's hand caressed her outer thigh then whispered across her downy curls, his gaze never leaving hers as he slipped a finger between her folds. Abby didn't want to respond, but his touch was expert.

"Get on the bed and straddle me." When she hesitated, he said, "I'll make you feel all better. Trust me."

Abby resisted another moment, and then did as he requested. She flinched as he took hold of her hips, thinking he would enter her. Instead, he slid his shaft between her cleft, rubbing back and forth with teasing strokes, the friction against her clitoris making her moan.

"Kiss me," he softly ordered.

Abby leaned down and pressed her mouth to his, without intimacy, too afraid of what might happen, of provoking the volatility that seemed to shimmer just below the surface of his skin.

He cupped the back of her head, holding her captive as his lips slanted over hers, hot, demanding, his tongue thrusting into her mouth in a carnal mating.

His other hand cradled her breast, molding, squeezing, and then pinching her nipples between his thumb and forefinger, applying enough pressure so that it bordered on painful.

Her traitorous body melted into him, and when his mouth moved to the sensitive tips and began to suckle deeply, the heat began to build at the core of her.

Then his hands slid down and grasped her hips again, easing her back and forth along his erection, teaching her the rhythm. "That's it, baby. Keep going with the motion." When his fingers returned to her nipples to resume their gentle plucking, Abby's movements became more frantic. "Slow, sugar. We've got all night."

Abby slowed her pace and reveled in each silken glide, feeling the ache building, the tension coiling around her, tightening every muscle.

"Stroke me," Stefan said in a husky murmur, taking her hand and wrapping it around his shaft.

Abby watched as her hand and body moved together, sweeping the full length of him, caressing the silky hardness, the extended contact eliciting dark guttural moans from him.

When her finger explored the small slit at the tip of his erection, he clenched his jaw and growled deep in his throat, the sound vibrating through her body and skittering along her nerves, making her bolder. Their actions became more frenzied with each passing minute.

"Faster," Stefan panted and Abby willingly obliged.

His back arched off the bed and he let out a primal groan as he found his release, spewing his seed over his stomach, leaving Abby to marvel over what her hands had wrought.

He slowly opened his eyes, his dark gaze impaling her. "Not done yet," he said in a way that raised goose bumps on her skin.

He tossed her none-too-gently onto her back and then loomed over her. She wanted a kiss. Instead his tongue curled around her nipple. "You haven't come yet," he whispered against her breast, sounding almost offended.

He pulled the nipple hard into his mouth and Abby cried out, but he soothed the pain in the next instant and then slid a finger over the swollen nub between her thighs, stroking fast as his mouth moved from one hard peak to the next, quickly bringing her back to a fevered pitch.

In the throes of the desire possessing her, Abby did not notice that he had moved between her thighs. All she knew was that she wanted him to end the torture, to help her find her release. She needed it so badly that tears ran unbidden down the sides of her face.

And when his teeth gently bit down on her nipple, her body splintered into a million pieces, the pulses coming deep and long.

Then, without warning, he stuck two fingers inside her and Abby nearly bucked off the bed. "Stop!" She tried to scoot away from him, but his hand clamped around her shoulder holding her still as his fingers pumped away inside her. "Don't!" she pleaded.

"Relax. I have something that will feel much better." He withdrew his fingers, wrapped his hands around her thighs and dragged her hard against his groin.

His hand guided his erection to her quivering flesh. She felt the tip of him ease into her, heard his groan and was seized by panic so raw, so severe that she didn't realize she had started pounding on his chest.

"No!" The word tore from her lips, from her very soul, and he immediately stilled.

"Oh, Jesus," he said, low and hoarse, swearing fluidly as he rolled off her and threw an arm over his eyes.

He might have spoken, might have said something in an attempt to soothe her, but Abby didn't know. She was lost to the terror, to the memory of feeling utterly helpless to a man.

She squeezed her eyes shut. "Get out!" she cried. "Get out, get out, get out!"

A moment later, the mattress sagged and she heard the door quietly open and close. Once Stefan was gone, she rolled to her side and hugged her knees to her chest and cried.

Stefan sat bolt upright in bed as the terrified scream pierced the night. He flung the covers back and hit the floor running, racing to the cabin Abby occupied.

He threw open the door to find her kneeling in the middle of the bed, her face bloodless, her eyes so wide the whites showed in terrible contrast. She had the pillow clutched to her chest and was rocking back and forth, whimpering like a wounded animal.

Stefan's gaze darted around the room, thinking perhaps someone had gotten onboard, but he saw no movement nor had any prickling sensation there was anyone else in the cabin besides him and Abby.

He had secured everything before he had gone to bed. And since he had done nothing more than stare up at the ceiling half the night, replaying the scene with Abby, not even an ant could had scurried past him without notice.

Cautiously, he approached the bed, afraid any sudden movement would startle her and set her to screaming again. She appeared almost childlike as those huge, unblinking eyes slid his way. She recoiled and scooted back against the headboard.

"Don't." She shook her head. "Don't."

"Ssh, honey. I only want to help. Let me help you." He continued toward the bed and sat down on the side opposite her, knowing it was best to keep some distance between them even though he wanted to wrap her in his arms and assuage whatever had frightened her.

Had he done this to her? Pushed her over the edge? God, he had been so angry, so full of impotent rage after finding out that he had been made a fool of that all he had been able to think about was lashing out at her, a razor-edged cruelty coiling around him that he could not rein in.

Never had he been so mindless with anger. And he hadn't wanted to admit why he had let her deception bother him so much, had refuted the truth with every breath, had tried to shake it off with each toss and turn, but harsh reality had followed him around like a vapor trail.

He had done everything to push it all away, but this moment, with the look in Abby's eyes, the full impact of the taut silence, eradicated all his hard work. Now he could no longer deny why he had acted like a cornered bull.

He had fallen in love with her, and when he had discovered her lie, his heart had felt like it had been ripped out.

He hadn't understood what had been happening to him because it had never happened before, not once, not even remotely. There had been women he cared for, but none of them had touched him like the woman now staring at him as if he were the devil.

And the same stupid anger that had set him on a course of destruction now choked him, sucking him down, condemning him to drown in her eyes.

"Tell me what happened, baby," he said softly. "What upset you?"

She shook her head and clutched the pillow tighter.

No matter what else she had done to him, she had not lied about her fear of men. In his heart, he had known she had been telling the truth. He could see it in her eyes, the way she spoke, how she had drawn inside herself as the terrible details of her attack were revealed.

But he had sought out her weakness, purposely used it against her to vindicate himself, and he had behaved no better than a common bastard.

"Did you have a bad dream?" he murmured, trying to draw her out, not realizing how much trust she had given him by opening up to him during these past few months. And callously, recklessly, he had tossed that trust and faith aside to pursue a vendetta.

What she had done had not been right. But what he had done had been worse, made even more despicable in light of what had happened to his sister.

God, how he wished she would tell him why she had lied. Maybe there had been a good reason. But to continue the pretense, even now after they had become intimate, hurt more than Stefan was prepared to acknowledge.

She eyed him warily, yet something had sparked in her eyes when he had asked her if she'd had a bad dream. He knew then that she had, and that somehow his actions had triggered it.

"Did someone try to hurt you in your dream, love?"

He thought she would not reply. Instead, she nodded her head. Progress.

He kept up. "Was someone chasing you? Were you trapped? Or—"

"He was pinning me down." Her voice was barely audible. Yet her words struck Stefan with the force as a runaway train.

His hands were trembling. He was almost afraid to ask her who had been holding her down, not sure he wanted to hear the answer. But he had to span this breach his anger had created.

"Who, *cara mia?*"

She rocked her head slowly back and forth. "I don't know. I—I can't see his face." A single tear slipped down her cheek and it was like a knife to Stefan's heart. "He just laughs and laughs." She clapped her hands over her ears. "Make him stop laughing!" she cried.

Stefan could no longer remain immobile. He crawled across the bed and gathered her up into his arms. She resisted at first, her limbs so stiff he thought they might very well snap. But as he crooned to her and gently stroked her hair, she began to relax against him.

"He won't hurt you anymore, baby," he promised. "You're safe with me."

"No." She shook her head. "You hurt me."

"I'm sorry." He laid his hands against her cheeks and eased her head back so that he could look into her eyes. "I went too far, tried to take something you didn't want to give. I was wrong."

"Why?" she asked in a small, choked voice. "Why did you do it?"

"Because I'm a bastard." No matter what else had happened, in this, he had gone too far. His heart told him to confess what he had found out about her, but his damnable pride wouldn't let him. He felt so much for her and he didn't want to believe it had all been a lie. He kept hoping she would tell him. He needed her to do it.

Those luminous eyes measured him, delved into the very depths of him, searching for something, though he knew not what. "Don't do it again," she whispered.

He leaned forward and brushed a kiss across her lips. "I won't."

She nodded and then surprised him by snuggling against his chest.

Stefan settled back against the pillows, having never felt so content with the simple pleasure of holding a woman in his arms.

"So do you want to tell me the rest of your dream?"

A few moments ticked passed before she said, "He knows where I am."

Stefan almost asked who, but then it came to him. "You mean the man who called you?"

"Yes." The word held a world of fear. "I know he's out there watching me, just waiting to come and get me."

"I won't let anyone get you," Stefan vowed, knowing he would do whatever was in his power to keep her safe.

She shifted her head and glanced up at him. "But what if you can't stop him?"

He didn't want to think about not being able to protect her. He had convinced himself earlier that because she had lied about who she was that she had lied about everything. He now knew how wrong his thinking had been. The threat was real. The truth was written plainly on her face and etched deep into her eyes.

"I'll just have to make sure I don't let you out of my sight. If he wants you, then he'll have to come through me first."

She sat up, her eyes widening. "No, I don't want you to get hurt because of me."

Stefan heard the sincerity in her voice and felt an

unseen hand give his heart a squeeze. "No one is going to hurt me. I'm a lot tougher than I look."

Her gaze roamed down his chest, as if to validate his claim. It also reminded Stefan that he was naked but for his briefs.

Her innocent glance caused his temperature to spike in record time. All she had to do was look at him and he was hard. Christ, he had to get himself under control.

"Don't do that, sweetheart."

Her gaze tilted to his. "Do what?"

"Look at me like that."

"Like what?"

Heaven help him, she was going to make this difficult. "Like you want to touch me."

She hesitated, not quite meeting his gaze. "Maybe I do."

How could she even look at him after what he had done? But he was thankful for whatever higher power had blessed him. Damn thankful.

"You do?" he said cautiously.

She nodded. "I love your chest. You've got all these hard planes." She ran a finger underneath his left pectoral. "And these taut ridges." Her finger slowly eased down over his stomach. "And your arms flex each time you move." That teasing finger slid up the center of his chest, to his shoulder, and then her hand closed around his bicep.

Stefan's entire body felt super-sensitive. Her breasts pressed against the side of his chest, and he longed to cup one full, firm globe. Instead he curled his fingers into his palm.

"Everywhere I look there are bulges. Especially

here." Her fingertip swirled above the edge of his briefs.

Stefan couldn't help himself. He groaned.

"Are you all right?"

"You're making me crazy, honey."

"Oh . . . I'm sorry."

Stefan gently took hold of her wrist as she moved her hand away. Her eyes locked with his. "That's not necessarily a bad thing, *cara*. It's just that when you look at me with those sweet eyes and touch me with those soft hands, all I can think about is making love to you."

She stared at him, as if she couldn't tell just how much he desired her. Shit, he could barely function these days; he had a hard-on so often. Her smile alone could make his cock rock solid in four seconds flat.

She glanced away. "Before . . . well, before you got rough earlier . . . I liked touching you there."

Stefan grimaced with her use of the word *rough,* hating what he had done. Yet his mind seemed inclined to focus more on her confession. He needed no definition of *there.*

Lord, he felt as if he were walking on eggshells. His mind evoked erotic images, picturing her legs wrapped tightly about his flanks as he plunged into her, her nipples scoring his chest, heard her soft moans, stroked her clitoris and felt her tight sheath gripping him as she came like a wet tide.

He was so lost in his fantasy that he hadn't immediately sensed where her hand was. He tensed when a solitary finger slipped beneath the elastic on his briefs, skimming the head of his penis with the barest caress. He clenched his teeth.

Abby glanced up at him. "I'd like to touch you again." In a soft, hesitant voice, she added, "May I?"

Stefan died in that moment, ten times over, six different ways. And there was no force in the universe that could keep him from saying, "Yes, dear God, yes."

She eased his briefs down and curled her palm around his shaft. The contact was so sensual, so unexpectedly jarring that his heart actually felt as if it stopped for a few moments.

"It's so soft," she murmured.

If Stefan weren't in the throes of a lust so rampant it beat at his brain, he might have chuckled. As it was, he could barely make the remark that was on the tip of his tongue.

"'Soft' is a word I'd rather not have you use in relation to my erection, love." He groaned then. "Yeah, that's right. A little harder."

Abby continued her fascinated observation of her hand gloving him. Watching her watch him only made Stefan that much crazier.

"Perhaps silky is a better word," she purred, leaning up on an elbow, her hair teasing his chest as her hand slid down and found his balls.

Stefan closed his eyes tight, his hard-won control beginning to slip. If he didn't stop her soon . . . ah, but God it felt so damn good. He had to touch her or he'd go mad.

He laid his hand on her bare thigh and ever-so-slowly eased her shirt up to her waist. He glanced up to see her studying him, a hint of wariness in her eyes.

He kept his gaze locked with hers as his hand slid under her shirt and molded her breast. She drew her bottom lip between her teeth and then released a wordless, breathy sound as his thumb played with her nipple.

He leaned up to give her a wet, tongue-to-tongue kiss, mating with her mouth, as another part of his anatomy wanted to do much lower.

She released him long enough for Stefan to drag the shirt over her head. In other ways, she might have deceived him, but in this . . . sweet heaven, in this she could not lie. Her body responded instantly and passionately.

He clasped her waist, holding her still so he could suckle her until her nipples were hard and distended. He pressed her breasts together and slid his tongue from one peak to the other.

Like a siren, she drifted to her back, massaging him, doing so with her left hand now so that he could have better access. "Stefan . . . please," she begged, then spread her legs.

He didn't hesitate. He gave her what she wanted, went where he knew she would allow him to go, gliding a finger between her moist delta and stroking the heated pearl within.

Her whimpers drove him to the brink and her hand pumped faster as he pushed her toward the ultimate pleasure. He captured her breathy cry with his mouth as they found their release together.

When he went to move his hand from her soft

nest of curls, she held it there, pressing his fingers against the spot where she throbbed.

"You can feel it if you want. A little," she hastened to add. "Just a little. Okay?"

She was giving him permission to put his finger inside her, the violation that had upset her hours earlier because he had been rough, uncaring. Stefan felt as if she had bestowed an unprecedented trust on him and he was humbled by it.

He smiled gently and then dropped a kiss on her lips. "Okay. Just a little." Then he eased a finger into her, shutting his eyes as she tightened around him, still pulsing.

Carefully, he moved his finger back and forth inside her and felt her respond. "Feel good?" he murmured, unable to believe he was getting hard again.

"Mmm."

He had never felt so insatiable, so primed. What excited him the most was how Abby responded to him, like everything was new to her.

Never had he so fully experienced the power of being a man, of bringing a woman pleasure, as when he was with her. Times like now he could almost forget the fact that she had misled him.

Almost.

With a groan, he reined in his passion and flopped back against the pillows, throwing a forearm over his eyes. A moment later, he felt Abby's head nestle against his shoulder, and he was a contented man.

"Sleepy?" he murmured.

She nodded, her fingers absently making circles on his chest.

Along with the contentment came renewed frustration. It welled up inside Stefan as he wondered when she planned to come clean and tell him why she had lied and what she and Michaela were up to. He had been allowing himself to believe that whatever their machinations it had nothing to do with him. But why all the secrecy then?

As his mind drifted back in time, he recalled wondering why Lowery had left Abby as the sole proprietor of *Bastion* when he hadn't seen her in years, while Michaela was living in New York with him. Stefan had been surprised by that twist in the will, along with the codicil Lowery had included about Stefan's future at *Bastion*.

What Stefan remembered most after discovering what Lowery had done was how relieved he had been that Michaela had not been given run of the magazine. And his relief had nothing to do with the fact that she would have gotten rid of him at the earliest opportunity. No, it stemmed from knowing she did not have the full power to drive the company into the ground.

So what had been Lowery's motivating factor? Guilt? It seemed a logical conclusion. Lowery had always lived under the mistaken assumption that material possessions could pacify all hurt. But Abby didn't strike Stefan as the type of woman who cared about such things.

She had lived on a farm, not under the jaded dome of a glittering cosmopolitan city. But could she possess the same characteristics as Michaela? He had never paid much attention to the nature versus nurture debate. Now he wished he had.

Either way, he knew he had to figure out how to make Abby divulge her secret. And as he slowly drifted off to sleep with her in his arms, his mind had already evoked several scenarios.

Sixteen

A strange restlessness dogged Abby for most of the following day, an underlying tension she could not dispel. She concluded her edginess stemmed from being cooped up. She had told Stefan it was ridiculous for her not to go into work. Certainly nothing would happen to her there. But he had held his ground on the issue, giving her a stern warning to remain on the boat, then tempering his command with a kiss that had burned the breath from her lungs before he left for the office.

As she made her way topside to sit on the deck, Abby recalled what she had been told by the police, that the empty apartment where she had first seen the mysterious man had belonged to Carol Elliot. Abby still could not fathom it.

Bits of memory started to come back to her. Micky's insinuation that their father could have been killed rather than dying from a heart attack. Then Carol uttering that cryptic comment about how Lowery had made the mistake of underestimating her.

Could the man now terrorizing her know something? Could he have been involved in some way?

Could her father have been murdered?

No. People died suddenly all the time. Even the doctor said her father had pursued the kind of lifestyle that could easily lead to an early coronary. No one had questioned his death. Why, then, should she?

Reaching the deck, Abby stared absently out at the calm, dark blue water. She wrapped her hands around the railing, feeling the need to hold on tightly to something as her life spiraled out of control, spinning on the head of her deception.

She had not told the police about Carol's threat initially because she had not seen any connection at the time. She had not told Stefan about what the police had revealed because she hadn't wanted him to worry needlessly. Instead she let him believe the detective had simply wanted to see her to find out if she could recall any more details about the man and woman she had viewed through the telescope so that an artist could do a sketch.

As the lies compounded, it became harder for Abby to confess to Stefan. She needed him so desperately right now. There was no one else for her to turn to, no one she could rely on. She was alone.

Abby knew that with each passing day she was falling more in love with Stefan. She finally felt as though she understood what true, encompassing love was: It was freedom. Stefan had released her from her fear of men, even though his roughness and strange behavior the evening before had set her back. She didn't understand what had come over him. But she had felt his regret. He had been genuinely ashamed of his actions.

It was hard for her to believe, but she was actually

contemplating taking their intimacy further. Stefan wanted to make love to her, and she was coming to see that she wanted that as well. She loved the way he touched her, how good he could make her feel. Never had she felt more alive than when she was with him. With all her heart, she wanted to believe he was thinking about her rather than Micky, that somewhere deep in his soul he knew the truth.

But there was more to consider than just the act. There was also the issue of his size. It was not his height or brawn that made her nervous anymore, but rather his other attributes.

The Lord had generously endowed him, and the idea of him inside her was more than a little intimidating. But for the first time in her life, desire had nearly edged out the fear.

A sharp pain suddenly pierced Abby's side, radiating a throbbing ache throughout her torso. Her knuckles whitened as her grip tightened on the railing. Then she doubled over and threw up over the bow of the boat.

It took nearly twenty minutes for the pain to abate, the bouts coming more frequently the past few weeks. She had been able to hide her condition thus far, but now other signs of her deterioration were beginning to show.

The swelling around her ankles, which she covered with socks, the slight tinge to her skin that makeup could not completely hide. That morning Stefan had told her she looked tired, and Abby had been fatigued, increasingly so. But the weariness went deeper than that.

Over the long months since she had gotten the

call, she had considered her options, the treatment she required. But she believed such measures would only be a temporary fix, even though the doctor had told her that with treatment and drugs she could very well make a full recovery, that running away without at least trying was akin to suicide.

But there had been her father's deathbed decree to consider and other things she had to take care of first. As well, she had seen the results of the remedial procedures and knew that she could spend precious time hoping things would turn out all right while the clock was ticking and life was passing her by, only to find out in the end that she was no better off. She had seen it happen before, during her mother's battle, and Abby knew the statistics.

She no longer wanted half a life. She had simply existed for so long, hoping things would change. Now she wanted, *needed,* all the things that had been refused her.

The shrill ring of the cell phone gave Abby a start. She figured it was Stefan. He told her he would be calling every half-hour to make sure everything was all right. Abby knew he was also checking up on her to see if she ignored his request to stay on board.

She moved to the cabana table and picked up the phone. "Hello?"

Silence met her greeting.

Silence that tolled like a death knell from the other end.

Abby's panic spiked, knowing who it was, knowing *he* had found her. "Please," she said in a hoarse whisper. "Please leave me alone."

"*Slut.*" The word hissed across the wire with the force of a gunshot. "Cunt. Bitch. Whore." The metallic rasp was like the crack of a whip across her back, each profanity flaying a piece of her flesh.

"Stop it!"

"Did he pet your pussy, little girl? Lick it until you writhed?"

"Shut up!"

"Were you thinking of my mouth on you? My dick inside you?"

With a cry of anguish, Abby disconnected the phone and threw it on to the table where it spun in a circle. She was panting, her whole body shaking violently.

Then the phone rang again.

Abby sank to her knees. "Go away," she whispered in a trembling voice, her gaze pinned to the phone. "Please go away." But it kept ringing and ringing and ringing until she thought she would go mad.

Then suddenly it stopped.

She closed her eyes, everything inside her caving in, collapsing, disintegrating. Long moments passed as she struggled toward some semblance of normalcy. But would her life ever be normal? Would she ever find the peace she had so desperately been seeking?

The phone rang again.

"No!" The cry pierced the air like the harsh splinter of shattering glass. Abby reached for the phone and shook it. "Stop! Please, dear God, make it stop."

But maybe this time it was Stefan? *Please,* she prayed. *Let it be Stefan.*

Abby clicked the button, and with her hand trembling beyond control, she put the phone to her ear. "Stefan . . . ?" The name was a benediction, a plea for salvation.

But there was none.

"Don't you ever hang up on me, you fucking cunt!" Then his voice modulated to the sadistic tone he had always used with her. "Do you want to know what I'm going to do to you when I get you alone?"

Tears of rage and despair rolled down Abby's cheeks. "Leave me alone," she said in a choked whisper.

"I'm going to handcuff your wrists to the head-board, then spread your legs wide and lash them to the bedposts."

"You won't touch me, you bastard!" Abby screamed into the phone, his threats breaking her down, corroding her until she wanted to curl into a ball and disappear.

Dark laughter echoed in her ears. "I won't? How will you stop me? You don't know when I'll strike. What day. What hour. You don't even know where I am. I could be watching you right now. Can you feel my eyes upon you? Feel my hands around your neck, you little prick tease?"

Abby whirled around on the deck, her gaze flash-ing on everything around her; the boats docked be-side *The Maria,* the wharf, the marina office so very far away. She felt isolated, as if she stood on a de-serted island and was being stalked by a predator she could not see.

He laughed again. "That's right. Be afraid. I could be standing at the bottom of the stairs on that pretty boat you're on right now."

Abby's heart slammed against her ribs. "No."
The word came out a horrified gasp as she jerked
toward the door leading to the galley and cabins.
She backed up until she stumbled into the bulk-
head.

"Have you ever heard of autoerotic asphyxiation?" he taunted. "While I'm fucking you, I'll wrap
my hands around your throat and squeeze until
you black out. It's the closest to heaven you'll ever
get without actually dying. And you never know,
maybe I'll keep on squeezing."

"No," Abby choked out. "Stefan won't let you
hurt me!"

"That cocksucker won't save you! You're mine,
and you always will be. I own you. Every time he
shoves his dick in you, you'll be thinking of me.
Soon we'll meet . . . very soon now."

Then the line went dead.

With a cry of anguish, Abby hurled the cell
phone across the deck, watching it shatter into a
hundred pieces, uncontrollable sobs shuddering
through her body as her legs slowly buckled beneath her. She wrapped her arms tightly around
her knees and rocked.

"I'm back, baby," Stefan called out as he came
down the stairs leading to the galley and sleeping
quarters—to the bed he and Abby had spent a
great deal of time in getting to know each other's
bodies the night before.

She'd had at least four orgasms before he had fi-

nally let her go to sleep, a fragile smile wreathing
her face as he cradled her in his arms.

Desire stirred as he thought about the moment
when she had decided to explore his erection with
her lips and tongue. Never had he experienced
such explosive lust, losing all control and nearly
coming in her mouth. During the throes of his
arousal, he had almost moaned her name out loud,
which would have been disastrous.

Looking back, he realized all the clues he had
missed that should have told him he wasn't dealing with Michaela. For one, his testosterone had
kicked in like never before, something that had
never happened with Michaela. He had been
reeled in by his own desire from the start, fighting his attraction by convincing himself he was
only trying to find out what was going on. But
Abby's sweetness and vulnerability had brought
out every protective instinct inside him while the
only reaction Michaela had every brought out in
him was fury.

So where was Michaela? And had she put Abby
up this? If so, why?

Stefan called out for Abby again. When his page
remained unanswered, he went to his cabin, thinking perhaps she was asleep, but he found the bed
made and no sign of her. He checked all the other
rooms, his palms starting to sweat when each place
turned up nothing.

Then he saw the last dying rays of sunset filtering
down the stairs that led to the upper deck. Of
course. She was enjoying the view. She did that
a lot.

On his drive back from the private investigator's office, where he had gone that afternoon to inquire about getting more information on Abby, Stefan had caught glimpses of the setting sun through the skyscrapers of Midtown.

When he had gotten out of his car in the marina parking lot, he had stood transfixed for a long moment, watching the sun's descent. He was glad he had returned in enough time to share it with Abby.

Tonight he planned to pretend as if no lie existed between them. He would cook her a nice dinner, open a vintage bottle of wine, and then perhaps lay out a blanket on deck so he could pleasure her under the moon and stars.

The thought made him randy and he took the stairs to the deck two at a time. But Stefan knew before he had crested the last step that she was not there.

"Where the hell is she?" he said, raking a hand through his hair. Obviously she had left the boat even after he had asked her not to. Damn it.

He turned to make his way back down the stairs, trying to think where she could have gone, when he spotted the cell phone he had given her smashed to bits in the corner. His mind processed the details and raced to an ugly conclusion, a conclusion he prayed was fifteen steps beyond what might have actually happened.

Yanking out his wallet, he retrieved the piece of paper with the telephone number he had gotten from Patty several days earlier. Then he pulled his cell phone from his jacket pocket and quickly dialed the number.

"This is Stefan Massari," he said, urgency in his tone. "Get me Detective Tremonte."

Abby wandered the backstreets of New York for hours, not seeing any of the people who passed her or paying attention to how far she had walked or where she was. She was numb.

It wasn't until darkness had completely encompassed the city that she began to come back to reality.

Where was she?

She wrapped her arms around herself and rubbed them, feeling suddenly chilled though the night was humid. The first cohesive thought that came to her was that she had to find Stefan.

She had fled the boat, terrified, not knowing where she was going, simply knowing she had to get out, get away. *He* had invaded the safety she had known there, corrupted it, just as he had tainted Micky's apartment, and now Abby wondered if there was anywhere she would feel safe.

Home, her mind whispered. *Go home.*

Idaho. The farm. The evil would not follow her there, would it? But nothing was waiting for her back home. Her mother was gone. The only hope Abby had for any kind of future lay here.

Here where someone wanted her dead.

It seemed surreal that the same place that could give her back her life could take it away as well.

Stefan. She had to find him.

Abby hailed a cab, hesitating on what address to give to the driver. She was afraid to go back to the boat. What if Stefan had not returned yet? What if someone was waiting for her in the dark?

No, she couldn't go back, not until she knew Stefan was there.

She got her bearings and discovered that she was actually closer to the office than the wharf. And when she discovered she only had six dollars on her, the decision was made. The cabbie trawled out into traffic and headed for Madison Avenue.

Abby felt as if she had come full circle as she stood on the sidewalk in front of the towering building that housed the magazine. Had it only been three months ago that she had arrived in New York? It seemed much longer. She felt like a different person than she had been when she arrived. In some aspects, she had grown. In others, she had toughened.

In one, she had lost her heart.

Abby pushed through the revolving doors and entered the building, heading for the elevators. She would call Stefan from Micky's office and stay where she was until he arrived.

The corridor was deserted as Abby stepped off the elevator; several of the bulbs in the overhead lights had burned out. One flickered above her head, and a moment later, extinguished, leaving a good part of the hallway steeped in shadows.

A realization struck her as she stared at the glass doors leading to *Bastion's* offices. "I don't have my key."

How could she have forgotten the doors would be locked this late at night? What would she do now? She was penniless and now farther away from the marina than she had been a half-hour ago.

In frustration, she rattled the doors. To her surprise, she discovered they were not locked. She frowned. The doors should not have been open . . . unless someone was still at work. But this late? It had to be nearly ten o'clock.

Stefan? Could he have lost track of the time? Perhaps he was trying to catch up on the work he had missed? Abby prayed that was the case. She needed desperately to feel his arms around her right now.

She stepped through the doors. The lights in the reception area were off, as were those in all of the offices—except for one, a wedge of yellow light breaking the blackness of the hallway.

Relief flooded Abby as she recognized that it was Stefan's office. He was here, and the tingle of fear that had raised the hairs on the back of her neck immediately dissipated. She practically ran down the corridor.

The back of his chair was facing the door as Abby entered his office, but he was not in it. She moved farther into the room, thinking perhaps he had stepped away. But where would he have gone?

"Stefan?" she called out, listening for his reply, but none was forthcoming.

Abby glanced back toward his desk, frowning when she saw a stack of papers littering the floor. Had he knocked them over? But what could have pulled him away so hastily that he had left his lights on and the front door open?

She told herself not to let her mind race needlessly. He would probably be back in a few minutes. In the interim, she would pick up his papers.

She knelt down in front of the mess, striving to arrange the stack into some semblance of order. She had just scooted her way around the edge of the desk when she spotted a thin red line rolling toward her. In stunned silence, she watched the line creep closer and closer until it began to seep under her sandal.

Her gaze followed the line back to its origin, to the spreading crimson puddle . . . the hand dangling over the edge of the chair.

Blood dripping from the fingertips.

A scream lodged in Abby's throat as she propelled herself upright, stumbling back until her shoulders pressed hard against the window, her lungs squeezed so tight she could not draw in air as she stared in horror at the body slumped in Stefan's chair . . . a glittering silver letter opener jammed into the neck.

But it wasn't until Abby's terrified gaze lifted and met the lifeless green eyes of the person who had once looked at her with such malevolence, whose threat had stalked her thoughts ever since the police had told her who had once occupied the empty apartment across the street.

Carol Elliot.

She was dead. Murdered. Taking whatever secrets she had to the grave.

Abby's mind scrambled for answers. But everything was a blur of confusion. She had to call the police. But the phone was close to Carol, too close.

She couldn't do it. She would have to go to her own office, but her limbs refused to move.

Then she heard a noise, a harsh clunk that seemed to come from everywhere and nowhere. Abby's gaze riveted to the doorway, her heart hammering.

Then the phone rang and her hands slammed back against the window in reaction. As though grasping a lifeline, she lunged for the phone.

"Help me!" she cried. "Please! Someone's been killed!"

"I know." The words were drawn out, slow and deadly like liquid nitroglycerine imbued with pure evil.

Abby's entire body froze in terror, her hand like an icy claw holding the receiver.

"Do you see what I did to Carol?" said the voice, filled with deadly intent. "That was for you."

"No." Abby shook her head wildly. "No, don't say that."

"It was all for you. You hated her. So I hated her." He chuckled darkly, sounding maniacal. "You should have seen her. She was rifling through your lover's file cabinet. She never even knew I was behind her until I grabbed her forehead and pulled her head back, the whites of her eyes huge as she looked up at me, gurgling as I stabbed her through the neck."

"No!"

"Now it's your turn," he taunted in a steel-edged whisper. "You've been a very bad girl and made me angry. So you have to pay."

"Please . . . please don't do this."

He inhaled a deep breath. "I can smell your pussy."

Terror closed around her throat, her gaze wildly darting about. Then she glanced down at the phone, life dissolving into sheer pinpoints of fear as she saw the digital readout telling her what she had dreaded.

The call was coming from inside the office.

Carol's extension.

Only six doors down.

"Are you ready for me?" His breathing quickened. "Do you remember what I said I was going to do?"

"Leave me alone!"

There was a pause and then: "I'm coming for you."

Abby's world faded in and out as footsteps sounded down the hallway, moving closer and closer. Coming for her . . . coming for her.

Her high-pitched scream pierced the air as a man appeared in the doorway. Blindly, frantically, she huddled back into the corner as Rick Faraday stood on the threshold.

"Stay away from me!" she sobbed.

Rick frowned at her. "What the hell's the matter with you?" he demanded, taking a step forward.

"No! Stay back!"

"Christ, you know how to hold a grudge. What's it been? Three months? Four? I only left you handcuffed to the bed for a few minutes while I peed. Shit, I drank a whole bottle of champagne. What did you expect? You got off three times. Doesn't that count for anything?"

Handcuffed to the bed. The words rotated through Abby's mind like a windmill. That's what *he* had said to her on the phone. Horror beat its own pulse beneath her skin.

"W-Why are you doing this?"

"What the fuck are you talking about? Jesus, are you overdoing the blow again? Or is there a new drug of choice? Damn, look at yourself. You're hysterical."

A movement behind Rick brought Abby's gaze jerking over his head as the lifeless eyes of the dark figure behind him stared right at her. In a single, horrible second, Abby knew. She knew.

"Rick! Behind you!"

"What?" He began to turn.

Through a queer distortion of time, Abby watched as the marble paperweight that had been on Carol's desk appeared in a brief flash before it cracked against Rick's temple with skull-breaking force. Like a rag doll, he slumped to the floor, his face turned toward her, showing a fist-sized section of mangled flesh and the blood matting his hair.

As though she dwelt in a nightmare, Abby's gaze slowly lifted to the man who had been stalking her over the phone and through a telescope. He was dressed all in black, his face covered by a leather mask, slits for his mouth and eyes. Those eyes, oh God, they were glittering disks of inhumanity, shining with pure madness.

"It's just you and me now," he said, his voice a muted rasp. Then he stepped over Rick's body and moved toward her with the slow, purposeful stride of a predatory animal that knew its prey could not escape. "Now we're going to have some fun."

Something tapped at Abby's subconscious, something she should know. But fear blocked off any thought besides escaping the evil closing in on her. Yet all the weeks of torment and verbal torture came crashing in on her, her head beginning to spin even as she tried frantically to stay within the realm of the conscious world.

And the last thing she saw before blackness engulfed her were the eyes of a killer.

Seventeen

Blood roared through Stefan's veins as he sped along Madison Avenue, his fear escalating with each passing mile, so that by the time he brought the Porsche to a tire-skidding halt in front of the office building, he was nearly out of his mind with panic.

Part of the street was corded off by the police. A row of cruisers stretched along the curb, red and blue lights flashing in some macabre special effect. Two ambulances waited with their bay doors open.

As Stefan leaped from his car, he saw paramedics wheeling a gurney from the building. Raw fear twisted his insides and sweat broke out on his body as he ran toward the gurney, praying he would not see Abby lying there.

A burly, gray-haired policeman stepped in front of him, blocking Stefan's path. When Stefan tried to go around him, the man grabbed his arms, restraining him.

"Goddamn it! Let go of me!"

"Who are you, pal?" the cop demanded, as two more men in blue closed in on Stefan, barring any movement. "And how did you get past the barrier?"

Stefan barely heard the man. "Where is she?" He

struggled against the hands holding him back, watching the gurney disappear toward one of the waiting ambulances. "Get the fuck off me!" he bellowed.

The officer unhooked a pair of handcuffs from his belt. "Look, buddy—"

"Let him go, Mills," a voice ordered from somewhere behind Stefan.

Stefan looked over his shoulder and saw a tall, well-built man, late thirties with sandy brown hair, striding toward him, blending in with the night in a navy blue suit and tie, the dark line broken only by his white shirt. He looked vaguely familiar.

"I'll take it from here," the man said. The officers nodded and dispersed. Then he introduced himself. "I'm Detective Tremonte."

"Where is she?" Stefan demanded.

"Ms. St. James is fine. Just shaken up."

Relief poured through Stefan like a flood. He had been going nuts looking for her, his mind building scenarios that he could barely bring himself to think about.

"I want to see her."

"You will." The detective extracted a pack of Marlboros from his inside jacket pocket, stuck one in his mouth then offered a cigarette to Stefan.

Stefan shook his head. "Why can't I see her now?"

"She's being looked at by one of the paramedics. I think he's going to give her a sedative to calm her down. Lady's been through a lot tonight."

Stefan needed to see her. He had to find out for himself if she was all right. He wouldn't know a moment's peace until he did, but it was clear he was going to be detained.

"Good thing you called us when you did," Tremonte remarked, taking a long drag of his cigarette and breathing out a stream of thick white smoke. "Otherwise I'm not sure what would have happened. As it was, the perp was still in the building when one of my men arrived. Damn rookie. Could have gotten his ass killed. His attention was sidetracked when he saw the bodies. Didn't even know the S.O.B. was hiding behind the door. The lights went out suddenly. Davidson shot a few rounds, but the guy got away."

An invisible hand squeezed Stefan's throat. "What bodies?"

Tremonte diverted his gaze, scanning the police activity around them. "One dead. One badly injured and might not survive the night. Your girlfriend found the murder victim and witnessed the second brutal attack."

"Jesus Christ," he said in a raw voice, feeling as if he had been blindsided.

"Do you know a Carol Elliot?" Tremonte then asked.

"Yes. She's the head of marketing."

"Not anymore."

Nausea roiled in Stefan's stomach.

"Do you have any idea what she might have been doing here tonight?" The question was framed in a casual tone, but the detective's gaze seemed to zero in on Stefan as if he might hold the key to this mystery.

"She was working late, I guess." Stefan raked a

hand through his hair, feeling disjointed, surreal. "I don't see any other reason she would still be here."

"What about"—the man flipped open a small notepad—"Rick Faraday?"

Stefan frowned. "Rick was here?"

Tremonte nodded, still watching Stefan closely. "The preliminary check on the phone shows a call from your office to Faraday's apartment at about nine. We've managed to round up a nightshift janitor who says he's seen Mr. Faraday and Ms. Elliot here several times late at night."

The look in the man's eyes told Stefan exactly what he was implying. "Are you saying they were carrying on some sort of affair?"

The detective shrugged. "Strictly off the record, I think they got their kicks out of doing it here in the office." Then he switched tacks. "Do you know what Ms. Elliot might have been doing in your office?"

"My office?"

"That's where she was found. Sitting in your chair."

The reality of the situation slammed into Stefan like a fist to the jaw. "No," he said hoarsely. "I have no idea what she was doing in my office." Then he asked a question of his own. "Am I a suspect?"

"Nope." Tremonte then added, "Not at the moment at least." He met Stefan's hard stare through a ring of smoke. "Unless you have something you want to confess?"

"I get it. I'm being subjected to the everyone-is-a-suspect routine. Is that it? Guilty until proved innocent."

"I wouldn't go that far," Tremonte returned noncommittally.

Stefan's jaw knotted. He'd had enough of this bastard's cryptic bullshit and power plays. "I want to see Abby. Now."

"Sure thing." The detective whistled through his teeth and waved over an officer. "Booker, take Mr. Massari up to see Ms. St. James." The patrolman nodded as he trudged toward them. Tremonte's gaze cut back to Stefan. "You do understand you'll have to stay out of your office for a while. Crime scene."

Stefan nodded. His only concern at that moment was taking care of Abby and making sure she would be all right.

"Will Ms. St. James be staying with you?" Tremonte then asked, a look in his partially hooded eyes that Stefan didn't like.

"Yes."

"Fine. Then I'll know where to find her when I need to ask more questions."

"Yeah, well don't need her too soon," Stefan told him in a clipped tone.

Tremonte made no promises. "I'd prefer it if neither of you left the city."

Stefan doubted *prefer* was the word the man wanted to use. "I don't intend to go anywhere unless Abby needs to."

"Just keep in mind, Mr. Massari, that Ms. St. James is a witness and the law frowns on witnesses being unavailable for questioning."

"You act as if Abby has a deeper involvement here than as just a witness."

Tremonte shrugged. "She saw a man being brutally attacked and she was also the first person to come upon Ms. Elliot's body. That seems pretty deep to me. You're also overlooking something."

"And what's that?"

"This wasn't just some random act of violence. The man who killed Ms. Elliot and nearly killed Mr. Faraday appears to be the same person who has been stalking your girlfriend." He flicked his cigarette to the pavement and ground it beneath his heel before meeting Stefan's eyes again. "Maybe there was some kind of love triangle going on here. Something kinky that got out of hand. What do you think?"

"I think I want to see Abby," Stefan said through clenched teeth.

Tremonte's expression was grim as he took Stefan's measure. Then he gave the go-ahead for Booker to take him up. Stefan turned and headed toward the building.

"Mr. Massari," the detective called out, stopping him halfway to the door.

Stefan spared him a brief glance over his shoulder. "What?"

"Just wondering. Were you in the office today?"

"No."

"Mind if I ask where you were?"

Stefan didn't know why the man had focused so intently on him, but if he didn't answer the questions here, he might have to answer them at the police station.

"I went to see a private investigator," he replied stiffly.

"I see. Mind if I ask why?"

As if it made any damn difference if Stefan minded. "For the same reason you're asking me all these bullshit questions. To find out what the hell is going on."

"No bullshit, Mr. Massari. Believe it or not, there's a method to what I do. I just thought I'd let you know that we also tracked a call made from your office to one of your cell phones today."

Stefan knew immediately which phone the detective was referring to, the one that had been smashed.

"Ms. St. James was visibly shaken by that call," the detective went on. "I wasn't able to get a whole lot of information from her, but the man apparently scared the shit out of her." His pause seemed purposeful and calculated. "A lot of people have your cell phone number?"

"Enough."

"Anybody stand out in your mind who might want to hurt Ms. St. James?"

Stefan thought of Abby, of what he knew of her, and thought no one could possibly want to hurt her. Then again, if he hadn't known she wasn't Micky, neither did other people.

Micky had made a number of enemies. Just about everyone in the office disliked her, and they had passed that dislike on to Abby, exactly as Stefan had. Tremonte was probably the only other person, besides Ida Gelman, who knew Abby was not Micky.

"Her sister was not very well liked," Stefan said.

"She was . . ." He hesitated, and the detective filled the void.

"A bitch? It's all right to say it. So does anyone stand out in your mind? Someone who might have had a personal vendetta against her?"

Plenty, Stefan almost replied. Then one unpleasant memory came to the forefront of his mind.

"There was an employee named Danny Matthews. Michaela fired him a couple of months ago. He wasn't too happy about it."

Tremonte nodded and made a note. "Why was he let go?"

"Performance issues."

"In bed, you mean?" Tremonte suggested, clearly reading between the lines.

"I wouldn't know."

"What about you, Mr. Massari? Did you have any 'performance issues' with Michaela St. James?"

Stefan's fingers curled into his palm, his control at the breaking point. "Is that relevant or just your insatiable curiosity speaking?"

"A little of both. So did you have sex with your girlfriend's sister?"

"No," Stefan ground out.

"But Michaela did get around sexually, correct? Three dead and wealthy husbands from what I understand."

"What's your point?"

"Just trying to better understand the hierarchy here, that's all."

Hierarchy, his ass. "Are you implying in some intricate, roundabout fashion that because Michaela enjoys sex her sister must be the same way and thereby invited this lunatic's attention?"

"Nothing of the sort. You read too much into my questions, Mr. Massari."

"I think I read you perfectly, Detective."

Tremonte's gaze briefly locked in silent combat with Stefan's before an imitation of a smile curled the man's lips. "Last question, then you can go," he said. "I'm curious to know how long you've realized you were dealing with Abigail St. James rather than her sister, Michaela."

"Not long."

"Why do you think she didn't tell you the truth about who she is?"

"I have no idea."

"But you do know that Abby, not her sister, is the sole owner of the magazine, correct?"

"Correct. But if you're trying to insinuate that I might have anything to gain by seeing Abby dead, you're wrong."

"I'm not suggesting any such thing. I'm simply endeavoring to get the facts. Although . . . up until recently, Michaela St. James was the sister who was running things while Abigail St. James had never been in the picture. Now that the power structure has changed, and Abigail St. James is here in New York, she could pull strings with the members of the board and get you fired. Isn't that right, Mr. Massari?"

A muscle worked in Stefan's jaw. "I'm not worried about it."

Tremonte lit up another cigarette. "Never said you were."

Prick, Stefan thought. Power-hungry prick.

"By the way, what is your yearly salary, Mr. Massari? Four million?"

"About that," Stefan replied tersely.

"Thanks. You can go now."

Stefan gritted his teeth and forced down his anger as he walked away, needing to focus his full attention on Abby and helping her get through this ordeal.

The elevator doors opened on the sixth floor and Stefan stepped out into a whirlwind of activity. The office was overrun with boys in blue. He scanned the sea of faces looking for only one.

Finally, he spotted Abby sitting on top of a secretary's desk halfway down the hall. Just seeing her made his heart ache. He wanted to take her out of there, block her from all this madness, but what he needed to do the most at that moment was remain calm. She would need all the strength he could offer her right now.

He came up behind the paramedic who was speaking to her and tried not to self-destruct at the sight of her pale, tearstained face. God, she looked as if she had been through hell.

"How's my girl doing?" he asked, hoping his voice didn't give away the emotions churning inside him.

Her gaze lifted to his and he watched her dissolve before his very eyes. "Stefan . . ." she said in a choked voice, the blanket draping her shoulders puddling around her as she opened her arms, silently beseeching him to hold her. Stefan needed no further prompt. This is what he had wanted.

He swept her tightly into his arms, pulling her close, feeling her body shudder as silently sobs wracked her. "It's all right, baby. It's all right. I've got you now and I won't ever let go." He glanced at the paramedic. "Will she be okay?"

He nodded, but his expression didn't hold the same assurance. "I've given her something to calm her nerves, but she's had quite a shock. I told her it might be best to spend a night at the hospital, but she doesn't want to go."

Stefan tipped her face up. Her eyes were glossy with unshed tears. "Is this true?"

"I . . . I j-just want to go home with you." She looked exhausted, and so wan it worried him. "Please, Stefan, take me away from here." The appeal in her eyes nearly unraveled him.

"All right, baby." He gently stroked her hair and transferred his gaze to the medic. "Are you done?"

The paramedic nodded.

Stefan didn't hesitate. He swept Abby up into his arms, oblivious to everything and everyone but the woman shielding her face against his shoulder.

He carried her all the way to the car. As though she were breakable, he carefully eased her into the passenger seat. Then he hustled to the driver's side, wanting to get her into bed as soon as possible.

He had just opened the door when a voice stopped him.

"Mr. Massari?"

Stefan's gut tightened when he spotted Detective Tremonte standing on the pavement not twenty feet away, smoking another cigarette. "What is it?" he bit out.

"Don't forget what I said. Please don't leave the city. I'll need to speak to Ms. St. James in the next day or two."

Stefan made no reply. Just hopped in his car and took off. But in his rearview mirror, he could see the detective stroll out into the middle of the street, watching as they drove away.

Eighteen

Stefan managed to hold off Tremonte for two weeks, much to the man's growing belligerence and threats. And during that time Stefan died a little more each day as he watched Abby drift through life instead of actually living, floating in a protective bubble that he could not penetrate and that only grew more impregnable whenever he tried to break through.

He kept believing she would pull out of the despair that engulfed her, as well as a kind of apathy, as though she simply had no more interest in the world and was merely waiting for everything to fall apart.

Along with growing more despondent mentally, she also seemed to decline physically. She had little appetite, and though Stefan was constantly trying to feed her, she only picked and started losing weight when she was already too thin.

Helplessly, he watched her, keeping a close eye, but feeling completely useless, as if he were navigating without a map. She spent countless hours sitting on the deck, staring out over the water, her knees drawn up to her chest, looking lost and alone even though she could have turned to him at any time for comfort and he would have willingly given it.

Whenever he tried to talk to her about going to see a doctor, she told him she was fine and then gave him that wan smile that made him feel as if his heart was permanently cracked.

He had wanted to lock out the Tremontes of the world for as long as it took Abby to get better, but he couldn't. When he had finally allowed the detective to question her, Stefan had hovered around, ignoring the man's blatant looks that conveyed his presence was not welcome.

It was during that initial interrogation that Stefan first heard the full story of Carol Elliot, how the apartment across the street, where Abby had first glimpsed the man, had once belonged to Carol.

Abby had never told him about that and he could only wonder why. But he wouldn't ask her, just like he wouldn't ask her why she had lied to him about who she was. Only a bastard would press her now.

But one truth seemed clear to Stefan even without the clarification of her identity, and that was that he could no longer bring himself to believe she had misled him for the sole purpose of deceit.

There was something else here, something she just couldn't tell him. It hurt him to think that she didn't feel she could trust him enough to be honest, but he was willing to be patient. Perhaps he would be rewarded.

Now, as he stood in the doorway leading to the deck, he tried to hold out hope, tried not to give into the threatening despair that had already ensnared Abby. But it was difficult. He felt its pull like a rope around his neck.

He didn't know if she sensed his presence, but that

was nothing new. Many days they did this dance. She, staring across the water. He, staring at her.

It was late September now, only a few days remaining until fall. In less than a month, the boat would be hauled out of the water and put in dry dock until the spring. The air already held a hint of autumn. The nights had become chillier.

Even now Stefan could feel a cool breeze kicking in as the sun began to set. He wondered if Abby noticed how spectacular the descending sun was—or even cared.

"Here, baby," he murmured, moving up beside her chair and holding out the sweatshirt he had brought for her. "Put this on."

Wordlessly, she did as he requested, as if saying no was too difficult, too much of an unknown variable to defy. He knew that slimy son of a bitch had done this to her, had taken the fight out of her.

Stefan dragged a chair over next to her, wishing he could dispel the anger inside him and the feeling that he had failed her, just as he had failed Maria. The look on Abby's face as she had numbly relayed to Tremonte what had precipitated her flight from the boat that terrible day still coiled around Stefan like red-hot metal.

Before Tremonte left, he had told Stefan in private that the perpetrator sounded obsessed and that he fell into the most dangerous category of sexual deviants.

A sadist.

After the detective was gone, Stefan went to the cabin he was sleeping in, alone, and punched a hole through the wall, bloodying his knuckles and fracturing one of his fingers. But he didn't care. He welcomed the pain.

Since that night, Abby had suffered recurring nightmares, but she wouldn't allow him to soothe her. Instead she turned her back on him, silently pushing him away.

The first few days after the murder had been the hardest. Stefan had needed his own lifeline, reaching out to his mother, seeking her guidance. She had always been a rock, just like his father, and she never failed to know what to say, how to ease whatever troubled him, or to simply be there to comfort him.

"Give her time, Stefano," she told him. "Lend her your strength and she'll come around. She has no one but you."

His mother's last remark had penetrated deeper than anything else. Abby didn't have anyone. And he was angry for her. Where the hell was her sister? It was just like Michaela to turn her back on someone who needed her.

Stefan watched the sun slowly dip beyond the horizon. He knew better than to talk. He had tried to at first, attempting to draw Abby out, but it cut too deeply when she would do no more than cast a sad look his way and touch his cheek, as if for one brief moment she remembered him, before turning her gaze back to the water.

So when she suddenly began to speak, Stefan felt as if daylight had dawned after a lifetime of darkness.

"My mother would have liked this boat," she said softly, not looking at him. "She used to love the water. We had a lake behind our old house." A wistful smile touched her lips. "I loved that house. I thought it was a fairy castle when I was growing up."

Stefan remained silent, afraid to say anything for fear she would wake up from her dream and revert back to the way she had been for the past two weeks.

"There was this tall staircase in the middle of the foyer. An Oriental carpet flowed down it like a river of exotic color. I used to believe someday that rug would detach from the stairs and become a magic carpet."

She stared down at her hands for a long moment, as if reliving memories, memories that were, perhaps, too painful to speak of aloud.

Stefan wished he could take on some of her heartache, ease whatever ghosts haunted her, but he couldn't. So he waited, knowing he would continue to do so for as long as it took.

She drew her knees in closer to her. "There were these huge windows at the top of the stairs that I thought I could fly my magic carpet through, like a portal to another dimension. I used to spend endless hours staring out those windows. There were so many trees, fir and sugar maple and orange-clad elms, and the grass was so green and thick, and the sky seemed to go on forever. There was no place on Earth quite like Hawthorne House. It was as if no one else existed but me and my family."

Stefan had once accepted an invitation from Lowery to an old-fashioned weekend party at Hawthorne House in upstate New York. It was reminiscent of the kind of country estate parties Stefan imagined were held in earlier centuries, where all the amenities were supplied and the edict of the day was to have a good time.

He knew the windows Abby spoke of, mammoth floor-to-ceiling panes of glass with a spectacular view. He had spent a good portion of his time that weekend looking out of them. The memory felt poignant now as he thought about her standing there as a little girl, waiting for her magic carpet to take her away.

The house, as Stefan recalled, had been willed to Michaela, and he vaguely remembered overhearing that she was in the process of trying to sell it.

"My father had a small boat anchored in the lake," Abby went on. "My mother and I would take it out so that we could go to the opposite shore where the water wasn't so deep and swim." For the first time since she started talking, she looked at Stefan. "Do you want to know what the boat was called?"

Stefan stared into the depths of her eyes and felt as if he were drowning. "What?"

"Pro Fortis."

Stefan's Latin was rusty. "What does that mean?"

"For honor." A short, humorless laugh followed that revelation. "Odd that a man who had no honor would name his boat such a thing."

Stefan heard longstanding bitterness, so softly spoken the words struck with the unexpected force of an invisible blade, slashing through the air without a sound, without a ripple, yet leaving a sense of devastation in its wake.

He thought about holding his tongue, remaining on the perimeter and looking in, but on some deeper level, he related to her pain, understood it. She had endured much since her parents' split.

Stefan knew that Lowery had never once gone to see his dying wife. No matter what had precipitated the breakup, Stefan couldn't condone Lowery's callous behavior toward his ex-wife—or his daughter.

Stefan had discovered through his private investigator that René St. James had been sick for many years and that Abby had been the primary caregiver, putting her life on hold.

He wanted to know about those years, understand the things that had shaped her life, but the last time he had brought up the subject of her mother, she'd closed up. He felt the need to try again.

"I was sorry to hear about your mother," he murmured, repeating the words he had spoken several months earlier.

He got the same reaction today as he did then. She stiffened. He thought that would be the end of the communication, that she would once more close herself off. She surprised him.

"My mother was sick for a long while," she said, seeming distant, as if she had gone somewhere else, to a place that allowed her to speak of things she could not bring herself to discuss without a protective barrier. "Sometimes I wished . . ." She paused, glancing down at her hands. "Sometimes I wished that death would have hurried and taken her rather than allow her to suffer."

Her confession wrung Stefan dry, twisted him and twisted him until he was without a single defense against the wound she was opening inside him.

He could understand how hard it was to watch someone you loved die. After more than thirty years of smoking Camel nonfilter cigarettes, his father had developed lung cancer. Within four months of his diagnosis, he was gone. His father had never stored much faith in doctors, and so he never went to see one when the initial symptoms had set in.

It seemed as if overnight his father went from a robust man to a wasted shell, and all Stefan could do was pray that when the time came his father would go quickly. To see him suffer was the hardest thing Stefan ever had to endure, next to his sister's suicide.

"What did your mother die from?" he gently asked.

She hugged herself, rubbing her hands over her arms as if she were cold even though the night still held some lingering warmth. "Acute diabetes escalated by end-stage renal failure." The words sounded as if they were spoken by rote. "She'd had diabetes for a long time. But after we moved to Idaho, she began smoking and drinking heavily and then developed high blood pressure."

Stefan wondered if Abby recognized that she had divulged who she truly was. He suspected she was so absorbed in her memories that she did not realize what she had unwittingly confessed.

For the first time, he felt as if he was seeing all of her, and he discovered that she was just as hurt and vulnerable and loving inside as he had come to believe.

"Those elements combined made her a perfect

candidate for kidney disease," she continued. "The doctors tried hemodialysis, peritoneal dialysis, and when neither worked, there had really been only one option left. Kidney transplantation."

Stefan recalled the physician's appointment card he had found in Abby's jeans. The doctor's title had been chief of nephrology—a specialist in diseases of the kidney. Things were beginning to make sense.

"The statistics for kidney recipients are low," she said. "When my mother became ill there were nearly fifty-five thousand people in the United States waiting for transplants and over six thousand people died that year because they didn't get one. Even if a person receives a kidney, they still run the risk of being mismatched because of time constraints and the variables of HLA markers."

It was clear she knew a great deal about the terrible disease her mother suffered from. Stefan's heart went out to her, having to go through that by herself. She had been so young when her life had been turned inside out.

"So did your mother get a kidney?" he asked.

"Yes." Her reply was barely audible. "But she died anyway. She was just too weak to fight." A single tear slipped down her cheek and Stefan ached to reach out and pull her into his arms. "I think . . . I think she simply wanted to die. After my father left, she seemed to give up on life. For a long time, I hated him. Hated men."

"And now?" Stefan ventured, needing desperately to know how she felt at this moment, if she might ever be able to open her heart to him.

Her eyes were glittering pools of pain when she

looked his way. "I'm numb. I thought I had let it go, forgiven my father, but sometimes . . ."—a stifled sob broke from her lips—"sometimes I don't think I can."

Stefan slipped out of his chair and knelt beside her, taking her cold hand into his warm one. "The hurt will lessen over time."

"No." She shook her head, the tears coming faster now. "He was my father. He was supposed to care about my mother. About me. It wasn't supposed to be this way. I . . . I want my life back," she wept in a small, broken voice. "I want . . . hope." Then she pulled her hand from his and pushed to her feet, running from the deck.

Stefan wanted to go after her, to tell her everything would all right. But who was he to dole out promises? He wanted to make her happy, to fix things for her, but could he? Did he know how? Instead of letting him in, it seemed as if she was shutting him out more each day and he didn't know why, didn't know how to fight what she was doing to him.

He loved her. Felt it with an intensity that frightened the hell out of him. Yet he was losing her and he felt powerless to stop what was happening.

Abby raced blindly to her cabin, trying to outdistance the emotions she had managed to keep at bay for so long, emotions that threatened to make her care, make her want to stay here with Stefan and forget about the rest of the world.

She shut the door, locked it, and slumped back

against the hard wood, sliding slowly to the floor where she put her face in her hands and wept for everything she had lost—and for things she wanted but would never have. A loving husband, messy-faced children. A new beginning. A future.

Couldn't Stefan see the truth yet? Did he really not know?

A stabbing pain seared Abby's midsection and she clutched her arms around her waist. "Please," she softly cried. "Just let it end."

What was left now? Why, after years of despair, had she endeavored to reach out for happiness? Too late, too late, too late. She had been allowed a glimpse through the keyhole, seen what was on the other side, but couldn't walk through the door.

She had denied Stefan and denied herself when all she had wanted to do when he had taken her from the building that night was hold him, keep him close, let him love her however he would and for however long.

But what did she have to offer him? What was left to give?

"I just want to be free. Just let me be free for this short time," she begged, crawling over to her purse, her hand groping blindly in the darkness for what she needed.

Then her fingers closed around the object. Pulling it out, she held the small brown bottle in front of her. *Take 2 pills when needed for pain,* the label read.

Finally, it had come to this.

Abby yanked off the white cap and spilled the pills into her shaking hand. They looked surreal there in her palm, and she thought, What difference would it make if I took the whole bottle? Then all the pain, the heartache, would go away.

She closed her eyes and choked down a sob. Why couldn't she just give up? Why did she continue to believe that the black cloud that had loomed over her most of her life would not always follow her around?

Because she had to. Something inside her wouldn't allow her to relinquish that small spark of hope or block out Stefan's face. It always pulled her from the desolation.

Abby stared down at the pills and then tossed two in her mouth, closing her eyes, trying to hold back the nausea that threatened as hot tears ran down her cheeks.

Then she curled up on the floor beside the bed, waiting for the drugs to take effect. And as they numbed her, she knew what she had to do, what she *must* do. There was no other choice.

Time had come full circle.

Nineteen

"Hello."

Stefan glanced up from the morning paper to find Abby poised on the threshold between the hallway and the galley. She appeared so fragile, it looked as if a strong wind could blow her away.

Her jeans hung loosely because of the weight she had lost, and he felt a nearly physical pain at the sight of her. He wanted to shake her and ask her what she was doing to herself about as much as he wanted to kiss her and make the world right for her again.

A fierce protectiveness surged through him, a renewed determination to pull her through this ordeal. He felt the first spark of hope when he noted the light dusting of color on her cheeks and her hair pulled back from her face in a shining ponytail.

He smiled gently at her and rose from his chair. "Hello." He came to stand in front of her. "Sleep well?"

She nodded, her eyes huge in her small face as she gazed up at him, surprising him by reaching up on tiptoe to brush a light kiss across his lips.

"I've missed you," she whispered.

A wellspring of emotions stirred inside Stefan,

and he felt as if he had just been given the best gift in the world. "I've missed you, too, baby."

He kissed her back then, capturing her face between his hands and slanting his mouth across hers, plunging his tongue into the sweet, moist recesses and smiling slightly when he tasted peppermint-flavored toothpaste.

He felt her small hands at the waistband of his jeans, her fingers skimming just inside until they met at the metal button in front, which she undid.

Stefan released her and opened his mouth to ask her what she was doing, but her hungry gaze impaled him, halted him as surely as a hand over his mouth. He fought himself, against the need he had for her that had only grown more intense the longer he was with her, but this was not about physical satisfaction. She had touched a place in him he had believed didn't exist.

He took hold of her wrist when she went to pull down his zipper. She was too weak to want this. She was so delicate that his rampant desire might crush her. She was doing this for him. He could see it in her eyes, and he didn't want it this way. Not like this.

"What's the matter?" she asked, looking hurt and bewildered. "Don't you want me?"

"More than you will ever know."

"Then why?"

"Because you don't really want me right now. But it's okay. I'll be here whenever you're ready."

"But I do want you." Color heated her cheeks as she admitted, "I want to kiss you . . . there." One slim finger uncurled and whispered over the bulge in his jeans.

Stefan's groin clenched in response, and it took every ounce of control he possessed not to think about having her mouth there, those sweet lips closing around him and drawing him deep. He willed back a groan.

"Sit down and let me give you something to eat."

"I don't want anything but you. Stefan . . ." She used his hold upon her wrists to lever herself up so that she could run her tongue across his lips. "Please . . ." She dropped hot kisses across his jaw and then down his throat.

Her breasts touched his chest and he could feel her hardened nipples through his shirt. She wriggled her hands free from his grip.

The sound of his zipper going down rocked Stefan like an explosion, the metallic zing multiplying and expanding in the quiet stillness of the galley. And when her soft hands slipped inside his boxers and wrapped around his shaft, he thought he would go straight through the roof.

Her head angled downward, both of them watching her hands slowly pumping his hardened length.

Then she dropped to her knees before him.

Stefan grabbed her shoulders. "Don't . . ." It was the only word he could get out before she went down on him, her hot, moist mouth tasting him, sucking, her tongue circling the tip.

He tried to pull her to her feet, but she whispered sweet pleas to let her continue. Stefan gave in to her, gave in to himself and sank his hands into her hair, hating himself and the burning need for her that sapped his sense, while he let her love him with her mouth.

Her inexperience only excited him, made him feel the thrum of blood rushing through his veins, sweat popping out on his brow. It felt so good because he loved her. The knowledge made every wet tug of her mouth, every lick of her tongue that much more intense . . . until he had to pull her away so that he didn't come in her mouth.

His release spurted from him in a torrent and he wished he was spilling his seed inside her, realizing with sudden clarity that he wanted to put his baby inside her, wanted to link her to him any way he could.

In the middle of all this craziness, he knew only one thing conclusively.

He wanted to marry Abby and face whatever happened in the future together.

But he could not ask her now because he knew she would believe he had proposed out of some twisted need to protect her, perhaps out of pity, both of which he felt, but neither of which motivated him.

Stefan hauled her to her feet and kissed her, hoping what he felt for her came through. When would she let him make love to her? When would she finally give that last piece of herself to him?

He maneuvered her back against the counter, grasping her waist, his hands skimming up her sides then moving in to cup her breasts, enjoying the weighty feel of the soft globes. She wore no bra. He swept his thumbs across her distended peaks.

He wanted to taste her. This time it was she who took hold of his wrists.

"Later," she whispered, a promise in her eyes. "After Patty's wedding."

Stefan stared at her, perplexed. "Patty's wedding?" He had forgotten all about it. Granted, he had told Patty he would attend, but he doubted she would still expect him to come after everything that had happened.

"I told her I would be there," Abby said, the set of her jaw telling Stefan she would be stubborn about the subject.

"She'll understand."

"I see no reason we shouldn't go."

Stefan couldn't put his finger on what it was that made him uneasy about Abby's sudden interest in going to the wedding when he had barely been able to get her to leave the boat.

But did he want to deny her simply because he felt anxious? He had been waiting, hoping, she would shake off the lassitude that had cloaked her since the night of Carol Elliot's murder. Now she was expressing an interest in something. If she wanted to go, how could he refuse her?

He dropped a kiss on her forehead. "All right. We'll go."

She smiled, and it held gratitude and a certain wistfulness. "I'll have to buy something to wear."

"Fine. I'll take you shopping." She nodded and turned to go, but Stefan took hold of her arm, bringing her back around to face him. He wanted to tell her how he felt about her. Instead he said,

"Since the reception's at the Plaza, how about we stay the night?"

"I'd like that," she murmured.

Then she was gone, leaving Stefan to stare after her, unable to shake the feeling that things were not as they seemed.

The wedding ceremony was beautiful.

The church was alive with the sound of the organ, filling every crevice, wafting through the rafters. Flowers adorned every conceivable spot as late-afternoon sunlight pierced the stained-glass windows in prisms that dappled the floor in jeweled tones of ruby, sapphire, and gold.

Through it all, Abby's tears fell silently. Onlookers would think her moved by the union of the happy couple as they vowed to love, honor, and obey, when what she truly felt was a keen sense of emptiness.

But she wanted these last precious hours with Stefan to be something he would remember. Everything had to be right, special, and a wedding was both.

Now, as the reception got underway and Stefan swept her out onto the softly lit dance floor, his strong arms closing around her, Abby could pretend that they had been the ones married today, and this was their reception, their start of a bright future together.

And that tonight would be their wedding night.

She would hold nothing back, but rather be as

free as she could ever hope to be, live while there was living to be done and rejoice in each moment.

The morning would bring reality. Then she would consult with her father's lawyers about the magazine's future and stay with Ida until everything was finalized. Cowardice kept Abby from returning to Micky's apartment.

Cowardice also kept her from telling Stefan her plans. But soon enough he would know why she had left. He would know and it would be over.

"Have I told you yet how beautiful you look?"

Abby glanced up to find Stefan smiling down at her. He was so handsome, he took her breath away. How could so simple a smile and so tender a look make her feel as if she floated a foot above the earth? She would never regret stealing this time, for pretending to be Cinderella as time ticked away toward the moment she would be exposed as a fraud.

But until the clock struck midnight, the fairy tale was hers and she would hold fast to it.

She pressed her body nearer to Stefan's as they danced, wanting to be as close to him as possible. "You've told me at least ten times," she said with a smile.

"And I'll probably tell you another ten times before the night is through," he murmured close to her ear, wrapping his arms tighter around her waist.

Abby closed her eyes and laid her cheek against his chest, breathing deeply, enveloped by the masculine scent of him, drowning in his heat.

The song drew to an end, and Stefan's fingers laced through hers. "Let's get out of here."

Abby did not protest. She wanted to be alone with him.

They issued their farewells to the joyous bride and groom, and Patty gave her an encouraging smile and a wink before Stefan tugged her toward the door.

When they got on the elevator, Abby thought they were going back to their room, but the elevator passed their floor. "Where are we going?" she asked.

He gave her a melting half-grin. "It's a surprise."

The blinking light ticked off one number after the next until they were at the top floor. The doors opened and Stefan led her to a steel portal with a sign that read: AUTHORIZED PERSONNEL ONLY. ALL OTHERS KEEP OUT.

Abby halted, tugging him back when he went to open the door. "We can't go in there. That leads to the roof."

"I know." A hint of amusement tinged his voice as he proceeded through the door.

Abby had promised herself that tonight she would be unfettered by worldly concerns, but she didn't want Stefan to be sent to jail for breaking the law.

"Stefan . . ." She pulled on his hand.

He glanced over his shoulder at her. "Don't worry, love. The hotel manager is a friend of mine. No one will bother us."

Abby gnawed her bottom lip. "Well, if you're sure . . ."

"I'm sure. Now come here and look at this view."

She climbed the remaining stairs and stood unmoving, awed by the spectacular panorama set out before them. Three hundred and sixty degrees of sky. It was as if they hovered on the top of the world and all she had to do was reach up on tiptoe to touch heaven or capture a star in the palm of her hand or pull down the moon.

Below them were thousands and thousands of lights glittering like gold jewels and beneath this halo was an ebb and flow of humanity that she and Stefan watched as though they were immortals marveling at the wonders God had created.

In that moment, Abby was almost able to believe the world could stop just for them, that the morning would never come and they could remain there cradled in the night until the end of time.

Stefan moved behind her, his arms circling her waist. "Do you like it?"

"I love it."

"There's more."

Abby followed his gaze to where a blanket was laid out on the ground along with a bottle of champagne chilling in a silver bucket and two fluted crystal glasses glimmering in the light of the moon.

"It's beautiful." She turned to look up at him, glimpsing something in his eyes that stole her breath away.

He kissed her then as if he never intended to let her go, as if everything she felt for him he returned, and so much more. By the time they separated, they were both breathing hard.

"Champagne?" he asked.

She nodded and he led her to the blanket. He

took the bottle from the ice and picked up the corkscrew lying beside the bucket.

He poured them both a glass and then held his up. "To a brave and beautiful woman. May she get everything her heart desires." Then he clinked his glass to hers.

There was only one thing Abby desired, but she was too afraid to reach out for it, too afraid it would be taken from her like everything else she had ever wanted.

She put the crystal to her lips and drank deeply while Stefan watched her intently over the rim of his glass. It was carnal, his look, and full of heated promise.

The night wind was warm, as if the heavens had conspired to produce a sultry breeze just for them. Or perhaps it was not the design of a higher being, but simply the heat radiating from their bodies, pushing away any chill.

Stefan opened his arms and Abby melted into them. They shared another kiss that annihilated her senses and lay siege to her heart. He pulled away and turned her in his arms so that her head was cradled against his chest.

Content in his embrace, she pointed out the constellations while he told her amusing stories about growing up in a big family, making her laugh in a way she hadn't in a long time. Then the conversation drifted in other directions.

"So did you always want to work at the magazine?" he asked, idly fanning a lock of her hair through his fingers.

"No," she said without thinking. Micky had always

loved the magazine, but Abby had never had an interest. She had seen the way it had consumed her father's life, leaving little time for his family.

"What did you want to do, then?"

"You'll probably laugh." Abby wondered how wise it was to open up to him like this. She had never let anyone get too close. But here under the moonlight, the lure was too strong. This would be the last opportunity she would have to share a part of herself with him.

"I give my word as a Boy Scout that I won't laugh," he vowed, placing a hand over his heart.

His warm smile and playful demeanor loosened her tongue. "Well, if you really want to know, I aspired to be a schoolteacher." And for a short while she had lived a bit of that dream, working part time at a nursery school. Then her mother's illness grew worse and Abby couldn't be gone for any extended period.

When she had tried to talk to her mother about hiring a home healthcare nurse, her mother had adamantly refused, telling Abby that she didn't want some stranger in her house, and didn't her own daughter love her enough to take care of her? The guilt had worked the way it always had, and Abby had given up her job.

"So what happened?" Stefan quietly asked.

"Other things came along." She stared out into the night sky, feeling Stefan's regard but not wanting him to see what was in her eyes, the remnants of a longing for a dream she had no chance of recapturing.

"You must like children a lot if you wanted to be a teacher."

"I love them." The only dream that had ever been substantial to Abby was that of being a mother someday. "There's something about the innocence of a child that nothing else can compare to, when their lives are being shaped and nothing taints their view of the world."

Stefan's fingers whispered along her neck, making her shiver with yearning. "And what things shaped your life, *cara mia?*"

"The same things that shaped everyone's life, I suppose."

"You suppose?"

Absently, Abby took hold of his hand, holding it up in front of her, sketching the lines of his palm, thinking how Ida had once done the same thing to her. The integral difference was that Ida had been able to glimpse something inside Abby while Abby could see nothing but dissecting lines on a hand she fervently wished would touch her.

"I was never like other girls," she heard herself admit, feeling as though nothing could hurt her as long as she was in Stefan's arms. "I always felt like a butterfly beating my wings against the inside of a glass jar. Always looking out. Always waiting to be released."

Stefan's hands settled on her waist and turned her to face him. "You're free now, love, and you can be whatever you want to be."

Abby wanted to believe him. But she wasn't free. Not really. Life seemed to take joy in placing hurdles in front of her, mounting them higher and higher until there was no chance of succeeding, and no reason to keep trying.

But she didn't want to think about those things. Not tonight.

"Make love to me, Stefan," she murmured. "Right here, beneath the stars." So the moment would be captured forever within the universe and she could pull down the memory whenever she desired.

"Are you sure that's what you want?" He looked so uncertain, so boyishly vulnerable that Abby's heart filled with a love she had never thought imaginable.

"I've never been more sure of anything in my life."

Twenty

Abby sat back on her knees and prayed shyness would not overcome her now. She wanted nothing to mar the memory of this night.

She had purposely bought the sexiest dress she could find, the front dipping low, clinging provocatively to her bare breasts. In what seemed another lifetime, she would never have been brave enough to wear something so blatantly sexual. But she wanted tonight to be perfect. And the effort had been well worth the reward. The heated look Stefan had sent her when she had emerged from his room with it on still sent a shiver down her spine.

With shaking hands, she reached around to the zipper, her eyes locking with Stefan's as the straps floated off her shoulders and the material pooled around her waist. Shimmering moonlight slanted across her bare torso, bathing her breasts in its luminescent glow.

As he stared, self-doubt rose up inside her and she automatically lifted her hands to cover herself, thinking he had found her lacking in some way.

He took hold of her arms and lowered them. "You're beautiful. Don't ever hide yourself from me."

His words banished the last remnants of her fear. "Touch me, Stefan."

He hesitated only a hairbreadth and then cupped her breast, lifting it high and taking the peak into his mouth. A moan rose in her throat as delicious sensations floated through her.

He wrapped a hand around her waist and held her there while he bathed her nipples with his mouth and tongue, pulling her under the spell of his sensual ministrations.

Abby fumbled with his tie, loosening it and easing the silky fabric from his collar. Then she shoved his jacket from his shoulders. His mouth never left her breasts as she tried to unbutton his shirt. Her hands were shaking badly with need and excitement and the craving to fulfill this dream.

He put an arm behind her back and slowly eased her down to the blanket. Then he knelt beside her, the moon washing his chiseled features, making him look like a pagan god come to teach the mortal world about physical love.

He tugged his shirt from the waistband of his trousers, tossing it negligently to the side. Abby's fascinated gaze skimmed the hard, sculpted planes of his chest, reaching out to stroke one satiny brown nipple, his muscles tightening as her finger whispered over him.

He took hold of her wrist, bringing her hand to his lips to kiss her palm and each of her fingertips, before working his way up her arm, to her shoulder, her collarbone, his tongue dipping into the hollow at the base of her neck, skimming up to her ear, gently tugging the lobe between his lips before moving to her jaw.

And when their eyes collided, his mouth lowered to hers, stealing reason, leaving only a desperate hunger and the imprint of his touch to consume her.

His hands molded her breasts, squeezing, finding her nipples and playing until she writhed beneath him. She moaned, begging him to stop, not to stop, to help her find the place she longed to go.

He suckled her deeply, making her nipples ache. And she wanted to feel the pleasure/pain he was so adept at evoking. He had left her clad in the silk panties she had secretly bought that afternoon, her thigh-high stockings, and black pumps.

She squirmed restively as his body slid down between her legs, his head moving between her thighs, a sweet throbbing centering there, her body quivering in anticipation, knowing what he was going to do.

A gasp of pleasure broke from her lips as he pressed his hot, wet mouth to the silk covering her mound, pushing against her until she could feel his tongue on her clitoris. His teeth sank gently down on the engorged nub and her back came off the ground.

Then he slipped a finger beneath the lacy edge of her panties and groaned at finding her ready. He eased the finger inside her and she instinctively clenched him.

"You're killing me, baby," he said, sounding tortured as he made quick work of removing her panties.

He kneed her legs farther apart and then knelt

between her thighs, stroking her, making her watch him, see everything that he was doing to her.

Then he leaned forward and laved her nipples. "Touch yourself," he said in a husky voice. "Feel how soft and sweet you are."

Abby hesitated, something inside holding her back from doing as he requested, as if laying her hands upon her own body she would look too wanton, too wild.

His hot tongue bathed the sensitive tips again. "Do it for me."

For him. Abby acquiesced, placing her shaking hands on top of her breasts while Stefan continued to tease the hot pulse point between her cleft, watching her with dark, sultry eyes.

"Play with your nipples." His voice was a deep purr, washing over her like warm honey. When she hesitated, he put his hand on top of hers and made her stroke the hardened peaks. "Feel good?"

Abby wanted to deny it, wanted to say that the feel of her own hands on her breasts was not erotic. But it was. Oh, God, it was. She closed her eyes and enjoyed it.

"Sweet Jesus," he groaned a few moments later, pushing her hands aside and latching on to her nipple, his tongue flicking the peak while his finger teased her clitoris, his movements growing more and more frenzied until her orgasm tore from the very depths of her.

But she had wanted Stefan inside her, wanted to know what it was like to have his hardness sheathed within her when she found her release, to be one with a man in a way she never had been before.

"Stefan . . ." Abby unbuttoned his trousers and undid his zipper, finding him hard and hot and throbbing.

"See what you do to me." He groaned deep in his throat as she began to massage him, moistening her fingers with the beads of liquid that escaped from the tip of his penis.

He allowed her to play for a few minutes, holding himself tightly under control, the muscles in his jaw clenching and unclenching, until finally he grabbed hold of her wrists and pulled her on top of him.

He sat her up so that she straddled him. Then he gripped her thighs and slid beneath her until his head was directly below her nest of curls.

He stared up at her, his eyes dark and wicked as his tongue found her sensitive nub, spearing just the tip with expert precision and then slowly circling.

Abby's back arched, her body tensing, her entire sphere of comprehension centered on what Stefan was doing to her, washing her away in a whole new flood of feelings and sensations.

It took Stefan less than two minutes to have her on the verge of coming again. "Please," she begged, no longer drifting in the world of mortal beings, but floating outside herself.

He had her on the pinnacle, the barest edge, so that he could have blown a whisper across her clitoris and she would have dissolved into a thousand pieces. Instead, he slid up until his erection was between her spread lower lips.

He rocked back and forth, solid friction against the engorged nub, once, twice, three times . . .

"Yes . . . Yes . . ."

Her body stiffened, and as the hot flood began, Stefan lifted her . . . and impaled her to the hilt on his shaft. She cried out, feeling as if she had been split in two.

"Oh, Jesus Christ," he swore, low and fierce. "Jesus, Jesus, Jesus . . . why didn't you tell me?"

He was inside her, fully, completely. He had made them one, and the ache was so small in comparison to the miracle he had wrought.

He took hold of her upper arms and shook her lightly. "Why, damn it? Why didn't you tell me you were a virgin?"

Because then he would have known the truth. That she was not Micky. He would have left her, and that she couldn't bear. Jimmy Bodine had violated her, but he had not succeeded in taking the only thing Abby could offer to the man she loved. The security guard's sudden arrival had saved her.

"Don't stop," she pleaded, not realizing tears coursed down her cheeks, only seeing the tormented look in Stefan's eyes. "Please, I need you."

"God, if I had known . . ."

She wanted no words now, no recriminations. No pledges it would not happen again or that it shouldn't have happened in the first place. She prayed he would surrender to his need and forgive her for not being the woman he had believed her to be.

"Stefan . . ." His name caught on a sob.

"Sweet God, forgive me," he said in a raw voice.

"But I have to have you." Then he grasped her hips and drove upward, completely submerging himself inside her, leaving her flushed and trembling, her body burning with pleasure as he taught her the rhythm.

And as he began rocking her more feverishly, Abby gazed up at the stars overhead, knowing she would never be closer to heaven then she was at that moment.

Abby awoke in the dark, heated dreams of Stefan making her surface to the real world where he existed in the flesh.

For a moment, she wasn't sure where she was. She had expected to see the endless black expanse of the sky above her, broken only by the radiant sphere of the moon. Instead she looked up at a ceiling. And she was no longer lying on a blanket on the roof, but tucked under the covers in a king-size bed.

The hotel room, her mind recalled.

But how did she get back here? The last thing she remembered was falling asleep in Stefan's arms. He must have carried her back to the room. She was sorry to have missed it.

She glanced at the clock on the bedside table. Two minutes to midnight. The witching hour. When Cinderella reverted back to a lonely peasant girl. Soon, she would have to go. How she wished she could make time stand still and have this night go on forever. But Ida would be waiting for her.

Abby turned her head on the pillow, thinking to

find Stefan asleep beside her, but he was not there, nor was there any indication that he had lain beside her at all since they had returned to the room.

A bead of alarm raced down her spine, her eyes scanning the darkness. A frightened gasp burst from her lips when she saw a large figure standing in the shadowed corner of the room by the window.

The person turned upon hearing her and took a single step forward. Abby backed up against the headboard, fear closing off her throat. Then he took another half step, moving into a slim beam of moonlight pouring through the panes, illuminating his face.

Stefan.

He stood there, naked to the waist and so devastatingly handsome that Abby felt a rush of warmth just looking at him. She wanted to burn the picture of him into her brain, to hold it to her heart during the hard times to come.

"Sorry," he murmured. "I didn't mean to wake you."

"I wasn't that tired." Although a short while ago, she had been so exhausted that she had fallen asleep on the hotel roof only minutes after Stefan had made love to her.

The champagne they drank combined with her pain medication had caught up with her, forcing her into a deep slumber when she had wanted nothing more than to savor these last few hours in Stefan's arms.

She sat up against the pillows, wincing slightly from the ache between her thighs, a delicious throbbing that made her feel more alive than she had ever felt before.

Stefan remained unmoving at the window and a sense of unease began to grow in the pit of Abby's belly. "What's wrong?" she asked.

"Why?" The word whispered across the distance separating them. "Why didn't you tell me?"

She closed her eyes. Here it was at last. The truth was out. The reality she had been hiding from in her quest to never have this dream end. But she would not regret her decision to make love to Stefan.

And yet, knowing all that, why did she desperately wish she had more time?

She had always counted on time, time to make things right, time to heal old wounds, time to come to grips with what life had in store for her. There seemed to be so much more of it once.

"I didn't know how to tell you," she replied, unable to look at him.

"You didn't know how to say, 'Stefan, I've never been with a man. Please be gentle with me?' Jesus, how difficult is that?"

Abby's head snapped up. He was talking about her being a virgin? She had thought he'd been referring to her deception. Certainly he had to know now that she wasn't Micky. Her sister had been married three times, after all.

"But what about—"

"We'll talk about that in a minute." He walked over to the bed. The mattress sagged as he sat down beside her. Abby thought he might very well shake her, he looked so angry. But instead, he brushed the hair from her face, his knuckles skimming her cheek. "God, the last thing I wanted to do was hurt you."

Abby felt like weeping at his concern. He wasn't angry with her. He was angry with himself. "You didn't," she said. "Well, maybe a little. But only for a moment and it felt so good after that."

A reluctant half-grin twisted his lips. "You humble me, do you know that? No woman has ever done that to me. But with you . . . God, I just wish I had known."

Abby glanced down at her hands. "I was afraid."

"Afraid of what? You must know by now that I would never hurt you. Not intentionally."

"I know. I guess I thought if you knew the truth that you . . . you wouldn't want me."

"Not want you? Look at me, love." He tipped her head up. "I've done nothing *but* want you for months. You don't know how many nights I laid awake thinking about being deep inside you, hearing you moan my name as I stroked in and out of you. Every morning I had to take a cold shower to keep my libido in check so that you wouldn't think I was some horny bastard. Christ, I thought I would go insane there for a while."

A smile tugged at the corner of Abby's lips. "You did?"

He nodded. "Certifiable. Straight to Bellevue." His expression sobered then. "Thank you for the gift you gave me tonight. Lord knows I didn't deserve it."

Abby laid her hand on his cheek, enjoying the slight roughness of his whiskers, knowing no mo-

ment would ever be more real than this one.
"You're the only man I've ever wanted to make love
to. Always remember that."

He took hold of the hand against his face, kissing
her palm. "I'll never forget, Abby."

There it was, out on the table, the thing she had
dreaded. Her lie coming full circle. And for the
barest heartbeat, she wanted to deny his words, remain in the safe world of her pretense. But it had
to end.

"I'm sorry." Sorry for so many things she could
barely speak of them. She had thought herself prepared. But how could she ever have prepared herself for the love she felt for him?

"Why didn't you tell me who you were? Didn't
you trust me?" He took her hand and held it over
his heart, letting her feel its steady beat. "Was there
something going on here between you and your sister? Did you set out to trick me?"

Abby shook her head vehemently. "No. No, I
never meant to deceive you. Things just . . . happened, and then I couldn't stop them."

"What did I do to make you afraid to tell me who
you really were?"

"Nothing. It was me. I wanted to be like Micky. I
wanted to be strong and confident and fearless. I've
spent my whole life wanting to be someone else
and hiding the real me. So I hid again, this time behind my sister's name. But even that I messed up. I
didn't know how to be like her."

"Why would you want to? God, don't you know
how special you are? You don't need to hide behind
anyone."

"But Micky is so sexy and men love her. *You* loved her and that made me want to be like her." Tears built behind Abby's eyes. "I wanted you for myself. I was selfish."

He closed his eyes and dropped his head, and Abby thought she had finally and irrevocably lost him. He now knew her shame, knew her to be a liar, a thief of his affection, and it would end. It had to end, after all.

Even though the truth was out now, it still didn't change things. She could never subject him to half a life, half a woman. Never tie him down the way her mother had tied her down.

The moment she had set herself on the course of action she had taken tonight, she knew she would have to let him go. Nothing had really changed. Only now her conscience was clean.

Stefan glanced up at her then and his eyes were not filled with hate or mistrust, but rather an emotion Abby was too scared to look at too closely. "I never loved Micky."

"You didn't? But she said that you and she—"

"Whatever she said was a lie. We didn't get along from day one. I'll admit, she tried to seduce me a few times, but nothing ever happened."

"Nothing?"

"Nothing. There's only been one woman who has touched my heart. And that's you." He took hold of her hand. "I love you."

The tears that Abby had held in check would no longer be contained. They spilled down her cheeks and over Stefan's fingers as he fervently tried to brush them away. Something she had never known before expanded inside her, and in a moment of utter clarity, she knew what it was.

Courage.

Stefan's love had given her the courage to face whatever came next, and there were not enough words to express her gratitude.

She kissed him then, pouring forth all the love that was in her heart, telling him with actions rather than words how she felt.

He broke the kiss first, breathing heavily as he dropped down to his side behind her, pulling her back against his chest, her buttocks pressed tightly against his groin, his arousal intimately nudging against her.

"I remember you," he murmured, his breath warm on her neck as he feathered light kisses across her skin. "From twelve years ago."

"You do?"

"I was just starting at the magazine and was already full of myself."

"I had such a crush on you."

"You did, did you?" She could hear the smile in his voice and the cocky edge to his words.

"Yes, but I got over it," she teased.

"Are you sure?"

Abby had to bite her lip to keep from moaning when he slipped his hand beneath her arm and cupped her breast, his finger slowly circling her nipple but refusing to touch the sensitive peak. She squirmed, trying to get his finger to move, but he continued to torture her in degrees.

"Is there anything I can do to bring back that loving feeling?" He dipped his finger into her mouth and returned to her breast to stroke the wetness across her nipple, still toying with her.

"I'm . . . *umm,* not sure." Abby was slowly liquefying under his calculated onslaught. "What . . . *aah* . . . did you have in mind?"

"Oh, I don't know." His hand whispered over her stomach and slid between her thighs, finding her already wet. "I'm sure I can think of something."

Abby couldn't take it anymore. She surrendered and rolled over to face him. "Well, then"—she boldly laid her hand over the huge bulge in his briefs, delighting in his swift intake of breath as she started massaging him—"what are you waiting for?"

Twenty-one

Michaela St. James checked her reflection in the mirror of her compact as her limousine rolled toward Manhattan. She grimaced at what she saw. Four months of indulgence in Paris showed quite plainly on her face. The end result of too much cocaine, too much booze, and too many parties that went on until dawn.

Even though it was after midnight, she dropped her sunglasses back into place to cover the damage and decided the first thing she would do in the morning was call her plastic surgeon and schedule an eye lift. The second thing she would do was book her sister into a hotel, preferably across town. The less they saw of each other, the better.

Micky had not told Abby she would be returning. She hadn't spoken to the Holy Vessel in at least two months, not since those first few conversations shortly after Sister Dear had arrived in New York and started to probe into matters that were none of her damn business.

Abby had had the audacity to question Micky's decisions, when *she* had been working at the magazine on and off for years. Micky had solved the problem by simply making herself as unavailable to her sister as possible.

That same method of avoidance had been the reason she had jetted off to Europe in the first place, so her sister could do her little stint in the office—compliments of dear old Daddy's will—before oh, so graciously handing *Bastion* over to Micky. If Abby wanted to be noble—and wasn't she always?—then who was Micky to complain?

Micky wasn't sure what had prompted her sister to give up all her shares of the company rather than splitting it fifty-fifty. But why look a gift horse in the mouth?

Besides, the magazine should have been Micky's in the first place. She would never forgive her father, the bastard, for viciously turning on her and throwing her lifestyle up in her face shortly before he died. How dare he question her morals when he had been led around by his dick his whole life.

What a fool she had been to stay with him after he had divorced her mother. He had always thought she had stayed for the money, pretended loyalty to get his millions. And maybe he was right. After all, what had he done for her?

He had never wanted a daughter. He had wanted a token child. Someone he could toss a credit card to instead of giving a pat on the back, buy a car rather than confer an ounce of his affection. And what had she done in return? Worked harder and harder to win his love, but nothing she did was ever good enough.

Abby, who had never made any pretense of how

she felt about him, who had often been outright disdainful, had been the one he had chosen to leave the magazine to—and that blow had only made Micky resent her sister that much more.

Sweet Abby who could do no wrong, who gave up a good portion of her life to take care of their ailing mother, who had never bitched, never felt any self-pity, who had been a stoic little trooper through it all. Bravo. She deserved a fucking medal.

Abby had always been the good twin, forever casting Micky in the role of the bad twin, and Micky had played that role to the hilt. She did not need or want anyone. What did it get her anyway? Disillusionment and more bitterness.

Yet there had been times over the years when she had found herself wondering what her life might have been like if she had chosen to live with her mother instead of staying in New York with her father.

A bitter laugh escaped Micky, picturing herself as a replica of Abby, princess of Bumfuck, Idaho, sporting overalls instead of Valentino originals, and talking with Betty Jo and Bobby Sue about who made better peach cobbler. Shit, what a prospect.

And yet, maybe she might have found some measure of happiness in all that simplistic crap. But it seemed that every time she had come to a fork in the road, forces propelled her down the wrong path.

Christ, what did it matter anymore? Her life was her life and it was too late for what-ifs or to go back and start over.

The limo pulled up at the curb and her driver retrieved her luggage from the trunk. She was home. Time to slip back into the role she had perfected.

She adjusted the obscenely expensive wide-brimmed hat she had purchased from a French milliner, knowing people would stare once she stepped from the limo, wondering if perhaps she was some movie star. And that's exactly what Micky craved. Speculation. Adoration.

Attention.

The security guard raised his head as she whisked by him without a word and headed toward the glass elevator leading to the owner's suites. God, how she loathed Hans. Bloody moral prick. He had been a blue-collar worker all his miserable little life and he had the nerve to look down his nose at her.

Micky knew he thought she was too promiscuous. The accusation was there in his eyes. He had watched the procession of men who had come to visit her, even during the years when she had been married and whatever husband was away on business.

She didn't need a shrink to tell her that she substituted sex for love. But who the hell was fucking Hans to judge her? Was his life so perfect? Was he so upright and God-fearing?

In time, he had stopped checking her visitors. She could have gotten him fired for that, but then he would have known he had gotten the better of her—and no one ever got the better of Michaela St. James.

She couldn't believe her hands were trembling as the elevator worked its way up to the sixtieth floor. How could she possibly be afraid of seeing her sister?

Micky immediately scoffed at the ridiculous thought. Afraid of Abby? Please. The shakes were just a mild reaction from withdrawal. She hadn't had a toot in nearly twenty-four hours.

She dismissed her driver as soon as he had deposited her luggage in her bedroom. She looked around the old homestead. Still a masterpiece of marvelous taste, she thought, tossing her sunglasses on a side table.

Now where was her darling sibling? Most likely in bed. It was after one o'clock in the morning and dear Abby the Saint probably adhered to the old adage, Early to bed, early to rise.

Micky wondered if she could coax the little prude into doing a line or two of blow. Perhaps smoke a joint? Probably not. But what a kick it would be to see Abby stoned. She would probably turn six shades of gray.

Regardless of Abby's hang-ups, Micky intended to enjoy a few snorts from her stash before turning in for the night. The dope always helped her relax—and during sex, it made her orgasms really intense.

She took off her four-hundred-dollar hat and discarded it on the table. Then she undid the pins holding her hair in its elegant coiffure and finger-fluffed the long length. It fell nearly to her waist. Men loved it when she used it to toy with their cocks.

She kicked off her shoes and glanced around. "Now where the hell is Sheba?" Usually her cat was twining in and out of her legs by now, begging to be picked up. "Probably got a fur ball up her ass because I've been gone so long."

Micky shrugged and began to peel off her clothes, shucking items as she padded into the kitchen to mix herself a welcome-home rum and Coke. She was down to her skimpy bra and matching thong by the time she made it to the liquor cabinet to grab the bottle of Bacardi.

"What the hell is this?" She stared in mounting anger at the six-hundred-dollar Porthault sheets covering the windows, obscuring her magnificent view. Had to be fucking Abby's work. God forbid the world should get a glimpse of her tits.

Micky took a long gulp of her drink and turned away in disgust. She grabbed her purse, pulled out the vial with her coke, tapped out a line on the table, and snorted it up with a hundred-dollar bill. Nirvana.

She sighed and closed her eyes. "As pure as the driven snow."

After a few minutes, she drifted toward her bedroom, flipping on the stereo and filling the room with the soulful sounds of Creed.

She ignored the closed door to the guest room where Abby was probably fast asleep, dreaming she was Heidi frolicking in a fucking meadow on the Swiss Alps or Shirley Temple on the Good Ship *Lollipop*.

Micky peeled off her bra and dropped it outside her bedroom door. She would call her housekeeper, Marta, in the morning and let her know the boss was back in town and to hustle her underpaid Haitian behind over.

Ah, sweet, young, starry-eyed Marta, all wrapped up in her dreams of America the beautiful, land of the free and home of the brave, a golden-tinted paradise that would someday make her a bonafide citizen and lift her from her life of poverty to a life of slightly less poverty, where she could go forth and multiply ad nauseam and produce a passel of kids she couldn't afford. Until that day, however, they could share a dildo and a little afternoon delight.

Micky turned on the shower. Four massaging jets instantly spewed a mountain of water. A heady languor descended over her as the coke and booze worked that voodoo that they do so well.

She toyed with her nipples while waiting for the water to get to the perfect temperature. Then she peeled off her thong and grabbed the stool she used when she wanted to sit directly in front of one of the pulsating streams and let it massage her clit until she got off. Sometimes masturbation was so much better than a man. Got right to the heart of the matter and cut out the machismo crap and endless "Oh, yeah, baby. Give it to me."

Micky stayed in the shower a long time, climaxing three times before the water began to get cold and her pussy grew sore from the pounding jets. God, it was good to be home.

She wrapped a towel around her hair, dried herself off with another and then left both of them in the middle of the bathroom floor. She was ready to slip naked between her sheets and let obscenely expensive fibers caress her body.

She stopped in her tracks when she saw what was propped against the pillow on her bed. "Shit," she swore with renewed irritation as she stared at the single red rose. "The man doesn't know how to take a hint."

When had he left his signature calling card? And how? She had gotten her keys back from him when she had broken off their affair before she left for Europe.

Could he have made a duplicate set? She wouldn't put it past him. That was part of the reason she had dumped him. He was too controlling, too overpowering, liked to dominate her in bed and enjoyed S&M more than she did, wearing that black leather mask over his face and the leather straps around his cock and balls. The sex had been fun at first, kinky, hot, but it had quickly grown old. So had his possessive behavior.

Micky remembered when Abby called asking if she knew anything about a perverted voyeur with a red rose fetish. She hadn't been exactly truthful when Abby told her about the little surprise that had been left on her doorstep. But Micky figured Snow White deserved a hard dose of reality. Might snap her out of that puritanical acid trip she'd been milking since birth.

Moving to her bed, she picked up the rose and frowned. It looked fresh, almost dewy. How long had it been there? A few hours or a few days? She had been so doped up she couldn't recall if it had been there when she walked into the room.

"Prick." She tossed the rose across the room, the petals breaking off and drifting to the floor.

Tomorrow she was calling a locksmith. Then she would corner Hans and make sure the little Nazi understood that he better start doing his job and not allow people up to her floor who weren't on her goddamn list of acceptable visitors or else she would get his pasty old ass canned.

If that didn't keep her ex-lover away, then she would have to resort to her threat to call his boss. Surely New York's finest wouldn't want a scandal on their hands—however long acquainted with scandal they may be.

"Hello, love."

Startled, Micky whirled around, staring in shock at the man she had mentally consigned to a slow, painful death in the bowels of hell.

"Welcome home," he said with a faintly mocking smile, fondling the black leather whip he had bought her months ago, latex gloves covering his hands. "I've missed you."

"What the hell are you doing here?" she demanded, fury overriding her fear.

"Miss me?"

"Yeah, about as much as I miss any fucking psychotic."

His dark eyes glittered. "I don't like that kind of talk."

"I don't give a shit what you like. Now get the hell out of my apartment!"

He smiled then and it sent a frisson of foreboding rushing through her veins. Then, without a word, he swung the whip, sending the tip cracking across her waist.

"Stop it!" she demanded, falling back onto the bed. "What are you doing?"

He lunged for her, pulling a pair of handcuffs from the clip on his belt and locking one of her wrists to the headboard.

Micky yanked against her bond. "Let me go, damn you!"

He unbuttoned his shirt and tossed it to the floor, his gaze crudely raking her naked form. "I see you're ready to play. I watched you in the shower."

"Stop this, you bastard! I'm not amused."

"Oh, but you will be. I promise." He tugged something from his back pocket. It was the black leather mask. He pulled it over his head. Then he unhooked another set of handcuffs.

Micky screamed and he clamped a hand over her mouth. She struggled, kicking out at him, catching him in the groin.

"Bitch!" he exploded, his hand cracking across her face, the coppery taste of blood filling her mouth. She groaned in pain, blackness threatening to engulf her.

"Now she what you've made me do?" he growled darkly. "You've been a bad girl and bad girls must be punished." He grabbed hold of her left leg and yanked it across the bed, using one of her scarves to tie her ankle to the post. Then he did the same to her other ankle. His black eyes surveyed her, and they were empty, without mercy. "Now that's the way you should always be for your master."

"Please . . ." she rasped through her split lip.

"That's right. Beg me for it." He let his pants drop to the floor and stroked his erection. "Like what you see? It's all for you." He unrolled a condom and slipped it on. "Don't want to leave any evidence now, do I? That's the joy of being a cop; no one ever looks at you like you're a suspect and all the intel you could ever want is at your fingertips, like phone records and airline reservations and security guard snitches to fill me in on people's comings and goings. No one ever bars a door to a cop or tells a cop where he can or can't go. So you see, you can't get away from me. You're mine . . . and you always will be."

He stroked the whip between her mound and then trailed it up to flick a nipple. She flinched. "It was fun playing with your sister while you were gone. I'm going to enjoy fucking her as well. See whose pussy is tighter. Maybe I'll even give it to her up the ass."

"Piss off, you sick fuck."

He backhanded her, sending another gush of blood into her mouth. "Now, I'm going to give it to you good and hard the way you like it." He bent down and retrieved something from his pants pocket. "I even brought your favorite toy to heighten the pleasure."

"No!" she cried, struggling against her bonds as he came toward her with a pair of nipple clamps. Pain lanced through her as he clipped them on and gave a tug.

"But before the pleasure begins, I have to first teach you what happens when you disobey me." He stepped away from the bed.

Then he raised the whip over his head, the
room filling with the sound of leather as it hissed
through the air.

Abby stood next to the bed and stared down
at Stefan as he slept. He lay on his back, his silky
black hair tousled, one arm across his stomach
and the other above his head. He was so beautiful, so perfectly formed that he should be carved
in stone and put on display for the whole world
to see.

She knew the strongest urge to trace the muscles of his chest with her finger, as she had done
earlier in the night, when he allowed her up for
air in between making love. He was insatiable. She
was insatiable. They couldn't get enough of each
other.

Even now as she drank him in, looking her fill,
she wanted him. Without doing a thing, he made
her long to slide back under the sheets and press
her body close to his, to fall asleep to the sound
of his heart beating beneath her ear.

But she had stolen all the time she could, made
it theirs. She now had new memories to replace
all the old painful ones and she would cherish
them. He had freed her.

And now she would free him.

She had not understood until that moment how
wonderful the simple act of letting go could be,
not truly fathomed the sacrifice of walking away
from someone you loved because it was the right
thing to do.

Now she understood.

Gently, she swept a lock of hair from his fore-head. Then she leaned down and brushed a light kiss across his temple. "I love you," she whispered, finally saying the words out loud.

Then she turned and quietly walked to the door. She did not look back.

"Oh, dear girl. I was worried about you!"

Abby forced a smile of greeting to her face as she walked into Ida's apartment, trying to act as if nothing was wrong, as if she didn't already feel as though an eternity had sprung up in the short space of time since she had left Stefan at the hotel.

But she knew she was doing the right thing, as much as she knew walking away from Stefan would be hard. She just hadn't figured how hard—or that she would miss him this intensely, this soon.

"I'm sorry, Ida," she said, feeling physically and emotionally drained. "I should have called to let you know I would be late."

"Well, come in. Come in. Did you have a good time, I hope?"

Abby could feel the poignancy of her own expression. "I had the best time of my life." And nothing could ever take that away from her.

Ida beamed like a proud parent. "Wonderful." Then she beckoned Abby toward the kitchen. "Tea?" She filled a kettle and put it on the burner as if it wasn't the middle of the night.

"No, thank you. I think I'm just going to go to sleep if that's all right." She was exhausted and her stomach was beginning to throb again. Over the past two weeks, she had been forced to take ever-increasing doses of her pills to get the same amount of relief.

"Certainly, my dear. I fetched a few items for you from your sister's apartment this afternoon with the spare key you left me."

"I appreciate that, Ida. Thank you."

"You're more than welcome." Then, as if Abby had not just indicated she wanted to go to bed, Ida said, "So do you want to tell me why you've deserted that luscious Italian to stay with an eccentric old Jewish woman?"

Stefan was the last subject Abby wished to discuss. The minute she had walked out of the hotel room, she had vowed to put her feelings for him behind her, to move forward and not look back.

"You're not eccentric, Ida. Nor are you old," Abby replied, hoping to evade the real question.

"And you, my dear, are very sweet. But I'm too wily to be put off that easily, no matter how politely you attempt to change the subject. Now, what happened between you and Stefan?"

"Nothing, Ida. He's wonderful. Everything I had ever hoped for in a man."

Abby pictured him as she had last seen him, asleep, endearing, very sexy, the single sheet hugging his waist, outlining his sex, making a slow burn begin inside her as she remembered the heights he had taken her to, how superbly he had used the endowments God had blessed him with to bring her such joy.

"Well," Ida said, "what's the matter then? Why

didn't you stay with him? Not that I mind your company. Not at all. But if I had a man like that, I don't think I'd ever leave his side."

If things had been different, Abby knew no force on Earth could have made her leave Stefan. But it seemed as though she was fated to spend her life on the outside looking in, watching the world roll by, occasionally tapping on the glass and hoping someone would let her in. And when she had finally given up hope that that would ever happen, she had been granted a short pardon. She would always be grateful for that.

"I love Stefan," she said quietly, wanting at least one person to know, so that no one could ever dispute it. "I love him with all my heart. He brought me sunshine when I thought never to see it again."

Ida laid her hand over Abby's. "He loves you, too. I just know it."

Abby knew it, too. Stefan had said the words, but he had not fully understood what he was getting into at the time. Reality would change everything, and she could not bear to have that happen.

"I shouldn't have gotten him involved in my trouble, Ida. If he was hurt because of me, I would never be able to forgive myself. I have to take care of this on my own."

"He's a big boy, my dear. He can handle himself."

Abby knew that was true, but she also knew Stefan would do whatever was necessary to protect her. And she had taken advantage of that, relied on his strength, never considering how she had turned his life upside down. He wasn't expecting this, hadn't asked for it. Yet she had thrust the burden on him.

"I have to do this alone, Ida. Please understand."

"Are you sure there isn't more here, Abby? Something you're not telling me?"

"Isn't it simply enough that I don't want him to get hurt?"

"I wish I could understand what moves you. Why you seem so determined to keep people at arm's length."

"I didn't realize that was what I did." But she knew she lied. "Besides, my stay here in New York was only meant to be temporary."

"I still don't see a problem. If you dislike New York, and I certainly can understand why you might considering what you've been through, then there are some lovely little towns outside the city."

"I can't stay here. Please understand."

Ida gave her a kindly smile and patted her hand. "All right, dear. I know when I'm pushing. I just hope you know what you're doing. I'd hate to see you making a mistake you'll regret."

There would be no regrets. Abby had promised herself. She would not leave what she had shared with Stefan behind. She would take it with her and keep it close to her heart.

"I know what I'm doing."

Ida nodded, not looking entirely convinced. "I'll see you to your room." She started walking out of the kitchen and then halted abruptly. "Oh! I almost forgot to tell you!" She turned around. "Your sister is back. I saw her come in a short while ago."

A surge of heart-stopping panic sluiced through Abby.

Micky was home? And alone in the apartment?

Visions assailed her, memories of the man who had been terrorizing her, who had vowed to kill her—who had murdered Carol Elliot because of her, flashed like a macabre strobe light in Abby's mind.

"Oh, God," she choked out through the tight knot in her throat. "She shouldn't be over there alone."

"Calm down." Ida wrapped an arm around her shoulders. "Security has been apprised of the situation and things have been tightened up. I've even seen that police officer friend of hers around here, checking on things. I feel safer already."

Abby's gaze jerked to Ida's. "What police officer friend?"

"I don't know his name, but I've seen him a few times. I think I caught a glimpse of him tonight, as a matter of fact, though I can't be sure."

Abby could not quell her unease. Something inside her rang with an urgency to see Micky now. It was as if . . . as if her sister was calling for her. She couldn't quite explain the feeling. But it was there.

Abby rifled through her purse and pulled out her keys. "I'm going over there, Ida. I have to see Micky and make sure she's all right. I never told her how dangerous the situation has become."

A wrinkle of concern creased Ida's brow. "Maybe I should come with you."

"No, you stay here. I'm sure everything's fine and

I'm worrying for nothing." So why couldn't she convince herself of that? She wouldn't know a moment's relief until she saw Micky.

"All right. But I want your promise that you will call me from there. If I don't hear from you in ten minutes, I'm coming over."

"I promise." Abby hastened to the front door. "Ten minutes."

Twenty-two

Stefan awoke with a jolt, his body covered in a thin layer of sweat. He felt disoriented, but more than that, he felt an overwhelming sense of apprehension. Something wasn't right.

His gaze jerked sideways, searching for Abby, but she wasn't beside him on the bed, and when he laid his hand on the empty space, it was cold.

He threw the covers back and jumped to his feet. "Abby?" he called out, hoping she was just in the bathroom.

No reply greeted his ears. His concern began to escalate and the uneasy feeling inside him expanded.

He glanced around and noted her clothes were gone. She had left him. He knew it for a fact. But why? What had he done? She loved him, damn it! Why would she leave? And where had she gone in the middle of the night? Didn't she realize that maniac was out there waiting for his opportunity to strike? Dear God, why would she risk getting herself killed?

Her defection tore at him because he suddenly realized why she had gone, knew the answer without the words having to be spoken.

She didn't want him getting hurt. The little fool thought she was protecting him.

Didn't she understand that his life would be meaningless without her? That she was a part of him now and he couldn't lose her?

He had to find her. Had to tell her. Before she got any more idiotic notions in her head. But where could she have gone? She wouldn't have returned to the boat. That left only one place.

Micky's apartment.

But would she go back there alone? He didn't think so. Perhaps she had taken another room in the hotel or gone to different hotel?

He raked a hand through his hair, on the verge of losing control. Then he glimpsed a folded piece of paper propped by the lamp. He swiped it off the table and opened it.

Dear Stefan,

I couldn't leave without telling you how much these last few months have meant to me. Never in my wildest dreams did I think I would find someone like you. I owe you so much. You have given me back my life, and for that, I thank you.

I know you won't understand why I left, but believe me when I say I have my reasons. I knew when things began to develop between us that I couldn't stay here, that another life awaited me elsewhere. I should have told you, but I was selfish. I wanted to steal this time with you. For that, I was wrong, and I pray someday you'll forgive me.

Please don't worry about me. I'm in good hands. If you truly care for me as you have said, I beg you to

*let me go and trust that I am doing the right thing for
both of us.*

Abby

Stefan crumpled the note, his insides feeling as if
they were being twisted with a wrench. She wanted
him to let her go. Did she think she could just walk
away without an explanation? But would it have
mattered? Either way, he wasn't giving her up without a fight.

So where could she have gone? She said she was
in good hands, so that told him she had to be staying with someone. Then the answer dawned on
him.

Ida. It made sense.

He rushed to the door, buttoning his shirt as he
went, not allowing himself to contemplate the possibility that he could have jumped to the wrong
conclusion, that he might not find her.

Because he had to find her.

Abby stood in front of Micky's apartment door
debating the wisdom of disturbing her. She was
probably asleep and would think Abby was nuts if
she roused her for the sole purpose of making sure
she was all right.

Yet something gnawed at Abby, a sensation that
would not be ignored. She tried to tell herself that
her distress was simply a product of residual anxi-
ety, of returning to the place where her troubles
had begun, where that first fateful glance through
a telescope had dissolved into a nightmare.

Abby clutched the keys in her hand and then slid

the one she needed into the lock and entered the apartment. She heard music coming from the stereo, confirming that Micky was home and possibly still awake.

Clothes littered the floor. The disarray was comforting, making Abby think all her worrying had been for nothing. There was certainly nothing sinister in untidiness.

She glanced toward her sister's bedroom at the end of the long hallway. The light was still on.

"Micky?" she called out, walking over to the stereo and turning it off.

No reply greeted her. Maybe she was in the shower? Or perhaps she had fallen asleep with the light on?

Abby headed out of the living room and stopped, an unexpected chill sweeping down her spine as she noticed her sister's bedroom light was now off. She told herself not to jump to conclusions. Micky probably hadn't heard her calling and was just turning in for the night.

She should leave. Certainly her conversation with her sister could wait until the morning. It was only a few hours away.

Abby dismissed the idea as quickly as it came. She wouldn't be able to sleep until she told Micky about what had been going on and made her sister understand that the threat was real and not simply a matter of Abby "toughening up."

Her decision made, she walked toward her sister's partially closed bedroom door. "Micky?" she called out again. She thought she heard a sound. Footsteps?

Stopping in front of her sister's door, Abby knocked lightly. "Micky? It's me." Slowly, she pushed the door open. "Micky?"

Abby stepped inside the room, squinting into the darkness, trying to discern a shape beneath the bedcovers. The light from the living room was dim, but she could just make out a faint outline.

"Micky?" Abby moved farther into the room. "I need to talk to you. It's important." No response came back to her. A bead of foreboding worked its way down her spine as she progressed toward her sister's bed. "Mick?"

The faintest whimper caught Abby's ear, a sound so slight she wouldn't have heard it had her ears not been attuned to a heightened awareness. Her foreboding blossomed into rising fear.

She stumbled across something in front of her, nearly falling into the end table, reaching out to catch the lamp as it teetered. Her fingers searched for the switch and clicked it on, bathing the room in a soft glow.

She turned toward the bed . . . and a choking sound of horror lodged in her throat.

"Oh God . . . Micky." The words came out an anguished whisper, the world swirling dizzily around Abby as she looked down at her sister's beaten body.

Micky's face was so battered it was nearly unrecognizable. Across her stomach and chest were bleeding whip marks, and around her neck . . . around her neck were horrible purplish bruises.

The kind of marks made by someone's hands.

Have you ever heard of autoerotic asphyxiation? While

I'm fucking you, I'll wrap my hands around your throat and squeeze . . .

With a strangled cry of despair, Abby reached blindly for the handcuffs holding her sister's wrists to the bed, but there was no way she could open them. "Micky," she sobbed. "Oh, dear God, Micky."

She tried to breathe, tried to think as she stumbled to the end of the bed, her hands shaking uncontrollably as she struggled to undo the bindings holding Micky's legs open.

"It's all right. I'm here." Tears streamed down Abby's face. "Just hold on. Please, hold on."

Call for an ambulance, her mind screamed. *Call the police.*

Abby grabbed the cordless phone . . . but there was no dial tone. "No!"

A groan brought her gaze swinging around to Micky. "Abby . . ." Her name came out on a thin, raspy whisper.

"Don't try to talk."

Another moan issued from her sister's cracked, bleeding lips. "Go . . . Now." She tried to open her eyes, but they were too swollen. "Go . . ."

"I'll get help." Ida's apartment. She'd call from there. *Oh, please, God . . .*

Abby turned to run from the room . . . and screamed.

Standing in the threshold was a man, his obsidian eyes glinting through the slits in his black leather mask. The same evil eyes that had stared at her across the length of Stefan's office.

The eyes of a killer.

"We meet again." Something about his voice rang

familiar, but Abby could not wrap her mind around it. Terror eclipsed everything. Terror . . . and the need to save her sister.

"Don't come near us! I've called the police!"

He laughed, that same dark, hideous laugh she had been hearing in her dreams for months. "You did? Without the telephone wire?"

Abby's gaze whipped to the telephone and saw there was no cord running out the back. Her attention flew back to the man now turning a razor-edged dagger in his hands.

His hands. That voice. Suddenly everything clicked.

"Detective Tremonte." The name was spoken in a horrible murmur of recognition.

"Smart girl. Bad timing. You interrupted me. I was at the final stage of teaching your sister a lesson about teasing a man, which would account for the missing wire in case you were wondering. I had to use it around her neck. She was giving me a hard time. And I don't like women who give me a hard time."

Bile rose in Abby's throat like acid. "You bastard," she spat in a raw voice.

His eyes glittered dangerously. "Don't make me have to hurt you more than is necessary."

Abby knew she should be afraid. She had little doubt the man intended to rape her, kill her. She could see it in those cold eyes. But no man would ever make her cower again.

"Why, damn you? Why did you do this to my sister?"

"Because women need to learn their place. Your

sister was a cock-tease. I tried to warn her that she
could only push a man so far, that he would eventually crack. But she didn't listen. You can see the
result." His slitted gaze shifted briefly to Micky's
prone, unconscious form.

"That was you across the street, wasn't it? And
on the phone. All you."

He nodded, his thumb running along the edge
of the knife, drawing a drop of bright red blood.
He didn't seem to notice. "I didn't realize at first
that your sister had slipped from my grasp and
out of the country. So I ended up playing the
game with you and then grew to like it too much
to stop. Your sister used to watch through the telescope while Carol Elliot serviced me." He ran a
hand over his groin. "She told me the whore deserved to be used. And I got off knowing she was
watching."

"You're lying! Micky would never do something
like that."

"You don't know your sister, then. She's a kinky
bitch who likes her drugs a bit too much. That's
how we met. I caught her snorting a line of coke off
the hood of her limo. She offered her pussy as a
bribe to keep from being arrested and I took it. I
knew she spread her legs for everyone, but I also
knew she would be different now that she had me,
that she would give it to me *and only me.* I told her
not to test me. She chose to ignore my warning. So
you see, this is really all her fault."

Anguish for her sister threatened to choke Abby.
"You're crazy."

"A crazy man would have left a trail. I didn't. All

the evidence points to other people, like your lover, for example. He had a motive to want you gone, after all. You held the key to his future at the magazine. As for your sister, it's well known he could barely tolerate her. She was constantly causing him problems."

"No one would ever believe Stefan was capable of hurting anyone."

Tremonte shrugged. "If that possibility didn't fly, there were plenty of other potential suspects. Your sister was universally hated. The precinct would be lining up perps from here to hell.

"As for Carol's fate, your actions caused her death the minute you called about what you witnessed across the street. I couldn't take the chance the silly bitch would let something slip now, could I?"

"You could have ended this and left us all alone."

He went on as if she hadn't spoken. "Then you showed up that night at the magazine and surprised me. I was going to frame the office lover boy, Rick Faraday. The cocky bastard was a perfect scapegoat.

"Then I toyed with the idea of manufacturing evidence to make it look as if you killed Carol. You hated her just as much as your sister. She stole your father, and as any prosecutor would point out, you were bitter because she was the direct cause of your family splitting up. Hence, motive.

"Most people also knew that your sister was having an affair with Rick and that he was fucking Carol on the side—a scandalous love triangle that caused a big blow up between the two. So you see, there are suspects coming out the asshole, and I am the least likely candidate in this scenario."

"You won't get away with this."

"We both know I will. Cops watch out for cops. You and Sis will just be another statistic, a pair of raunchy twins who took their love play too far and ended up on a cold slab in the morgue. Another tragic tale in a city full of them."

He held the blade up then; it glinted wickedly, like molten silver. "As I've said, you really have bad timing. A few more minutes and I would have had your sister's throat slit, cleaned up all the evidence, and then conveniently been here during the investigation to see what turned up. But your arrival is merely a blip in my plan. In some ways this is even better because now I'll get to test-drive your sweet ass and see which sister is the better fuck. A million men's fantasy."

Thoughts spiraled one on top of the next in Abby's head, her mind wildly searching for ways to delay him, knowing time might be the only thing that would save her and Micky.

Only one thing was clear at that moment.

This man wanted to see her cower, needed to see her fear. It was reflected in his eyes. It excited him. Giving into her fear would only build his strength. She knew then what she had to do.

Abby forced herself to look directly into those empty eyes. "Is this the only way you know how to be a man? By terrorizing women?"

His body tensed. "I'm more man than you could ever handle. And I'm going to show you dark delights you've never experienced before."

Cautiously, Abby slid her hand behind her back, feeling for the edge of the end table, knowing there was a pair of scissors in the drawer.

"You're not a man," she taunted. "You're a weakling. A coward. What was it you said to me on the phone? That I'm the only woman who makes you hard? Well, look at you." She pointed to his partial erection, trying to deflect his attention. "You can't even get it up like a normal man."

"That's because you're a whore!" he growled, his knuckles growing white as he gripped the knife. "You and your sister let any dick inside you."

"It's not us. It's you. Can't you see? You don't function normally."

"Shut up!"

"You want to blame women for your problem because you're half a man."

"Shut your fucking mouth!"

"You make me sick. You make all women sick." Abby pulled the drawer open and felt blindly for the scissors. "You're a freak. And you hate women because you can't perform. We make you feel inadequate—especially a woman like my sister, who is vibrant and strong and sexual. You can't stand it." Abby forced a laugh. "You're a pathetic excuse for a man!"

His face mottled with rage, spittle coming out of his mouth as his control snapped. He lunged at her, wildly swinging the knife, the blade hissing through the air. She jumped back, hitting the end table, the lamp crashing to the floor.

Her fingers wrapped around the scissors just as he

arced the knife back over his head. She screamed
and closed her eyes.

Ramming the scissors into his chest.

The Porsche was half on the sidewalk in front of
Trump Towers when Stefan jumped out, flying past
the doorman who called after him to stop. But Stefan's entire world was absorbed with one consuming thought.

Finding Abby.

She needed him. He knew it, could feel it in his
bones.

On the floor that led to the owner's suites, he
raced passed the security guard, who came after
him, grabbing his arm as Stefan got into the elevator.

"Come back here!" he ordered, but Stefan gave
him a quick shove right before the elevator doors
banged shut.

It seemed as if time stood still in the two minutes
it took the elevator to reach the sixtieth floor. Stefan pried his hands between the doors as soon as
they began to open and pushed his way through.

He ran to Ida's apartment and found the door
open. "Abby!" he barked as he entered.

Ida appeared, her face stricken. "Oh, thank God
you've come!" she cried, hastening toward him.

"What's the matter? Where's Abby?"

"She's gone . . ."

A spike of alarm slammed through Stefan. "What
do you mean she's gone? Where did she go?"

Ida's body trembled uncontrollably. "Micky," she

said. "She's in Micky's apartment. Oh, God, I told her I would come over in ten minutes, but the door was locked and I left the key here. Then I heard the scream and I tried to wake up the neighbors . . ." A choked sob broke from her lips. "Please, you must help her!"

The words hit Stefan with the force of a wrecking ball. He swung toward the door.

"Wait! The key." She pressed the apartment key into his hand. Then she pulled a revolver from her skirt pocket. "It was Bernard's. I was going to try . . . Here. Take it. And dear God, be careful."

Stefan grabbed the gun. "Call the police." Then he turned and ran down the hallway.

Tremonte howled in pain as the scissors sank into his flesh.

Abby's eyes snapped open and found the instrument impaled two inches into the middle of his chest, blood spewing from the wound. His gaze was fixed on the scissors as if he couldn't believe what he saw.

Then, slowly, his head elevated. Abby's eyes widened in terror as their gazes locked. His lip curled, his face a mask of impotent rage as he grasped the handle of the scissors and yanked them from his chest, squirting blood on her.

"Now you're going to die, bitch."

Abby screamed, ducking as his arms closed around her. She shouldered him to the side and ran for the bedroom door, hearing him pounding directly behind her, knowing she would never make it to the front door.

His hand wrapped around her hair, jerking her back. She saw the edge of the knife he still held as it came down over her shoulder.

She rammed her elbow into his stomach with every ounce of strength she possessed. She heard his grunt. His fingers loosened and she took off.

She only got two feet before his arm snaked around her waist, his punishing grip forcing the air from her lungs as they hurtled headlong toward the floor. She grappled with him, but he was too strong. He pinned her arms to the floor.

He raised the knife above his head. "See you in hell!"

A scream lodged in Abby's throat, her gaze glued to the descent of the blade, her mind numbed to the sound of the front door crashing against the wall.

"No!"

Stefan? she thought, a moment before she felt the burning sensation of the knife ripping into her upper chest, searing her with pain unlike anything she had ever known.

A gunshot tore through the air, the bullet blasting into her attacker's skull, the impact sending him flying back, leaving his limbs at odd angles and his body twitching with death spasms.

Abby felt herself losing consciousness. She glimpsed Stefan through a haze as he came to a running stop beside her and dropped to his knees.

"Stefan . . . ?"

"It's me, baby. I'm here. Just hold on. Please, dear God, just hold on."

She could see his face through the center of the fog shrouding her eyes. He was crying. She reached her hand up to cup his cheek.

"I love you, Stefan," she whispered as the pain squeezed her lungs and stole her breath. She had finally said the words. Everything would be all right now. She could move on. The numbness was taking away the hurt. The fear.

At last, she was free.

Twenty-three

Stefan ranged the lobby of University Hospital waiting for word on Abby's condition.

For hours he had been reliving those few agonizing seconds in Micky's apartment when he had thrown open the door and seen Abby sprawled out on the floor, a madman pinning her down—a knife descending toward her heart.

He hadn't had more than a second to think, react, no more than a moment to wonder if his aim would be true as he leveled the gun.

The report of the revolver as he had clipped off a single round echoed through his head, as did the vision of what he had seen when he had dropped down beside Abby.

Blood . . . so damn much of it, and her face had been pale as death. He had been too late. One fucking moment too late to keep the bastard from hurting her.

God . . . if he lost her . . .

Visions bombarded him. Abby dancing around in her bare feet in Micky's office, and seeking his approval about ideas for the magazine, and savoring cannolis, and blossoming under their first kiss, and honoring him with her virginity.

And telling him that no one ever saw her.

God, he did see her. Would he ever get to tell her?

Anger began to build inside Stefan. Anger at himself. At life. At circumstances that had propelled him and Abby toward this end, the same impotent rage he felt when his sister had been taken from him, swept away into a nightmare of bureaucracy, deal making, and torment.

He still couldn't believe what had been revealed this night, the face beneath the black leather mask, a man who had vowed to protect and serve. Detective Tremonte. A cold-blooded killer and sexual sadist.

Stefan finally remembered why Tremonte had looked familiar. He had seen him with Michaela once, briefly, many months earlier. He just hadn't connected the pieces. But how could he have connected them? Would he have immediately thought a cop was the one behind all the sick shit that had been happening to Abby?

And Christ, Michaela . . . Stefan had caught a glimpse of her being rolled out on a gurney. The twisted son of a bitch had beaten her until she was barely recognizable.

Stefan stared down the long corridor toward the double doors of the trauma unit. Somewhere back there they had Abby. A medical team had rushed her straight to surgery and all Stefan had gotten from a nurse was that she would let him know as soon as there was any information.

So he waited. And prayed.

Every time he heard footsteps coming down the

hallway he jumped, wracked with a nearly unbearable tension as he watched another person walk by, none of them stopping to give him word about Abby's condition. His world, his very existence, was collapsing in on itself.

He looked down at the dried red stains on the sleeve of his shirt. Abby's blood. It had been seeping out of her chest as he applied pressure to the wound while he raged to the heavens not to let her die, not to take the only woman he had ever loved. He had vowed he would sell his soul to the devil if it would keep her alive.

He leaned a shaking hand against the window and stared out at the street below. The sun had come up a half-hour earlier.

Until Abby had come along, he had never truly appreciated the glory of a sunrise or the power of a sunset. She had opened his eyes. Now it was as if all the color had been siphoned away, leaving only an endless stretch of gray.

"Mr. Massari?"

Stefan jerked around.

"I'm sorry. I didn't mean to startle you. I'm Doctor Bladen." He was tall and slim, somewhere in his late fifties with white hair and thin-rimmed glasses. He still wore his scrubs and looked exhausted. "I'm head of the surgical team that worked on Ms. St. James."

"How is she?"

"Stable," he replied, easing his shoulders back. "We managed to get the bleeding under control. Another inch in any direction and I don't think she would have made it."

Stefan closed his eyes and held back the wave of emotions engulfing him. Abby had made it through. God had granted them another chance.

He opened his eyes, knowing his feelings for her were written plainly on his face. "Thank you," he said in a hoarse voice.

"Don't thank me yet. She's not out of the woods. Though the stab wound will heal and shouldn't leave any permanent effects other than a scar, it has exacerbated her other problem. With the use of only one kidney, and that kidney malfunctioning, she runs a greater risk of infection and a potential poisonous buildup of fluids."

Stefan felt as if the floor had cracked open, sending him hurtling headlong into blackness. One kidney? Christ. All this time she hadn't said a word. Why? Why would she keep such information from him?

He remembered now the scar on her stomach. He hadn't thought to ask where she had gotten it. His senses had been too full of her, his body too desperate for hers, his need to protect her too consuming.

"You didn't know, did you?" Bladen asked.

"No."

The doctor shook his head. "I'm sorry. You shouldn't have found out this way."

"What else don't I know?"

"I've already divulged more than I should. I'll have to assume Ms. St. James has kept her illness private for a reason. Therefore I'll leave it up to her to tell you. If you'll excuse me?" He turned to walk away.

Stefan stepped in front of the man, blocking his path. "Tell me what?" he demanded.

"I'm sorry—"

"Damn it! I don't want to hear you're sorry. I want to know what the hell is the matter with her. You can't just tell me she has a malfunctioning kidney and then leave me here wondering what that's going to mean for her."

"You're not her husband or a member of her immediate family. I'm not at liberty to say more."

"The only immediate family she has is her sister—and you've already seen her."

The slight wince on the doctor's face told Stefan the man had been affected by what had rolled into his trauma bay.

"I'm all Abby has." Stefan heard the pleading note in his voice.

"I can't say more. Please try to understand."

Bladen began to walk away again and Stefan grabbed his arm this time. "Understand?" he bit out in a raw voice. "Understand that the woman I love is ill and no one will tell me a goddamn thing? Would you understand that, Doctor? Would you sit back and accept that answer? Wouldn't you want to tear everyone apart who told you to understand while your whole world is shattering before your very eyes? Now, please, dear God, tell me what I need to know."

The doctor hesitated, glancing down at his hands and then back up at Stefan, his gaze very direct. And very serious. "What Ms. St. James is suffering from is far worse than that of a stab wound."

"What are you saying?"

"She's dying, Mr. Massari. She has kidney cancer."

The words were like point-blank bullets to the brain, sending Stefan reeling from the impact. "No." He shook his head. "She can't be dying. Her mother . . . You're thinking of her mother. She died of renal failure. But Abby . . . No. Not Abby."

"She's a very courageous young woman. She gave up a kidney for her mother, which is why she has only one left."

Stefan remembered the way Abby had spoken of her mother, of the disease that had finally taken the life of René St. James. And then there was the appointment card for a Dr. Samuel Dressler.

Dated six months earlier.

Abby's mother had died more than a year before that.

He had missed it. And it had been right in front of his damn eyes.

Abby had given up one of her kidneys to save her mother and now cancer was killing the remaining one. It was a savage twist of fate, and Stefan's heart was slowly and irrevocably bleeding to death.

"You can treat her, can't you?" he asked desperately. "You know, shrink the cancer, make it go into remission?"

"No," Bladen said solemnly. "I'm afraid we can't. She didn't get the necessary treatment when she should have and now the cancer has metastasized. There is one thing in her favor, however. The cancer does not seem to have spread beyond the kidney at this point, and the initial CT scan and ultrasonogram have not shown any tumors in the bones or lungs."

"That's good then, right?"

"All it means is that the cancer is confined to one area at present, the remaining kidney."

"Aren't there any drugs you can give her? Chemotherapy or something?"

"We're past that point, I'm afraid. Had she started treatment immediately upon diagnosis, we would have had more of a fighting chance. We could have tried radiation therapy, or biological therapy, or perhaps arterial embolization. One of those treatments might have been successful in putting the cancer into remission. Unfortunately, those methods are no longer open to us."

"So that's it? You're giving up? I thought you were a doctor! You're supposed to save lives!"

"That's what I try to do every day, Mr. Massari, to the best of my ability. Saving lives is why I became a doctor. I wanted to make a difference."

"So save her. There's got to be a way."

Bladen hesitated. "There is an option open to us."

"What?"

"A nephrectomy. It's the only thing that might keep the cancer from spreading any further."

"What does it entail?"

"Removing her kidney."

"But you said she only had one."

"Which would mean a dialysis machine would have to do the work for her kidneys until a donor could be found."

"And how long will that take?"

"I won't lie to you. Organ donations have decreased over the past five years. The only positive

thing is that the powers-that-be are finally seeing
this as a real problem and are launching campaigns
to get people to donate. But results won't come
overnight. The current predictions are a three to
five year turnaround."

The answer left Stefan feeling as if he had been
stripped bare and staked out in the bright, searing
light of day. He knew Abby was strong, but she
would never survive being hooked up to a machine. It would destroy her spirit.

"This nephrectomy . . . could it . . ." Stefan
couldn't bring himself to say the words.

"There is every possible Ms. St. James might not
survive the procedure, but that's the risk in almost
every type of surgery. At this juncture, we would
have to wait until she's stronger to even consider it.
Now if you'll excuse me? I have to get back and
check on her and her sister."

Numbly, Stefan nodded and then said, "When
can I see her?"

"As soon as she's settled into her room, but she
probably won't be awake for a few hours. I'll come
and get you when she's situated."

Stefan sat at Abby's bedside for hours, watching
her as she slept, counting each rise and fall of her
chest, trying not to think about how sick she was or
notice how pale her face was or how fragile she
looked swallowed up in the hospital bed, machines
monitoring her vital statistics, bleeping and click-
ing off digital numbers.

This was reality, this disease, this place. Stark.

Gritty. Harsh. And all of it damn hard to come to grips with. Even having Micky in the next bed was surreal.

Life ticked by in a peripheral blur, his thoughts one sphere of focus. When the nurse came to tell him it was time for him to leave, he begged to stay. He had to be there when Abby opened her eyes. He didn't want her to be alone, afraid.

"All right," the nurse relented. "A little while longer."

Stefan held Abby's hand and talked to her, telling her how he felt, how she had to get better so that they could get married, pouring out every emotion in his heart and praying for a response.

At some point, he dozed fitfully in the chair, Abby's hand clutched in his. He woke up to the sound of her scream reverberating in his ears.

But her eyes were closed, her position unchanged, the machines still bleeping, and life going on as usual beyond the small realm in which they existed. The scream he had heard had been in his mind.

He watched her for a long time, endeavoring to fight off the heavy pull of weariness, knowing what sleep would bring, the visions that loomed each time he shut his eyes, mocking him that he had been too late to help her. But his body refused to obey his mind, and his eyes closed, dragging him down into that looming abyss.

This time when he awoke, he discovered a blanket draped over his shoulders. And when his gaze jerked to Abby's face, he found her beautiful eyes fixed on him.

His heart beat thickly as he rose to his feet and

brushed his lips against the back of her hand. "Welcome back."

"Where am I?" she whispered, her voice sounding raw and unused.

"In the hospital."

She looked confused for a moment, and then the horror of her ordeal dawned on her face. "Oh, God . . ."

"It's all right. It's over now."

Her hand tightened around his. "Micky?"

"Is going to be fine." Stefan nodded toward the curtain separating Abby's bed from her sister's. "She's right over there."

Abby's attention shifted to the curtain, staring at it for long moments before turning back to Stefan, meeting his gaze for only a second, allowing him to see her pain and torment before looking away. "He's dead, isn't he?"

"Yes," Stefan quietly replied.

Her gaze lifted to his and he saw everything, each piece he had missed, all the complexities that made up this woman that he loved.

"Why?" she asked in a barely audible voice. "Why did he do it?"

Stefan shook his head. "I'm not sure. He was obsessed, I guess. People like Tremonte don't have a normal reason for their actions and you can't allow yourself to delve too deeply into what motivated him. He's gone now and that's all that matters. I want you to put him out of your mind."

"I don't think I can."

"You can. I'll help you. Think about something else. Like us."

"Us?"

"As in you and me."

"Is there a you and me?"

Stefan smiled down at her. "Without a doubt. And this time I don't plan on letting you slip through my fingers." His voice sobered. "I was frantic when I awoke in the hotel and you were gone."

Her gaze dropped to his throat. "I'm sorry. I wanted to tell you myself how much our time together meant to me, but I couldn't." She flicked luminous eyes up at him. "You're very special, Stefan, and I hope you never change."

"I don't foresee that happening any time soon, love. As long as I have you, I have everything."

"Stefan . . ."

"I'm not letting you go, Abby, so don't say it. I love you. Doesn't that mean anything?"

She briefly closed her eyes and when she opened them, they were glossy with unshed tears. "It means more to me than you will ever know."

"Do you love me, Abby?"

She hesitated, as if willing herself to say nothing, but losing the battle. "Yes."

"Then say it. Tell me how you feel."

"I love you, Stefan. I'll always love you."

The tension he had been carting around deflated at her words, knowing he had overcome his first obstacle. "Then marry me, Abby, and make me a happy man."

"Marry you?"

"I had planned to ask you last night, but you ran away before I had the chance. And no, my proposing has nothing to do with your getting hurt. But

God," he said, a thread of remembered anguish tightening his insides, "I wish I could have gotten to you sooner. I'm sorry, baby. I failed you."

"No. You didn't fail me. You could never do that."

She may have forgiven him, but Stefan knew it would be a long time before his guilt faded. "So what do you say?" he asked, keeping his voice light. "Will you have me? I know I'm not much, but I'll give you all that's within my power to give and do my best to make you happy."

She reached up and cupped his cheek. "Any woman would love to have you, and you've always made me happy."

"But not just any woman would make me happy, Abby. I want you."

She gave him a sad smile. "I don't know what I did to deserve you. I feel as if I've waited a lifetime to find you and here you are now when . . ." She stopped. But she didn't need to finish the sentence for Stefan to know what she had been about to say. That she had found him now that it was too late. But it wasn't too late. He wouldn't let it be. "I think I'm dreaming and you aren't really here asking me to be your wife."

"You're not dreaming."

"I know. And that's what's so amazing. I didn't believe God would ever give me such a gift. But I've come to realize that miracles happen when you aren't looking for them."

"So say the words, Abby. Say you'll marry me."

She shook her head, the look in her eyes heartbreaking. "I can't."

Stefan had thought himself prepared for that answer. He wasn't. "You can. You love me."

"And that will never change."

"So why aren't you giving us a chance, then?"

"Please . . . don't make this any harder than it has to be."

"You're the one making it hard. Not me. Give in. Let me love you. Let me take care of you."

Haunted eyes jerked to his, her whispered words an accusation. "You know."

Stefan thought of issuing a denial. But what purpose would it serve? He didn't want to play these games. Each moment was too important to waste. He wanted the reality of her illness out in the open and for them to deal with whatever came next together.

"Yes. I know."

"How?"

"It's not important. The only thing that matters is that I love you and that we were meant for each other. Let me be there for you, Abby."

The tears that she had been holding back began to flow. "I don't want your pity."

"Do you think that's what I'm doing? Couldn't it be possible that I admire your bravery, the way you have struggled through adversity when other people might have chosen to hide away? I don't pity you, Abby. I respect you, and that's not something I give easily."

She turned her head away, her tears dampening the pillow beneath her. "Just go away, Stefan. Please."

He cupped her chin and turned her to face him. "I'm not going away. We're in this together."

"I don't want you to be in this!" she sobbed. "Don't you understand? I don't want to marry you. I don't want to see you. I just want you to go away and leave me alone! Just . . ." Her voice broke. "Just leave me alone."

"Is everything all right in here?"

Stefan turned to find the nurse standing in the doorway, her gaze taking in his haggard expression and Abby's tear-streaked face.

Abby tugged her chin from his grip and turned away from him again. "Please," she said in an anguished voice. "Go away."

"Abby," he pleaded. "Don't do this."

"I'm sorry, sir," the nurse said, "I'll have to ask you to leave."

Stefan wanted to fight, to rail, to shake Abby and tell her that he had no intention of giving up, which is what he knew she wanted him to do because she was afraid and hurting inside. He needed to allow her some time to think, to let it sink in that he wasn't going anywhere.

"Fine," he said. "I'll be back later."

"Don't," Abby told him.

Anger began to uncoil in the pit of Stefan's belly. "I'm coming back, Abby, and if you refuse to see me, then you better make sure the hospital posts guards to restrain me." Then he turned on his heel and left.

Twenty-four

Abby watched Stefan's retreating back until he was gone from sight, part of her wanting to call him back, to ask him to hold her and promise he would never let go.

But it was better this way, a clean break. He felt an obligation toward her, nothing more. He didn't really want to marry her. He couldn't. He would be making the biggest mistake of his life if he did, and then he would regret it.

"Jesus, that was stupid."

Abby started at the sound of her sister's voice. "Micky?"

"In the flesh." A short, bitter laugh followed.

"How are you feeling?"

"Like I've been run over. But I'll survive. What about you?"

"I'm fine." And physically that was true, but emotionally, spiritually, Abby was bereft. Telling Stefan to leave had been the hardest thing she had ever done, and the process of ending what was between them, of trying to sever the feelings she knew would be just as strong a year from now as they were today, was like dying one small bit at a time.

"Doesn't sound that way from what I just heard. Obviously you've been busy while I've been away."

"It's nothing."

"Give me more credit than that. No matter what other things pain me, my hearing is perfectly fine."

"Stefan and I are friends. Nothing more."

"So did you two 'friends' fuck?"

"Micky!"

Micky gave a harsh laugh. "Christ, this is priceless. Sweet little Abby got laid. Hallelujah. After all these years of mooning over the man from afar, you've finally landed him. Congratulations."

"I haven't landed him." It was easier to pretend that she hadn't just forfeited any possibility of a future. What could she have ever given Stefan anyway? A sick wife.

A wife who would never be able to bear his children.

That truth was the most soul-destroying element of her disease and the main reason Abby had always wanted to work with children. It was the closest she would ever come to having any of her own.

She knew there was always adoption, that plenty of deserving, beautiful kids needed a loving home. And she had love to give. So much of it that it threatened to overwhelm her at times.

But what man would not long for a child of his own? A product of his flesh and blood? Stefan would eventually grow to resent her for not being able to give him a son or daughter. And how could she even consider being anyone's mother when she didn't know if she would live long enough to see that child reach adulthood?

Abby closed her eyes. She had no choice. Even if her heart longed for Stefan, railed at her to grasp what he was offering and hold on for dear life, it was impossible. She was too afraid. Losing him would be worse than dying.

"Hello?" Micky said impatiently. "Are you still with me?"

"Yes."

"Thinking about the one you let get away?"

"No." Abby forced back the image of Stefan's haggard face after she told him she would not marry him. Now she had to concentrate on trying to fix the only thing in her life that she might have any control over. Her relationship with her sister. "I'm sorry, Micky."

"Sorry? For what?"

"For not getting to you sooner."

"Jesus Christ, Abby. What the hell could you have done? It wasn't as if you asked that prick to rape and beat me."

The rancor in her sister's voice scored Abby. What had she done to earn such hostility? All she had ever wanted was to bridge the divide that separated her and Micky, to heal old wounds before it was too late. Perhaps it was already too late.

"You're my sister. I worry about you."

"Yeah? Well don't. I'm a big girl now." Micky changed the subject. "So why aren't you going to marry Mr. Tall, Dark, and Guido?"

Abby didn't want to discuss Stefan, but she knew Micky would not let the matter drop until she gave her some kind of answer. "We're too . . . different."

Micky snorted. "As if I believe that. Now tell me

the real reason. The man's gorgeous, worth a bun-
dle, and probably has a shlong that would make a
pornographer salivate."

Abby winced at her sister's crudity. But Micky's
words gave something away. Stefan had been telling
the truth. He had not slept with Micky, otherwise
she would have known how well endowed he was.

"So what's the scoop, Snow White?" Micky
pressed. "Afraid he's more man than a little old
country girl like you can handle?"

Abby's anger began to rise at her sister's continued sarcasm and prodding. "Whatever my reasons,
they're none of your damn business."

"What's this? Sister Christian has a temper. Call
fucking Guinness."

"You know, Micky. I came here to see if you and I
could find our way back to the friends we once
were, perhaps start over again."

"So typical of you, Saint Abby."

"Forgive me for forgetting that you don't know
how to act like a functioning member of the
human race. God, Micky. You're the only family I
have left. Doesn't that mean anything to you?"

"Fewer gifts to buy at Christmas?"

"If your anger stems from the fact that Dad left
the company to me—"

"So there it is. The big revelation. Please, don't
get on your pedestal and preach to the masses. I
could give a flying fuck what the old bastard did
with the company. I have better things to do with
my time."

"I think you're lying. In fact, I think it hurt you a

great deal when Dad didn't leave the magazine to you. And you have every right to be hurt."

"How gracious of you to give me your permission to be upset," Micky said dryly. "Now I can go on living."

"You don't have to always hide your feelings from me, Micky."

"Oh, great, now we're going to discuss how I feel? You don't know one damn thing about how I feel, so why don't you just drop it?"

"You're right. I don't know how you feel. I didn't know whether my coming here was a good idea or not. But I was willing to try. I still want to try."

"Look, I hate to tell you this, but I didn't need dear old Dad, and I sure as hell don't need you. I don't need anybody. So get off my back."

Micky's words rang with cutting finality. Abby said no more. And for the first time she allowed herself to believe that perhaps she and Micky had passed the point of no return, that too much separated them—lost years and distance and leading different lives.

Never had Abby felt more alone in the world.

When Stefan returned to the hospital later that day, he found Abby gone and her bed made up, nothing left to prove she had ever been there at all.

A surge of panic nearly brought him to his knees, images of her lying on a cold slab in the morgue, complications of her injuries, her illness.

Oh, Jesus God, why did he leave?

"Relax, lover boy. Saint Abigail is fine."

Stefan swung around at the sound of Micky's voice and found her coming up behind him in a wheelchair, a nurse returning her to the room.

The left side of her face was swollen and painted with dark bruises, one eye still puffy and closed. Her other eye, however, was fastened on him, mockery shining clearly.

"Where is she?"

"Getting an MRI." Micky shrugged off the nurse's help as she got back into bed, her battered body moving slowly. Stefan caught the grimace of pain she couldn't quite hide. Once settled against the pillows, she rudely dismissed the nurse and smirked at him. "Guess my darling sibling thought she was Wonder Woman, wrestling with that twisted shit who did this to my face. Pretty, huh?"

Stefan's concern for Abby was momentarily eclipsed by the anger he felt toward her sister. "Christ, you're incredible, you know that?"

"So I've heard. But it's too late for you and me, lover. You've already been in my sister's panties, which means you've been tainted by her sugary lovemaking and wouldn't know how to please a woman like me."

Stefan had to remind himself that Micky was injured. "If I had wanted a woman like you," he said tightly, "I would have taken you up on your sexual offers. If you recall, I didn't."

She shrugged. "Your loss."

"You really are a piece of work. Your sister risked her life to save you and you can't even get the words 'thank you' out of your mouth."

"Good old martyred Abby, protector of the underdog. I swear, she should be canonized. Did you have to get a papal blessing before you shoved your dick into her?"

Stefan's jaw tightened. "I always thought it was just me you hated. But you hate the world."

"There are plenty of people I like. Just not you or my sister."

"I could care less if you like me. It's Abby I'm concerned about. For some reason, she loves you and needs to have you in her life. She doesn't understand you were born without a heart."

Her eyes flickered with fury, but her words were smug. "Now, now. There's no need for all this hostility. We're practically kin."

"You know, all this anger you've directed at Abby makes me wonder what caused it. There's only one answer I can come up with."

"Oh? And what's that?"

"You're jealous of her."

"Jealous!" Micky gave a short bark of laughter. "You've gone off the deep end. The girl has not an ounce of fashion sense, is clueless about hair and makeup, and is so teeth-gnashingly innocent I want to slash my wrists."

"And I bet you want to be just like her."

Micky's hands fisted in the bed linens. "You don't want to play this game with me. I'll flay you alive."

Stefan realized he had struck a nerve and he intended to keep chiseling away to hit pay dirt. "I think you're mad as hell, too."

"Why? Because Abby screwed you and I didn't? Don't flatter yourself, stud. You could be replaced by an inflatable doll, and I'd probably enjoy myself more."

"That's not why you're angry."

"I guess you're going to enlighten me now?" Her bored stare couldn't mask the tension simmering just below the surface.

"I think you're pissed because Abby saved you."

"What!"

"I think you wanted to die."

"Don't be an ass."

"Admit it, Micky. You wanted that bastard to kill you because you couldn't find a way to kill yourself."

"You don't know what you're talking about."

"My sister was raped and the shame of it caused her to take her life. You were violated, used against your will. You're angry and you're hurting and you want to lash out at everyone. But you can't show those emotions because you think people might find out you're not as tough as you want them to believe."

"You're full of shit," she spat, her knuckles white where she gripped the sheets.

"I think you're just a scared little girl beneath all those fancy clothes and that shellacked sex appeal."

"Shut up!"

"You're frightened and lonely and put on an act so that no one will get too close or else they might find out that you're a fake."

"*Shut up, I said!*"

"You didn't do anything to deserve what happened to you. No man has the right to force himself on you, Micky. No man. No matter how you have conducted your life, the choice is still yours."

Her eyes were squeezed shut, but a single tear escaped, and the sight of it cut right through Stefan, telling him that his assumption had been correct, that much of her behavior was an act, a protective shell to keep the world at bay.

He disliked his methods, more so because he had his own selfish reasons for wanting to prick Michaela's unyielding hide. Abby needed her right now, perhaps more than she needed him. Stefan wondered if the sisters realized how very much alike they were.

He raked a hand through his hair, guilt assailing him. "I'm sorry. I shouldn't have said all that."

"Go to hell," she choked out.

"The whole world isn't again you, Micky. You have Abby. She's your family and she's reaching out to you. Don't be so damn pigheaded that your anger causes you to sever something that could still be salvaged."

She made no reply. Stefan figured she wouldn't. He had hoped he had pierced her armor, perhaps made a difference, but he could see now that he hadn't.

He sighed and turned to leave, intending to go in search of Abby, but Micky's words stopped him.

"You really love her, don't you?" She was looking at him now, allowing him to glimpse the pain she had so carefully kept hidden.

"Yes . . . I really do. But she needs you."

Micky seemed to digest the words as if finally

hearing and understanding them. "She needs you, too," she said quietly, surprising Stefan.

"I have no intention of going anywhere."

"Why won't she marry you?"

Stefan wasn't sure how to answer that question. He wanted to tell her that he suspected Abby didn't want to burden him with her illness, that her foolish sense of nobility was keeping her from allowing him to help. But did he have the right to tell Micky something that should really come from Abby?

Yes.

The answer came that swiftly. Abby would not open up to her sister with the wall that sat squarely between them. She had kept the information from him, hadn't she? Micky deserved to know what her sister was going through.

"She's very sick," he said.

"You mean from the stab wound?"

"No." Emotions that Stefan had managed to keep below the surface started pushing against him, threatening to annihilate his resolve. "She's dying, Micky. She has kidney cancer."

Beneath the bruises, Micky's face paled. "Dying?" The horror of the word, of what it meant, reverberated in that single breath of sound. "No." She shook her head, disbelief rapidly following, as it had with Stefan. "Not Abby. She's never been sick a day in her life. She . . . she's always been the strong one, the one everybody leaned on. I don't believe it."

"It's true."

"Why didn't she tell me?"

"Would you have listened?"

She met his stare for another moment and then lowered her head. "No, probably not." Her fingers splayed against the sheets. "She's been trying to talk to me for so long but I was avoiding her. God," she said in a pained voice, "this can't be happening. Not to Abby."

"I didn't want to believe it either. But wishing won't change reality." He knew. He had tried.

"Isn't there anything the doctors can do for her?"

Stefan remembered posing the same question to Doctor Bladen and hearing the terrible news, that they would have to remove Abby's kidney and put her on dialysis until a donor could be found.

He couldn't recall all the things that had run through his head at the time, besides the pain, but he imagined that was when he had made the decision to give Abby one of his kidneys. He just hadn't acknowledged it until his shock had ebbed far enough for him to think clearly. He intended to question the doctor today and see if he was a match.

"The doctor says her kidney needs to be removed," he told Micky.

"And then she'll be all right?"

"No. She only has one kidney."

"One?"

"Didn't you know?"

"No," she said quietly. "I didn't."

Stefan could now see just how vast the chasm was between the sisters. "When you mother's diabetes escalated, so did the trouble with her kidneys."

"So Abby gave up one of her kidneys, right?"

Stefan nodded.

"God, that's so like her." Micky's words were edged with anger. "She always was selfless, and now she's dying because of it."

Stefan could almost relate to Micky in that moment, wanting to blame someone, anyone, to rail against fate and the unfairness of the situation. But what good would it do? Would it change anything? Make Abby well again? No. So now they had to proceed in the best way possible for Abby.

"What will happen if the doctors remove her kidney?" Micky asked.

"She'll have to be put on a machine that will do the work of her kidneys until a donor organ can be found."

"And how long will that take?"

"Maybe a few months. A few years. For some . . . never."

Micky closed her eyes. "Dear God," she whispered. "After all these years of hating her and believing she was the reason my father could never love me, thinking all the bad things that happened in my life were in some way tied up in her existence, that if I could have been an only child my life would have been different." She opened her eyes and looked at him. "She's all the family I have left. Now it's too late."

"It's never too late."

"But what can I do?"

"Just be there for her."

A sound at the doorway had Stefan turning around. The nurse who had been abruptly dismissed by Micky wheeled Abby into the room.

Abby's eyes widened upon seeing him, briefly flickering with something that resembled happiness, but she quickly averted her gaze.

Stefan went over to lend a hand as she rose from the wheelchair. She tugged her arm from his grasp. "I can do it."

It was hard, but Stefan let go, fighting the urge to pick her up and settle her in the bed instead of watching her struggle. But he would only alienate himself from her further should he help.

Once she was propped up in the bed and the nurse had departed, she said, "What are you doing here, Stefan? I told you I didn't want you to come back."

"And I told you that I would. And I'll continue to come back every day for as long as it takes. I'm with you for good or bad, in sickness or in health, until death do us part. I don't need to say the words before a priest to validate how I feel about you."

"Don't do this," she softly pleaded, glancing toward the curtain separating her and Micky.

"Don't do what? Love you? It's too late for that."

She closed her eyes. "I'm tired. Please go."

"Fine. But I'll be here when you wake up."

She looked as though she was gearing up to protest. Then she nodded and rolled to her side, away from him.

When Abby awoke a few hours later, she was surprised to find Micky sitting in a wheelchair at the corner of her bed, watching her.

"Is everything all right?" she said groggily, trying to blink the sleep from her eyes.

"I want to help you."

Abby pushed herself up against her pillows and struggled to clear the fog from her head caused by the pain medication the nurse had given her.

"Help me with what?"

"I want to give you one of my kidneys."

Abby came instantly awake. She didn't need to ask to know how Micky had found out about her illness. Stefan. She wanted to rail at him for his interference, and yet, the look in her sister's eyes was one Abby hadn't seen in a very long time.

But why did the specter of impending death have to be the tie that binds? Why was it always the component that brought people together, compelled by some inner need to set things right when there was no desire to do so before?

Micky had been forced to contemplate her own mortality, to have reality brought to the forefront of her mind, and come face-to-face with a fear most people tried to block out. That of dying.

Abby wasn't as scared of death as she had once been. It was inevitable, after all. Death was the easy part. It was living that was hard.

"Will you let me do this for you, Abby?"

"Why, Micky? Just tell me why."

"Because I need to."

"That's not a reason."

"I'm your sister. Does there have to be anything else?"

"You have no idea what you are getting in to, no clue as to what this could mean for you."

"Did you think about what it could mean for you when you agreed to give Mom one of your kidneys?"

Stefan hadn't missed a thing. He had managed to wring an emotion out of Micky that Abby never had. And every piece of himself that he left behind made it that much harder for her to walk away.

"What I did for Mom was different, Micky."

"How so? Because you were the one giving something up instead of me? Do you think you're the only person with the capacity to do something noble?"

"No. I don't think that. I've always known you were a good person and that you had a lot of gifts to give, if you'd only open your eyes and see them."

"Maybe I didn't have the same faith in myself that you did. Maybe I still don't." Abby was not prepared for the tears that suddenly formed in Micky's eyes, or the possibility that they could break her heart. "But I'll never know unless you let me help you. Please, Abby. Give me a chance to do something right."

"Micky . . ."

"You're all I have left in the world. What will I do without you?"

In her entire life, Abby had never seen her sister cry. Now fat tears coursed freely down Micky's cheeks. Abby reached out and took hold of her sister's hand.

"If anything should happen to you . . ."

"Nothing will happen."

It was so hard to say the words Abby wanted to

say, to hold on tight to her sister's offer and pray for the best for both of them.

"I don't know if you would be a match . . ."

Micky plucked a tissue from a box on the table beside her. "Is that a yes?"

"I want you to talk to Doctor Bladen first and understand what you're getting yourself into. I don't want you to have any regrets."

"That's fair. But what if the doctor talks to me and I still want to move forward?"

Abby took a deep breath and released it slowly, knowing what she was about to say could irrevocably change both their lives forever.

"Well, then . . . I guess I'd say yes."

Twenty-five

Tension ran high after the tests had been taken, but the results had not been much of a surprise to the doctor. Micky was not only a relative, but Abby's twin, making her a perfect match.

Stefan could only thank whatever power had compelled Micky to make her offer, more so after he found out that he was excluded from being a donor.

He leaned against the door frame of Abby's hospital room watching her sleep. It seemed as if he was always watching her. He couldn't get enough of her. He wanted to capture every moment, each nuance, and hold on to them. She didn't know it, but she gave him strength, and he would need all he could summon in the hours to come.

It was 6 A.M. In less than two hours she and Micky would be heading to surgery. The nurses hadn't stopped him when he had shown up before visiting hours, and they no longer roused him when he fell asleep in the chair beside Abby's bed.

His hair now dusted his shoulders and most of the time his face was covered with a five o'clock shadow as shaving seemed too formidable a task to challenge every day. When he looked at himself in the mirror, he wondered if his face would be the only one staring back at him from now on. Reality was too hard to meet head-on so he blocked it out, shut it off, and simply existed.

Abby had yet to give up trying to convince him to leave, telling him that what they had shared was over. There were days Stefan actually believed her, when he was sure she would never let him into her heart again, that he would never get to hold her again, or kiss her, or feel her body aching for his. But one thing would always pull him back from his anguish.

She loved him. And love didn't simply fade away at the first test of its strength. They would make it through this. He wouldn't allow himself to believe otherwise.

"Stefan . . ."

Stefan came away from the door with a start, his gaze snapping to Abby's sleepy eyes. "I'm here, baby." He moved to the bed and took hold of her hand. She didn't resist.

"What time is it?"

He checked his watch. "A little after six-thirty. How are you feeling?"

"All right, I suppose." Her grip tightened on his hand. He wondered if she noticed. "I . . . I'm afraid."

"I know, baby. I know. But everything will be fine. Doctor Bladen is one of the best surgeons in the country. You and Micky will be in good hands, and I'll be right here waiting for you when it's over."

"Stefan—"

He pressed a finger to her lips. "Please don't say

it's best if I leave. What's best for me is being here with you."

"What can I do to make you understand?" A single tear slipped from between her lashes. Stefan wiped it away with his thumb. "I can't give you anything."

"You can give me yourself. That's all I'll ever want."

"No." She shook her head. "You say that now, but you can't mean it."

"I do mean it."

"I can't have any children." Her admission came out a tortured whisper and Stefan's heart broke for her. "I won't ever be able to give you a son or daughter of your own." She opened her eyes and they were liquid pools of pain.

"Do you think that's all that matters to me? Having children? I want to share my life with you, whatever life that may be. If we had children, that would be wonderful. If we didn't have children, that would be fine, too, because I have you. You're what makes me happy. Why won't you believe me?"

"Because I couldn't bear to lose you. I . . ." Her voice broke on a sob. "I couldn't bear it."

"Oh, God, baby. You won't lose me." He brought her hand to his lips.

"No." Her tears slipped onto the pillow. "It won't work."

"Give us a chance, for the love of God. Give *me* a chance."

She closed her eyes, silent sobs wracking her body as she whispered, "Good-bye, Stefan."

A nurse walked in then. "I have to get the ladies prepped for surgery now."

A tear rolled down Stefan's face as he kissed Abby's palm. "I love you. I always will." He closed his eyes, trying to hold back the riptide of emotions inside him. "I never wanted it to be this way. I really thought I could make you happy, that if I pushed hard enough everything would be all right. But I see now that I can't force something from you that you don't want to give. I can't make you want me . . . want us."

He opened his eyes and looked at her, knowing it could be the last time, his gaze skimming over her face, taking in every detail. He would never forget her tears or the sorrow reflected in her eyes. "I want you to be happy. That's all I ever wanted. And once I know you're all right, I'll leave you alone. I'll walk away, Abby, and give you what you want." He leaned down and brushed his lips across hers. "You'll always have my heart," he whispered and then he let her go.

Stefan stared out at the water as he stood on the deck of *The Maria.* The air had grown cold and nearly every slip was empty. Most of the boats had been dry-docked now that it was almost November.

He couldn't bring himself to have his boat hauled from the water. Some of the best days of his life had been spent here. His most vivid memories of Abby came to life on this deck. At times, he could almost feel her in his arms, hear each laugh, each breathy whisper of his name when he touched her, see each tear she shed.

The surgery had been a success. The sisters were

both doing well. All the hours he had spent pacing the hospital corridors had given him time to reflect, to hope that Abby would open her eyes and smile and tell him that everything would be all right, that they had a chance to make it.

She didn't.

So he had kept his vow and left her alone, maintaining a solitary vigil on his boat, feeling a keen sense of grief at his loss, as the woman he loved slipped farther and farther away from him.

Life went on back at the office and he functioned as best as he could, trying to block out the memories that lingered even there.

Abby had split the company with her sister, making them equal partners, rebuilding the bond that had been severed all those years ago. Stefan was happy for her. This is what she had wanted.

If only she had wanted a future for the two of them as much.

Soon Micky would be returning to the office to take up where she had left off and Stefan would walk away from everything he had known. It was no longer a matter of not being able to work with her. He understood her better now. Or perhaps it was simply that he understood himself better. Either way, it didn't really matter. Seeing Micky every day would just remind him too much of Abby, of what he had lost.

It was time to move on.

Janelle Harrison had been after him to come on board, to build *Posh* the way he had built *Bastion*, and Stefan had finally accepted her offer.

That morning, he had forwarded his resignation

letter to Abby at Hawthorne House, where she and
Micky were recuperating. The messenger had acknowledged it had been received.

It was really over.

A crew would be arriving within the hour to put
The Maria away for the winter. This was the last time
Stefan would be standing in this spot for a long
while. Now he had to gather up the last of his be-
longings and try to put this part of his life behind
him as best he could.

He turned to head down the stairs to the cabins,
the dying rays of the autumn sun glinting in his
eyes, blurring his vision.

Then he saw her.

She was standing at the other end of the dock,
the setting sun her backdrop, gilding her features
with gold, making her look like an angel.

Afraid she might vanish, that she was simply a fig-
ment of his imagination, Stefan slowly moved toward the back of the boat, his gaze never leaving
her as he stepped onto the pier, facing her across
the distance.

He wasn't sure how long they stood there or
which of them moved first, but the space closed between them until they met somewhere in the middle.

She had grown thinner and her face was slightly
drawn, but Abby was still heartbreakingly beautiful
to him and very much alive. He wanted to kiss her,
hold her close, end the pain that just seeing her
had caused, opening up a wound that was still raw.

"I knew I'd find you here," she murmured, her

gaze skimming over his face with a tenderness that nearly brought him to his knees.

"Is everything all right?" he asked.

She nodded. "The doctor says I'm doing fine. And Micky, well, she always was able to bounce back easily. She came with me."

Stefan's gaze lifted and finally noticed the limousine slanted across the deserted parking lot. Then his attention returned to Abby. "Why are you here?"

A flash of uncertainty crossed her face before she lowered her head, her hand dipping into her purse and pulling out an envelope. His resignation letter. "I can't accept this." She held it out to him.

He didn't take it. "You have no choice."

"You can't leave."

"Why?"

"Because you are *Bastion*. You've made it into the company it is today. It's your life."

"No. It's not my life. I want more, Abby. What I have now won't work any longer."

"What do you want?"

"You know what I want. You."

"Still?"

"Always. And if I can't have you . . . then I want nothing." He turned and walked away from her, and leaving was no easier now than it had been the first time.

"I love you, Stefan."

Her words stopped him cold, stripped him to the bone and made hope begin to pound away in his veins. He faced her. "Then let go of the past and give us a future."

"I'm afraid," she said in a quiet voice, the unshed tears in her eyes wrenching at him. "There are so many things that could go wrong."

He took the four steps separating them and cupped her cheeks, smoothing his thumb across her skin. "We've been through the worst of it, and whatever the future holds, we'll face it together. Nothing is guaranteed, Abby. Life does not come without risks. But I'm willing to try."

"I pushed you away."

"But I didn't go far. Marry me, Abby. I love you."

Her tears rolled freely, bathing his fingers. "Yes," she whispered. "Yes."

He kissed her softly and then smiled down at her. "Take my hand."

"Where are we going?"

"Someplace we've never been before."

Her fingers entwined with his, holding tight. "And where is that?"

"Into the sunset."

A NOTE FROM THE AUTHOR

Dear Reader:

For those of you who have read my previous books, you know that I write more lighthearted stories, which I have thoroughly enjoyed doing and have every intention of continuing.

But when *TO DIE FOR* began to take shape, the characters came to me with emotional baggage and the story evolved into something darker, grittier, and more sexually charged than what you have read from me thus far. As you have always been so supportive of me, I felt you should know where my mind was when writing Stefan and Abby's story.

I can only hope you will take something positive away from this book. As always, I welcome your comments, and thank you for reading my books.

Warm regards,
Melanie George

ABOUT THE AUTHOR

Before she discovered romantic fiction, Melanie George was an executive search consultant. Her most important job, however, has always been that of mother to a much loved, sometimes vexing son and two precocious dogs, who sit with her in her office day after day, lending her uncompromising support.

When she is not writing, she is trying to restore her hundred-year-old house and marveling at the changes in the world since she last stepped out into the light of day. She looks forward to the release of her next novel in May 2003. You can visit Melanie at: www.melaniegeorge.com.